THE
TWINS

THE
TWINS

L.V. MATTHEWS

WELBECK

Published in 2022 by Welbeck Fiction Limited,
an imprint of Welbeck Publishing Group
Based in London and Sydney.
www.welbeckpublishing.com

A CIP catalogue record for this book is available from the
British Library

Paperback ISBN: 978-1-78739-917-4
Ebook ISBN: 978-1-78739-918-1

Printed and bound by CPI Group (UK) Ltd., Croydon, CR0 4YY

10 9 8 7 6 5 4 3 2 1

To Jen, who planted the idea of this book and then helped me water it

ONE

MARGO

The air smells of sea salt and cologne and money. I hear them all above deck, clinking champagne glasses, but I stay below in the galley and stare out of the huge porthole at a cut-glass blue horizon.

I never thought that this decadent lifestyle could be mine but here I am, floating on this luxury yacht on the Solent in the thick heat of summer, and arranging a seafood platter of crab tails, dressed lobster, and king scallops on a tray of ice. This evening, I'll have dinner at The Royal Hotel on the Isle of Wight, be sailed back to Southampton and then chauffeured all the way back to the six-bedroom house in Kensington. The twins will fall asleep in the car and we'll carry them gently up to bed and then, only then, I'll go and sit in my room and let myself breathe. I'll be able to tell myself that I've done it – I've made it through another day without mistakes.

I finish with the platter, wash and dry my hands. There's champagne in a tall-standing bucket and I don't want to drink it but there's something that begs for me to smell it and to see its bubbles race to the top of the glass. I pour some out into one of the crystal flutes, set it down on the table and look at it.

'Have you got a taste for the good stuff, Margo?'

One of the women, David's school friend possibly, has come down the stairs. I think her name is Barbara, or Barbie for short. She's long-legged under a violet sarong, bejewelled by rings and wears her black hair in a majestic-looking mass on top of her head. She's alarmed me and I'm embarrassed.

'Oh, I'm – I'm not going to drink it,' I say.

'You enjoy yourself, love,' she laughs. 'You've done a good job today.'

She smiles and one eye drifts a little. She's skittishly drunk, I can see, but that's the whole point of the day.

'I've come hunting out that coriander mayo you made for the chips,' she says.

I hand her a bowl. 'Here.'

She dips a slender finger straight in, licks it. 'Divine.'

She picks over the many other dishes to compliment the platter that I've laid on the kitchen top; smoked salmon and lemon pâté; arancini balls; teriyaki beef cups; Stilton and chutney rarebit bites. She pops an arancini ball into her mouth.

'Years ago,' she says, chewing. 'Before all the kids, we'd take this boat out to the Med. We'd strip off after too many drinks, go skinny dipping. Never knew whose body you were rubbing up against but that was the fun of it.'

She laughs and I laugh with her because I'm supposed to.

'Marie was telling me you used to be a dancer?' she asks.

Six-year-old Marie is my biggest fan and I love her for the pedestal she's put me on.

'I went to stage schools when I was little,' I reply. 'I've forgotten most of it now.'

'She told me that you've taught her some bits?'

'A couple of routines. She loves it.'

'I've always admired the discipline of ballet,' Barbara says. 'All that effort to look so effortless. Though their feet look like shit by the end though, don't they? Cut like ribbons.'

'Yes, that's true.'

'And so you decided against it as a career then?' she asks. 'Dancing? Because you like kids more?' She gives a shrill bark of laughter. 'That's a whole other load of punishment!'

I smile and she waits for me to say something more but I don't. Her anticipation of conversation is faltering and I don't know how to rescue it because small talk isn't what I'm good at. She claps her hands to signal the end and we're both glad of it.

'Well!' she says, nods to the bowl of mayonnaise in her hand. 'I'd better go before I eat it all! This is so incredible. You let me know if you're ever looking to come elsewhere, yes? I could lure you away. You'd choose me, wouldn't you? I don't even have children!'

Choose me.

I smile at her again, mute, and then she trots up the stairs and out of the hatch and I hear her speak to Emmeline.

'Doesn't say much, does she?'

3

'I think that's why I like her,' Emmeline replies and they both giggle but I don't mind what they say about me.

I take a white tray of sundae glasses filled with chocolate and salted caramel scoops out of the freezer, top them with sprinkles and vanilla wafers and walk up out of the galley. The children shout with delight when they see me. All ten of them are sitting on the front deck, wearing hooded towels over life-jackets, limbs bronzed and hair tangled.

'Ice cream!' one of them yells.

I take the tray in one hand and the sail rope with the other to balance myself as I step over it to get to them. It's not an easy move but precision is what's expected of me, today and all days. The children dive at the tray as I set it down, pick up silver spoons as I in turn pick up their discarded towels and hang on them on the rails before returning to the sunbathed saloon below deck. I look out of the porthole again. The sea is calm and I am safe here in this little space. I am safe with David and with Emmeline and the twins.

Being a nanny means knowing both when to be visible and invisible. It's living by another family's routine, abiding by their rules and wants. It's knowing to fold pyjamas over a hot-water bottle on cold winter nights before bedtime, it's remembering beloved bears for holidays, the hierarchy of china sets, and ticking off lists of Christmas presents for various relatives. It's updating the family calendar every week, cutting up boxes to make toy car garages, adding glitter to home-made cards and then tidying it all up again. It's being privy to an elite world where you are given a private corner of a house to observe it, where you don't ask questions when you come across conversations that you shouldn't.

My jobs provide me materially with everything I could ever want. The softest mattresses, Egyptian cotton linen, heavy blackout curtains for my bedrooms, cosy armchairs for my own lounges, organic food to cook, Le Creuset sets to cook in, Ottolenghi books to cook from. Sometimes it's hard to remember that none of it is really mine. At the end of a job I say goodbye to it all and I take away only memories and my limited wardrobe of clothing, and cash. Lots of cash, because families pay for outstanding service and they are also generous with donations as birthday or Christmas gifts. I don't even know how much I have in my account – I only know I have more than I would ever need. What would I ever buy myself? What do I like? I like going to the theatre and watching the dancers, to remind me of a life once lived.

I get a notebook from my bag and start making some lists whilst everyone is happy drinking champagne and eating ice cream in the sun. We have ten days before the new school year starts and I need to make triple sure I have everything organised. The summer holiday has been long, with a packed itinerary to satisfy the entire family: hosting barbeques for their friends, seeing family, countless day trips to Diggerland, Peppa Pig World, Legoland and zoos. David and Emmeline booked a week in Bali for the four of them and offered me a week off for my own pleasure and I smiled, pretended to be delighted and told them I would visit family. Instead I stayed in London in their house: bleached their shower heads, dusted tops of wardrobes, rotated the toys and tried to sleep as much as I could. I didn't want a holiday where I would sit on a balcony somewhere, thinking how lonely I really am.

I open my bag again, unscrew the lid of a little bottle that I keep zipped up in the secret compartment, swallow two of the white pills dry. They're running low so I add another line to my list to order more on express delivery.

'Margo!'

I startle at the shout and the lidless bottle pings up in my hand. Pills fall like little hailstones, click on the smart flooring and roll in every direction.

'Oh, sorry!'

It's Jonny, Marie's twin, at the stairs and he comes bounding down, crouches on the floor to help me pick them up.

'Don't worry, dove,' I say to him. 'It was an accident.'

I can hear that my voice is tight. These pills are my absolute lifeline.

'Is there any more ice cream?' he asks beside me.

'Yes, yes,' I say but I'm furiously pecking at them with my fingers. I don't want the children down here and picking them up, thinking they're sweets: they're far from it. I filter them inside the bottle.

'Jonny?' I ask. 'Did you get any?'

But I'm answered with silence and I turn my head, see that he's gone, already up and out of the hatch like a monkey. Has he taken any of the pills with him? I scramble up, panicking, and rush up the stairs. He's on deck, right next to Emmeline who is talking to another woman, and in the palm of his hand I can see that he's holding a dozen or so white pills and counting them. I go towards him.

I steer him towards the foredeck. 'Can I have those?'

'You can't eat things off the floor,' he says to me because that's what I'm always telling him.

'Wait—' I say but I watch him stretch his arm out over the rail and sprinkle the pills into the sea.

'There you go!'

He smiles because he thinks he's done the right thing, but I stare at the water in dismay. I have those pills shipped from America and I wonder how many days' worth I have left now in the bottle. Oh God, I've left them in full view down in the kitchen, and I need to get back down before anyone sees them. Don't panic, don't panic, I tell myself, but I feel sweat start to bead on my forehead.

'Great,' I manage and turn to go back. 'Thanks, darling.'

'Oh, Margo,' Barbie trills and I look to her. She waves an empty champagne flute at me, smiles drunkenly.

'I'll get a bottle,' I say.

'Can we have some more ice cream?' a child asks.

'I'll get some.'

I go back below deck, snatch up the bottle. I can see that I've only got a few left. Breathe. I can just order more, it's fine. I screw the lid on tightly, put the pills back in my bag, and I then look at the sea out of the porthole, exhale, and tell myself that I'm safe here. Looking after people is what

I'm good at: routine and order and consideration. There is no need to feel anxious.

'Margo?' someone calls from above. 'Can you bring up the oysters?'

'Absolutely.'

I busy myself with tending to the others. People don't realise you're not talking to them about your own life if you're putting food on their tables, if you're doing their laundry, if you're smiling at their stories. I like living their lives because it's easier than living my own.

My life has ghosts.

TWO

CORA

It's crowded in the bar. People are pressed against one another, there's sweat in the air and boozy breath too close to my cheeks but this is what I like: being at close quarters to these vibrant, sleek people with loud music thudding through my chest and coloured lights roving across my skin. This is the Saturday after-show party and I'm wired on it.

Nav leans in and I know that he's shouting in my ear but I can barely hear him.

'What?' I shout back.

He drags me off the dance floor.

'I said that arsehole Guy Harris is over there, and he's looking at you,' he says and points to a booth in the corner of the room where a man lounges with another dancer.

'I know,' I nod. 'I'm waiting for the right moment to speak to him.'

Nav makes a face over the music. 'Why?'

'He's the reason we're here.'

Guy Harris is a casting director renowned throughout the business for his tenacity and networking skills. He's also renowned for being tempestuous, promiscuous and lewd and I've seen all of these things, all at the same time.

'Are you serious?' Nav groans.

'One hundred per cent.'

'Oh God,' he says. 'I thought we were here for the free booze.'

'We are,' I reply. 'But also for favours to be exchanged.'

Both Nav and I are professional dancers and, especially between being signed-up, it's all about visibility. We're not even supposed to be at this party: we have nothing to do with this cast. A friend let us in but I have no idea where she went nor do I care.

'What kind of favours?' he says.

'There's a show that's going into production,' I say. 'And Guy is the person I need to talk to to get me an audition. Plus, he knows the choreographer really well.'

'Who's the choreographer?' Nav asks.

'Jean-Luc Laurent.'

His eyes widen because Jean-Luc is a big name in contemporary dance. 'What's the show?'

'It's not well known,' I say. 'But there's a part written for me.'

'You say that about every single role you're put up for.'

I dig into my bag, apply lipstick, and Nav rolls his eyes.

'Original,' he says. 'You're going to sleep with Guy to get an audition? Is sex your answer to everything?'

'Usually.'

'Can't your agent put you up for the audition?'

'I need something more than her good word,' I say. 'It's all about favours, Nav, I told you.'

'Is this a good idea? You're drunk.'

I pout at him with full red lips, flash my extended eyelashes. Everything about me is bigger and bolder tonight because one needs to stand out in a crowd as beautiful as this one.

'"*One should always be drunk*",' I say. '"*That's all that matters . . . But with what? With wine, with poetry, or with virtue, as you choose. But get drunk.*" Quote by Charles Baudelaire.'

'You're coming home with me tonight though, OK?' Nav says.

'Oh, relax. I'll meet you outside in ten minutes.'

I slip through the heaving mass of bodies on the dance floor, and feel hands catch my waist, strokes of fingertips on my arms and hot breath on my neck. Dancers are almost always tactile and I'm the best of them.

'Guy!' I exclaim as I reach his booth.

I reach over and kiss his cheek and then I sit on his lap. I see the other dancer raise her eyebrows.

Guy looks up at me through thick designer glasses and smiles slowly at the recognition. 'Cora Devaux,' he says.

My name oozes from his mouth like syrup. He's nearing fifty, has tanned skin and lines where they are handsome on men but not, according to cosmetic adverts, on women.

'Missed me?' I whisper into his ear.

He doesn't go to remove me and the dancer takes her cue, gets up and takes her drink with her.

'I haven't seen you in a while,' he says.

I shrug. 'I like to school people in the art of patience.'

He smiles again. 'Can I help you? I never see you unless you want something.'

'Oh! How you wound me,' I reply. 'But now you come to mention it, I'm interested in a show that's being cast at the moment.'

'And you think I can help you out?'

'I *know* you can.'

'If I can't?'

My thumb strokes the top of his hand as it's clasped within mine and he looks down at it.

'Then all the weight of Mondays would crush my shoulders,' I say. 'And shame on you because Mondays are the worst of the days.'

'I forgot that beautiful tongue,' he says, looking at my lips. 'You could charm the birds from the trees. What's the show?'

'*Mirror, Mirror.*'

He frowns. 'How do you know about it? Jean-Luc only announced it two days ago and not even widely.'

'Because I'm always looking for it,' I say. 'And I want to dance Eliza.'

He tilts his head at me. 'She's a fuck-up.'

'Exactly,' I say. 'But everyone likes a fuck-up, don't they?'

I move my hand from his and squeeze his thigh. He can feel my body through this ridiculous dress I'm wearing; a bright violet film of material ruched at the waist and stopping short just below my butt. He can see my toned calves; can see the lights making shadows across my collarbones. I use my body as a weapon.

'The part needs someone raw,' I say. 'Someone passionate; and that's me, isn't it?'

He grins. I can see the familiar excitement spark in his eyes. 'Could be.'

I smile. 'You could be credited for finding the star of this show and I could blow you kisses from the stage.'

'I'll see what I can do,' he says. 'But—'

'Of course,' I purr. 'Tit for tat. How's your wife?'

'Fuck off,' he says but he laughs.

I lean in, bite his bottom lip and his eyes widen in both surprise and then pleasure. Or is it pain?

Tit for tat. Is that enough, I wonder. I'm twenty-seven, he can have girls far younger than me who are more desperate for chances, but I have an edge a lot of them don't. He's panted it before, hot in my ears, as I've stared him down through a mask covered in feathers over his perspiring body.

'You're crazy, Cora Devaux,' he said once.

'Mad as a fucking hatter,' I'd replied. 'You want more?'

They always want more.

I hop from his lap. 'I'll sit in a cold corner and write desperately bad poetry in the hope of your call,' I say.

I hear him laugh again as I walk away. For all his failings – and there are many – I like the banter between us. Guy is always unapologetically himself and I find that liberating. I cross the dance floor, know he's watching as I go. People shout as I leave.

'Don't go, Cora!'

'You promised me a dance!'

'Send me your number, yeah?'

Did I kiss any of them tonight? All of them? I can't remember. I throw them all my best smile and then the door closes behind me.

Nav is waiting outside. The late August air is warm enough to walk barefooted even at this time of night and so I take my shoes off, feel the relief of the cool pavement beneath them. I swing my shoes by my side, can't see in the darkness how dirty my feet are getting.

'How did it go?' Nav asks.

'We'll see.'

He hands me a cigarette packet and I take my lighter from my bag and light one for him and one for myself. I hate cigarettes and so does Nav, and smoking them is a sure sign of a debauched night.

Nav and I met three years ago at a casting of a contemporary take of *Women of Troy* where he was dancing Paris because he's good-looking in an uncomplicated way; slim and dark with pearls in his mouth, and I was dancing Hecuba, the tragic heroine. Neither of us got the parts but we found each other and commiserated by drinking lychee margaritas at a Mexican bar and bitching about people in the industry. I liked his wit and his brutal honesty and he liked me for the very same reasons. I moved into his flat after six months and we've been inseparable ever since. It's good to live with someone else; I'd been living alone too long before that and I've decided I'm not as good on my own. I'm not as fun.

'That was a good party,' Nav says.

'I reckon top twenty.'

He drags on the cigarette. 'Agree. Look, I got some photos with Freddie Balaz. He's signed with Breaker Records.'

He shows me them as we walk. 'That one or that one for Insta?' he asks.

I look as he flicks from one picture to the other. 'I mean, they're both the same.'

'My lips look bigger in that one,' he says.

'That one then,' I say.

'But too big?'

'That one then,' I say and point to the other.

'But big enough?'

I roll my eyes though it's an effort because I must have reapplied my mascara five times in the space of only a few hours and my lashes feel heavy with it. My head is going to suffer tomorrow morning.

'Shit, I look dug up in this one here,' he says.

I lean to see. 'Send that to me *immediately*.'

'No fucking way.'

The cigarette is dry in my mouth; I need water. 'Nav,' I say. 'I see a golden and delicious archway that leads to fries and coke inside.'

I cross the road to the yellow-and-red shop front and I click my fingers for him to follow me.

'I'm not your dog,' he says.

'You're right,' I say. 'You're my bitch.'

I shimmy across threshold of the fast-food chain, see the late-night drunks and the groups of friends stop talking, stop what they're doing, to watch me. Someone wolf-whistles and the sound translates straight through me, to my hips and the muscles of my legs and I raise myself and spot the man who whistled me.

'Hello, gorgeous,' I say and pirouette once, twice, three times, and then I jump, back arched, to join the back of the queue to a round of applause and more whistling.

'Show off,' Nav tuts behind me.

He's right; I am a show off, an exhibitionist, an egotist. But to have people looking at me like they're looking at me right now is my fuel. My life is a show and I like it that way because it's the very opposite to *her* life. Margo got the luxury, the money and the safety, but I have the freedom.

'What's this play about anyway?' Nav says. 'The one you're tapping up Guy Harris for?'

'Rivalry,' I say.

I flash my best smile at the server as we move to order, and feel the ugly scar on the back of my neck tighten.

THREE

MARGO

It's Sunday and whilst David and Emmeline and the twins are eating the roast dinner that I prepared for them at home, I turn into the gravel drive of the Willows retirement village.

Granny's flat is on the ground floor because her legs are failing her now as well as her mind. She opens the door and smiles up at me and I feel guilty because I should make more effort to see her.

'Dove,' she says, because that's how she always greeted me and the warmness of her welcome makes me feel worse.

'Hello, Granny,' I say, and lean down to embrace her.

I remember when I was a girl that she was tall. Or is that my mind playing tricks? We're certain of a lot of things when we're younger but doubt ourselves later on. Are we truer when we're younger? Maybe Granny wasn't really so tall. I inhale her scent as I hug her and she smells of mothballs and lavender oil, and her white hair is thin in my face like spider silk.

'Come to the kitchen,' she says and I follow her along the thin corridor, to her tiny rose-wallpapered kitchen. 'Sit, sit – come and see my photo albums.'

On the small round table in the middle of the room is a hefty photograph album and I regard it with deep resignation. Granny loves looking at the photo albums. She has documented everything and everyone in her life with neat handwriting and it's a good thing too because she's forgotten where most of the pictures were taken, and who the people are in them, until I read them out aloud to her again. At least today she seems lucid – it's not always the case.

'I'll put the kettle on, Granny,' I say.

I'll need the caffeine to get through this next hour. My pills would have dulled the pain of looking through all these for the millionth time, but despite ordering an express ship-ment, they're now showing online as temporarily unavail-able. I ran out six days ago and I'm trying not to panic, but having them out of my system even for this short amount of time has resulted in a sharp and inclining headache and bouts of nausea.

'You're looking well,' Granny says admiringly. 'So smart with your hair done.'

I'm wearing a tailored navy jacket over a white shirt and skinny black jeans and glasses because my eyes are too sore to wear contacts – another side effect of being off the pills.

'I have to look nice for my job.'

I suppose it's because I'm a representative of an import-ant household. Occasionally Emmeline will have colleagues over for business meetings: leading professors in world economics, or we will entertain David's colleagues: barristers and judges. It's paramount that I am smart for every occasion they throw at me. Every six weeks I'm a new blonde, every year I have my teeth professionally whitened, every month my nails are done and three times every week, during term time, I swim, run or go to the gym.

'Are you a librarian, Margo?' Granny asks.

Not so lucid then. Perhaps it would help her if I saw more of her but I'm not sure it would help me.

'No, Granny. I'm a nanny. Remember? In Kensington?'

'Oh, yes,' she says.

I see her looking for her reading glasses and I reach for them on the little dresser behind her and hand them over. Everything in this little place came out of the 1970s house she lived in with Grandpa. The matching flower print crockery, her collection of jugs, the glass dresser with its tiny duck-egg blue drawers, the rickety oven that I pay extra for someone to clean and service before she can set fire to it. I look anew at it – there are tiny roses painted on the top. I've never noticed this detail before.

'Thank you, dove,' she says, putting on her glasses.

I put the kettle on, get out mugs.

'Your father rang me. From Switzerland. He said he might take up Nordic Walking.'

I busy myself making the tea but my heart swells for news of my parents. They've been in Switzerland for years though that hadn't been the original plan – they were grounded there unexpectedly. I'm glad they're getting out, getting fresh air. I remember the air in that house in the mountains became so stale.

'There you go, Granny,' I say, and put the cup on the table for her in case her fingers slip as I pass it. That's happened before.

'Get a biccie for us,' she says.

'I shouldn't.'

'There's nothing of you!'

I get the tin out of the cupboard. It's still the same one, round with illustrated ginger cats and rainbows. It was a present to her from me when I was seven and had saved my pocket money to buy it. The lid is bashed from years of use and doesn't close properly.

'Let me buy you a new tin?' I say.

She picks a biscuit that falls limp between her fingers. 'I like them soft. Oh! Did I tell you Julie died? She, Sybil and I are no longer the three musketeers. Six months ago. I must have told you?'

Has she told me? When did I last come? My visits here all slide into sepia recollections like all Granny's old albums. I look at her with pity – so many of her old friends are dying. It must be horrible to have your peers leave you; the loneliness must be crushing. I put my hand on hers, feel its softness. Granny's always looked after her hands.

'Are you OK?' I say.

She frowns. 'Why shouldn't I be?' she asks. 'Sit down and look at these pictures with me before our film.'

I can't delay the inevitable any longer. I pull up a chair and sit close to her.

'I got some new ones,' she says and she opens a page that she's bookmarked with a pizza delivery flier.

'You get takeaway pizzas here, Granny?' I smile at her.

'Is that what that is?' she says, vaguely.

She pulls out some loose photographs and hands them to me and I'm surprised to find that I haven't seen them before.

'Aren't they sweet? Look, that's you in the market when your dad was posted in Iran.'

I look closely. 'Oh yes.'

'And you on that horse you loaned at the stables when you were all in Doha,' she says. 'Or somewhere else? I can't remember where you all were and when.'

I can barely remember either. Dad had been a petroleum engineer and we were forever being posted somewhere exotic. Dad said moving around would broaden our childhood experience but I'm not sure it did anything but cause me anxiety. I look at the photograph of the girl on a bay horse. The horse was called Brew and she had a nasty attitude and kicked.

'Oh, you loved that horse,' Granny says.

'Yes.' I smile tightly but she can't see that it's not me.

'And you all with your mum,' she says. 'Not sure where that is.'

I look at the photo of us with our mother kneeling, enveloping us with her arms, and I'm hit by the memory of her smell – lemons and summer evenings.

'And this one,' Granny says. 'My favourite!'

It's a photograph of Cora and I can see why Granny likes it. Cora stands en pointe against a white brick wall, wearing a golden dress with thin straps and a skirt to the mid-calf. She's somewhere outside – the sun is in her eyes but the light enhances the amber in them.

'I remember your mother had this dress specially made,' Granny says. 'But for the life of me, I can't remember which performance it was for.'

There's something about this picture that I don't like. I stare harder at the dress and the gold of it flashes in my eye. 'I don't know either.'

'Well,' Granny beams. 'Isn't it nice to have these? Memories from a long time ago. I'll pop them into your bag, yes?'

'I—' But I trail off. 'OK.'

She gathers them up, and the photo disappears into the pile and into my bag.

FOUR

CORA

It's still dark but the rusty lights of the city bloom through the window and cast an orange glow around the room. My head is pounding. Did we drink a lot last night? Something hurts on my wrist and I see I've still got Guy's tie knotted tightly around it and my hand is a funny colour.

He enjoys tying me up to hotel bedposts: they all like my party trick, even the so-called gentlemen. The complexity of sexual desire is so intensely private and yet we crave to share it, to trust someone with our innermost fantasies. I'm the woman that can be trusted to say yes. Guy asked me if I wanted to be untied as we were falling asleep but I said no. I'm trained in keeping my body under control and the adult bladder can hold a lot of water. It's good practice for me to be disciplined, taut, and it unnerved him but I like unnerving people.

'Happy Tuesday,' I say.

'Good morning,' he says and he smiles without opening his eyes. 'What's the time?'

'Early,' I say, and gnaw at the binding. 'I'm going to fly out of the window in just a moment.'

He opens his eyes now and they're amber in this light. 'Like a witch?'

'Like a fucking lark, dick,' I say. 'It's a bird.'

He smiles. 'I know what a lark is.'

There's no pleading for me to stay but why would he? We both knew the arrangement when we met last night. I can't work the tie off my wrist so I lean over the bed and rummage in my bag with my free hand, pick up the penknife from inside and go to slit it.

'That's silk!' he protests.

'It *was* silk,' I correct.

'Why have you got a penknife in your bag?'

'For situations like this.'

The shreds of the tie slip to the floor and I twist my wrist around to get the blood flowing back to my hand before retrieving my clothes from around the room.

'You mean I'm not the only one?' he says, feigning hurt.

We both laugh, and I pull up my leggings, sling on my gold vest and leather jacket. I don't bother with my underwear, which I shove straight into my bag, because I dance better without underwear on.

'Good luck today,' he says.

'Thanks.'

'We have so much fun.'

'Call me,' I joke, and I shut the door behind me.

Out of the hotel I walk towards the main road. The silhouettes of the city are black against the rising dawn and I watch the sun waking up and changing the canvas of the sky from grey to indigo and then to pink. London is beautiful in this light. There are a few cyclists on the roads and people wearing gym clothes for early workouts.

Today is the day of the audition and I feel a shiver of excitement run through my body. I twist my wrist again. I'm lucky he didn't tie my legs. Did I want to be that person who slept their way to the top? No. I wanted to come to London and burst onto the stage like a shooting star, wanted to illuminate audiences with wonder and adoration. But I quickly came to rely on my charms over my talent. For me, the reliable way to keep visible was to literally claw up the trouser legs of important people. In return for a leg up in the industry, I gave both established and upcoming choreographers and directors a leg over. I stared them down in hotel rooms, glared at them in props cupboards whilst they shook with pleasure. I was good at being 'that girl'. I still am. Anything to enable me to dance.

I was four when my parents took us to see *The Nutcracker* on Christmas Eve in London. I remember that I sat mesmerised on my father's knee, in awe at the scenery and the costumes, but above all else, bewitched by the magic those dancers seemed to possess. My mother told me that I didn't talk until the theatre had all but emptied, that I had kept my eyes on the red velvet curtains in case the dancers came back. I remember willing them to reappear, but knowing that even if they didn't, I'd see them in my dreams that night and for every night after.

On Christmas Day I woke to the presents I'd asked for; a rainbow umbrella, a teddy with a locket around its neck, a doll on roller skates, but what I wanted above anything else, having seen that performance, was to learn how to dance.

My parents thought my obsession would be a passing phase but nonetheless indulged me and signed me up to a semester at a local stage school when we returned to Brazil, where we were then stationed. I fell in love with all the disciplines and I picked up routines and techniques quickly and with ease. I talked with my mouth full over dinner about dance. I read any book I could find about dancing, I put photographs up in my bedroom of all the famous dancers; Alessandra Ferri, Yvette Chauviré, Maria Alexandrova and Katherine Dunham. Every hour out of school I spent in studios and eventually my parents begun to realise that dance wasn't a phase; it was going to be my life. They bought me leotards to wear instead of leggings and training ballet shoes so I could practice pointe. They took me to the theatres to watch performances, let me watch infinite tutorial videos so I could practise steps at home. They took me to local competitions and I won them all.

I look up. How have I got myself here, to the Serpentine? Without the protection of brick and mortar, the wind kisses its cool breath on my face.

I see a woman ahead, sixties perhaps and comfortably rounded, standing by the edge of the lake. She's wearing a purple bathing suit and matching swimming hat that looks bruise-like against the white of her creped skin.

'Morning,' she says as I approach her.

'Hello.'

'Lovely morning for it.' She swings her arms above her shoulders in a circular motion. 'A swim at six-thirty and I'm set for the day.'

'I'm walking off a hangover.' And Guy. I have to walk him off like a hangover too.

She laughs. 'Careful of the edge then.'

'I'll be very careful,' I say, seriously.

'You don't swim?'

'I can swim,' I say because it's true; I've always liked the water, it's always felt safe to me. Surrounded, literally, in nature. 'But I don't like falling.'

She looks at me, oddly, and I wave goodbye.

The studio is large with light grey non-slip vinyl flooring, white walls, and a floor-to-ceiling mirror that spans the length of one side. There are six people already inside – three whose faces I see reflected in the mirror as I walk in, and three girls sitting along one wall in dance clothes. I look at them first because they're my competition, and my heart sinks because there's a girl I recognise here, Gisele Wu. She's a firecracker dancer, lithe and strong. We always seem to be up for the same parts and she seems to always get them. Beyond her is a blonde, like me, with brown polka-dot freckles on her face, and a girl with deep brown skin wearing a lime-green vest. I'm wearing a gold sequinned top and black leggings, my lucky gold bandanna, but how lucky will I be against them?

'Hello,' I say.

The three people on the chairs turn to look at me. Two women and a man that I know to be Jean-Luc.

'You're the wild card?' The older woman has spoken to me, looks to be in her late forties with an angular face and dyed plum hair pulled into an excellent tight chignon.

'Is that how Guy Harris described me?' I ask, amused.

'*Oui.*'

Jean-Luc is small and squat, bearded and bespectacled and wearing a farmer's flat cap and Nike trainers. He's nothing and everything I expected.

'Then, yes, I'm your wild card,' I say.

'*Bonjour.*'

'*Bonjour,*' I reply.

'You are French?' Jean-Luc asks, looks surprised.

'I'm a cocktail of English and Swiss-French.'

'You are unusual looking,' he says, sweeping his eyes over me.

Comments like this are commonplace in the industry. What you look like can tip the balance on whether or not you're awarded a part – a chorus line of girls must always match in height and weight, must melt into one another so that an audience is never jarred. A prima ballerina must have the looks to suit her role.

I flash Jean-Luc a smile because I can afford grace in my acceptance of his comment. Ice-white blonde with sepia eyes, high sharp cheekbones, and small straight teeth. I have confidence in the way I look, even though Nav tells

28

me it's not confidence but arrogance. Whatever it is I need to wring it dry by the end of this audition.

'*Bon*,' Jean-Luc says. 'Cora, meet Joanna, our director.'

The woman who described me as the 'wild card' is Joanna.

'And this is Rosa,' Jean-Luc gestures to the younger woman sitting beside him. 'She is narrating Eliza.'

Rosa is slightly younger than me but of similar build, slender and small with dark elvish features. She waves.

'*Salut*,' I say to the both of them.

'*Asseyez-vous*. Please sit.'

I walk quickly and soundlessly across the floor towards the other dancers.

'You are all here because you've been recommended for this role, *oui*? *Mirror, Mirror* is a little-known play about rivalry, deception and trickery, but above all – losing everything. It mirrors its turbulent decade, the Great Depression, a sense of oncoming war.'

No one talks of the great things of the 1930s, I think out of the blue. Amelia Earhart was the first woman to fly solo across the Atlantic Ocean, Monopoly was invented. It was the decade of Al Capone, Bonnie and Clyde, Superman made an appearance in a comic. *The Wizard of Oz* was made and the AA was founded. I know strange things.

'This is a stressful piece on the body,' Jean-Luc continues. 'It's outside the box for classical and neoclassical repertoire, so if any of you are successful in this audition, it means working harder on your cross training schedules, *d'accord*?

There's some interesting choreography but it's demanding on various muscle groups.'

We all nod.

'*Mirror, Mirror* is intimate; has only three speaking parts and three dancers. The speaking parts are static narrators, and the dancers are the expression of what the character is really feeling, *comprendez*? The dancer is the subconscious and the ego, it can be in rage even when the words are spoken as calm, *oui*? Today you are all here to dance, Eliza. She is the heart, the soul, the lead. Rosa here is Eliza's narrator.'

Eliza. My part. I already think of it as mine, it's been mine ever since my childhood dance mentor first told me its story.

'We're doing something a little different with this audition,' Joanna says. 'We want you dancers to interpret a scene we give you and choreograph yourselves. That's how we're going to decide this role. On technique and feeling the passion of the piece.'

I glance at the other dancers, and am pleased that they look uncertain at this. I, however, am delighted because I've spent years studying this play and wishing for it to be produced by someone like Jean-Luc, and now here is my chance.

Joanna gives us each a printed piece of paper and a pencil. 'The piece we've chosen for you to dance is where Eliza is going to meet her rival for the first time in years,' she says. 'You have fifteen minutes to read the text and plan a movement and then we start.'

I skim it quickly.

It is winter and my tongue is cold. I cannot tell this story alone. Sit down and warm my hands. You were there, you remember.

I love the rhythm of the piece, the words, the drama.

It could have been something wonderful, couldn't it? A life where we weren't locked in crisis.

Jean-Luc claps his hands. 'You must all go outside of the room and we will call you when we are ready, *oui*?'

We nod collectively and walk outside the studio with our paper and settle ourselves in various places along the corridor. I watch the others read through the script and make notes with their pencils, watch their arms move above their heads and their legs raise and flex to stretch and prepare for jumps. I do none of these things. I fold my script to make an origami crane. A long time ago a boy taught me how to make them and I've never forgotten how to do it, just like I've never forgotten him. He had green eyes and a smile that lit up my heart.

Fifteen minutes pass quickly and then we're called one by one to dance. I'm last to take the floor and I walk into the studio to see the other dancers sitting along the wall. I don't care if they're watching; in fact it makes it more dramatic for me to have an audience. I pick up a spare chair from the back of the room and walk to the middle of the room opposite Jean-Luc and Joanna, flick my origami crane over so that it lands at Jean-Luc's feet. I see him bend at the waist to retrieve it in curiosity.

'What is this?' he says.

'The Japanese refer to the crane as the "bird of happiness".'

31

'You are part Japanese too?' he says with an arch of a smile.

'It's believed that if you fold a thousand cranes your wishes will come true.'

'And what is your wish?' he says.

'That you pick me,' I grin.

Choose me.

I see the blonde girl raise her eyebrows. She's jealous of my trick and that's exactly what it is – a trick designed to create intrigue around me before I've even begun. You need to be remembered in this industry because there are always people backed up to replace you. Jean-Luc places the crane on his knee and then gestures to me that the floor is mine. I spin the chair on its leg three times and then place it down with a bang and then I sit on it and smile at Jean-Luc.

'OK?' he says.

'I'm ready,' I say.

I *know* this play. I am the girl who wears the gold silk dress.

'So,' he says, looks to Rosa who nods at him and then at me. 'Begin.'

Rosa begins. '*It is winter and my tongue is cold. I cannot tell this story alone. Sit down and warm my hands. You were there, you remember. It could have been something wonderful, couldn't it? A life where we weren't locked in crisis.*'

She speaks with a beautifully husky timbre, gives the words life. I could work with her, but I would work with anyone, given the chance.

I raise my knees from the floor and bend my head to them so I'm tucked on the chair seat before snapping my head up, looking squarely at Jean-Luc and then extend my arms outward and splaying my legs open.

'*Oh, mine was a life of a thousand possibilities but you took the one meant for me.*'

I pull my limbs in, ground my feet to the floor and then I lean forward and stand from the chair, twirl around it whilst my knuckles stay white around its back. I keep my eyes forward and then round it again, one working leg drawing a circular path. Rosa continues her monologue.

'*How were you the chosen one?*'

I turn my body into a question mark whilst en pointe.

Perhaps it's not your fault? Perhaps it's mine? Perhaps I would never have kept him tangled in silk sheets in my bed. Perhaps he would have always cut through them to get to you.

I turn my head, am stock-still.

But still, after all this time, I wonder how I can get him back. Sometimes I imagine that I cut you to get to him.

Oh, how this play mirrored so many feelings in my life. Something is building inside of me. I start moving across the entire room, switch leap into the air, and then a stag leap forward, straight into Jean-Luc and Joanna, up into their faces, and they sit back in alarm before I start spinning away again, face and arms upward to the ceiling.

Rosa sees the chaos of my movements and her intonation becomes angry.

He was everything and you took him.

I fall to the floor, my hands outwards and I move myself across the ground like liquid before I claw up to the chair, jump in second position behind it so my body resembles scissors.

Try to throw me beneath waves, try to drown me. But you owe me, friend.

Up and down the studio floor I dance with ferocity, with my very soul because what else have I got to convince them? What have I got to lose? I've never wanted anything as much as this. My muscles strain with every acute angle, every complex step, but I keep dancing until the flood tide; I lean forward and then snap backward, my body tugging against itself and then I hear someone screaming and the sound of something clattering to the floor. I stop dead and a beat passes before I realise the scream has come from me. I glance at Rosa but she's staring at me, isn't speaking any other lines. I can't even be sure she spoke any at all. There's silence and I blink, feel like I'm floating down into myself from a height. I'm on the floor, face up and spread, and my body is shaking.

'Wow.'

Who spoke? I try to extricate myself from the moment of being her, Eliza. I'm panting in the middle of a very still room and the lights are bright in my eyes. My skin prickles with gooseflesh, like I've returned fully from being elsewhere and not inside my own body. I sit up.

'Wow.'

The voice belonged to Jean-Luc.

'That was—' Joanna pauses. 'Incredible.'

'It worked,' Jean-Luc says. 'So did the chair throwing.'

I turn my head, see that there's an upside-down chair on the floor a metre from me. Where did it come from? I threw the chair? I've never done that before.

'Strong,' Jean-Luc says. 'Very strong.'

I smile at them. 'OK. Good.'

I walk to the wall for my bag where the other dancers sit and the black girl smiles at me.

'That's your part,' she says. 'No question.'

Yes, I think. *Yes*. I look to Jean-Luc who is staring at me.

'Thank you everyone for your time,' he says. 'We'll let you know as soon as we have decided.'

We all pick up our bags and start to leave the studio.

'Cora,' Jean-Luc calls. 'Can you wait behind a moment?'

I pause by the door, come back to stand in front of him and Joanna and Rosa.

'You've done your homework on this part,' Jean-Luc says.

'I love this play.'

'So I can see,' he says. 'But you see, we've also done our homework on *you*.'

I blink.

'And although you have talent – that much is obvious – we've been told you're "unreliable".'

I grit my teeth. Fucking Guy Harris had to tell them that? It's true that I've been cast in shows before and failed to see them through but there's always been a reason for why, not that I can ever explain it to anyone. The weakness I have is for me only to bear.

'Will you be unreliable with us?' he says.

35

'No.'

'Because I don't believe in second chances,' he says.

I do. That's why I'm here.

'But there is something . . .' He pauses. 'Special about you. This part . . . it would mean a lot to you?'

'Yes,' I say.

Because it's not only about wanting this part; it's about *needing* this part. Nine years ago, this *was* my part. I can close my eyes and still smell that theatre; the scent of hairspray blended with thick make-up, Tiger Balm and Deep Heat. I can smell sweat under lights, the dust of the stage. There were agents in the audience and they were all mine for the taking. I wore that gold dress when I was eighteen but I never danced the second act. I need to prove to myself that I can do it, need to prove it to Miss Patricia, my old dance mentor. I need to launch myself into the career I should have had all those years ago.

'Cora?'

I snap back to Jean-Luc.

'You are our Eliza.'

I beam at him and then at Joanna and Rosa. 'You won't regret it,' I say. 'I promise.'

'Gisele will understudy you. *Comprends?*'

I skip out of the door. I need to get high, I need someone to fuck me. I'll call Guy.

'Fuck you, world, and fuck you, Margo,' I whisper into the sky. 'It's my time and no one can stop me now.'

FIVE

MARGO

I put my hairbrush down, look at myself in the vanity mirror.

'You look nice,' a voice says.

Marie is standing at my door. Six years old and candy-floss sweet in rocket pyjamas that belong to her twin but that she prefers for herself.

'Thank you, lovely,' I say, though I feel far from it. I feel constantly sick from coming off the pills so suddenly, and although they now have an updated delivery date of two weeks' time, getting through each day without any has been excruciating. Last week I went to three pharmacies and bought over-the-counters, but they're not strong enough.

'Are you going out?' Marie asks.

'Yes,' I say. 'And you should be in bed.'

'Can you read to me? Before you go?'

I reach out to her. 'Come here.'

She comes over and together we sit on the chair that the children call 'The Duvet'. I don't know how it's ended up in my little room because it's expensive, a wedding present to David and Emmeline, but perhaps it looks too old now and isn't in keeping with the rest of the decor. It's cream and plush and has been sat in so many times that the seat is dented and the arms are frayed but it feels like a comforting friend and somewhere I can pull my feet up away from monsters. Which is a ridiculous thing to say because everything in this house is beyond what most people would describe as comfortable. And there aren't any monsters.

'What do you want to read?'

'St Faith's?' Marie suggests.

'It's not very representative of boarding school,' I say because I should know. No ginger beer or midnight swims in the pool or good-natured hockey games. No, there were competitive, ugly tricks. 'How about some poetry?'

She looks doubtful but then nods because she knows she's on borrowed time and should be in bed.

'OK,' she concedes.

I pick a book from the shelf. *The Book of Flowers.*

'How about this one,' I say. '*Gather the early dewdrops of summer and wear them like a crown. Run through the wilderness so your feet are stuck with earth. Find him in the harebell, and purple ragged robin, and you can make him your prince. Together you are invincible under cloud-scudded skies.*'

Something about this poem feels familiar.

'It doesn't rhyme?' Marie says.

'No,' I say.

'I don't like it. Can't we have St Faith's?'

I breathe in the scent of the vanilla-pod shampoo that I carefully washed through her beautiful dark hair in the bath tonight.

'Not St Faith's,' I say. 'Something else?'

'Can we have the book about the dancing mice?' she suggests. 'You like that one!'

'I do like that one.'

'It's because you know lots about dancing,' she says.

'I know some things.'

'I told Barbie you were a dancer,' she says and smiles up at me.

'Yes, she asked me about it on the boat. But remember, dove, that that was a long time ago and I've forgotten it all now.'

'Isn't it like riding a bike?' she asks. 'Why would you forget?'

'You need constant practice,' I say. 'Are you going to get the book?'

She slides from my lap. 'Or, we can dress up in some of the dancing dresses you have?'

'Not tonight—' I say but she's already bounding to my closet. 'Marie?'

'The red one in the box? Up at the top. Or the blue one with frills. The purple one? And the shoes, can we wear the shoes?'

The dresses are from cabaret shows, contemporary performance pieces and the shoes are tap shoes and she likes the clicking but they're not mine. I get up to close the closet because it's late and because I don't want to make up any more reasons why I don't dance any more, but before I can reach her she's spun away, a little bored sprite, whirling about my room with her hand splayed and jangling the porcelain blind pulls, tugging at the cord of my white towelling robe on the bedpost. I pick up everything after her, as always, until she stops.

'Oh!' she says. 'You look so pretty in this picture!'

She's at my bedside cabinet, has picked up a photo from the pile from Granny's. I know immediately without looking, which picture she's referring to.

'That's not me,' I say.

'Have you got this yellow dress in your box?' She's not listening. 'It's so pretty.'

'Marie?' Emmeline says.

Emmeline is standing at the doorway wearing a blue lace-capped dress and gold hoop earrings and bangles all the way up her arms; Tiffany, Pandora, Monica Vinader, lots of power women because she is a powerful woman.

'You should be in bed,' she says to Marie. 'Margo is going out.'

Marie knows when Emmeline's word is final. She hands me the photo and I shove it in the back of my jeans.

I look at Emmeline. 'I was—'

'She takes a mile, that one,' Emmeline says. 'Are you off out now?'

'Yes.'

'Thank you for your work on the meal tonight,' she says. 'The table looks beautiful.'

'You're welcome. I hope you enjoy it.'

Tonight David and Emmeline are hosting a dinner party for twelve. I've cooked a three-course meal, have laid the table in the dining room with the best porcelain and lit jasmine-scented candles. I've cleaned the house from top to bottom, have taken delivery of the five arrangements of flowers from the local florist, have hung out matching blue and white towels in the four bathrooms, have spot-checked for anything that could be out of place and now I loiter in my room, knowing that I'll have to leave soon because Emmeline has asked me to go out this evening.

'Right,' Emmeline says. 'I'm going down. I'll be leaving in the morning to see my sister in Suffolk. Her health has unfortunately taken a downturn.'

'Oh,' I say. 'I'm sorry.'

I don't ask questions; Emmeline finds it painful to talk about her sister's breakdown. I find it difficult to talk of my own. I used to have lots when I wasn't on the pills. I bite at my lip, immediately anxious I'll have some sort of paralyzing seizure when I'm out because they're still not here.

'Tomorrow David will take the kids out for breakfast but can you take them in the afternoon?' she asks. 'I know he's got some work to finish.'

'Sure.'

'Have a lovely evening.'

I nod enthusiastically but as she turns to leave, my heart sinks with the dread of going out. A Friday night in London is for groups of friends, for lovers, for raucous parties and not for loners. Does Emmeline think I have

41

friends? A lover? I want to ask her if I can stay in the house but she'll think that strange or she might take it as an invasion of their privacy or an insult to her generosity in giving me an evening to myself, and I can't afford to lose my place here with them. David and Emmeline and the children are too precious to me.

I take the bus to the city centre and queue for a ticket for *The Mask of Orpheus* at the Coliseum. I edge into the darkened auditorium, lower myself into the seat as it starts. I've bought a ticket for the first row so I can immerse myself in the production. I need to relax because I'm so tense. I'm over-thinking and over-analysing everything. Am I sitting too close to the woman next to me? Is my handbag in the way of anyone? Can I get out if I need to? I inhale, exhale. I'll be OK, I think, but I can feel myself beginning to overheat.

The orchestra finishes its introduction and I lean back to watch the chorus line of girls as they dance onto the stage, perfectly matched in white. Watching them feels like breathing clean air. Ballet has always been my favourite discipline because there are strict rules and there is also underlying secret pain. Ballet feels like how I feel in my own skin – outwardly calm, but on the inside, an anxious storm. I like knowing that however serene a dancer looks on stage, those innocent-looking silk shoes hide broken bones and stress fractures, which can get worse over time because self-treatment is normal in ballet – no one wants to be cast aside and lose their role. It's commonplace for dancers to wrap their feet in tape, to cover their toes with glue to make them stick when they're en pointe. Some even take scissors to their feet.

I miss dancing but I could never have handled it as a career. I couldn't have handled the extreme pressure, the rejections. I was never Cora, alive on stage and glittering.

People assume that identical twins are close but it's not so with Cora and me. I am the Yin to Cora's Yang, the shade to her sun, the introvert to her extrovert, and it was always this way from the moment we were born. I was the baby who sat still and watched as she clambered over furniture and tried to crawl up the fire chute. I was the toddler who looked both ways at the road when Cora leapt from the kerb, the little girl who listened to teachers when Cora wrote notes, the teenager who lied when Cora jumped from our dormitory window to meet boys. I'm the older twin by three minutes and I wonder if in those moments I made a pact with some god to take on the world's burdens so she wouldn't have to shoulder them. I remember her saying to me once that because I worried about everything so much, she was free of any of it. And I just agreed, didn't even try and unload some of the worry because what would be the use? I would worry that she wouldn't worry *enough* about the things that needed extra attention. So I worried for the both of us about the state of our bedroom, our homework, our exams, what she was eating, what she wasn't eating. I worried when she went riding her bike or a horse because she always rode both far too fast. I worried about her dancing. I worried when she submerged in the river when we were ten because we were trying to hold our breath. I worried when I didn't have anything to worry about.

The skin on the back of my neck prickles and I turn my head to the right, look down the row. Is someone watching me? But no, everyone is facing forward, lit up by lights. No one is watching me. I lean back again, heart thudding. No, I think. The theatre is my happy place, isn't it? Dancing, I loved dancing. I loved watching Cora dance.

At the end of the performance I clap hard, too hard for my hands because they feel tingly and raw, and when the curtains fall for the last time, I find my jaw hurts because I've clenched it throughout the show. As the lights come up I look at my watch, see that it's only ten-thirty, and feel anxious. Emmeline won't expect me back so soon. I go to the bar, order a glass of red wine and stare at my phone, hope to slip into invisibility. It's loud in here with conversation and perfume and that's good because I don't want silence.

'Great show.'

I look up at a man who's standing next to me at the bar.

'Yes,' I say. 'It was amazing.'

'Are you waiting for someone?' the man asks.

'I'm by myself.' I regret my admission because his eyes light up.

'Do you want to come over for a drink?'

He looks over his shoulder and I follow his eyes, see that he's come from a table of friends; two other men and a woman all of whom are beautifully dressed in tailored suits and dresses. I feel immediately intimidated, glance down at my jeans and cream blouse. Marie told me I looked nice but I feel self-conscious.

'Go on,' the man says. 'Join me in a glass of wine.'

'You get in first, and if there's room I'll join you,' I hear myself say.

He laughs. Perhaps he thinks that I've made this up myself when it was a quip from W.C. Fields. I'm not a funny person – humour was always Cora's comfort zone. I've answered how she would have done because I'm thinking of her.

The man reaches out his hand. 'Do you want to come?'

But I shake my head. 'No,' I say. 'I've got to go now.'

'OK. Social butterfly, are you?'

I smile, but his comment couldn't be further than the truth. I'm scared of butterflies. I recall visiting a zoo hot-house as a child, was excited to see the 'fairies' as our mother called them, but when we went inside, to my horror the butterflies were huge, exotic nightmares fluttering above my head and I ducked and screamed and swiped before Mother took me out, red-faced with embarrassment. Was it Mother? Granny? I can't remember. All I recall is the acute shame of being an embarrassment.

I slide from the stool and go outside, and as I walk I feel something crunch in my pocket; I'd forgotten that I'd pocketed the picture before I came out tonight. I take it out and stare at Cora wearing the beautiful gold silk dress. I can see her in my mind's eye, on stage in this dress, and I try to remember which dance this was from, but my mind draws a blank. I fold the photo, go to put it into my bag, when I see that there's writing on the back of it that sends a cold barb straight to my heart.

I know you will like this one. Axx

It's Annie's writing, but our little sister is dead.

SIX

CORA

I've been invited to a cast dinner at Jean-Luc's Pimlico house and I've dressed the part. I'm wearing a low-cut shimmering bronze dress that cost an arm and a leg, my black leather jacket, and have painted my eyes dark and smoky. I chain my bike to the black railings, flick my hair over my head to volumise my helmet hair, and fish out a bottle of wine whilst exchanging my trainers for six-inch blue heels. I walk up to a charcoal-painted door and ring its bell and, while I wait, I rub some cocaine onto my gums. I need to be on fire tonight and I don't have the energy to muster it myself.

The door opens just as I'm finished, and Jean-Luc smiles at me.

'You cycled over?' he says.

'I know.' I grimace. 'This dress is borderline offensive even without adding the bike to the mix.'

He laughs and I like the sound of it; a guttural toad-like rasp.

'*Entrez!*' he says. 'Come in out of the cold! You are the last.'

He kisses both my cheeks and the smell of expensive-brand aftershave applied with gusto inhibits my nose.

'Am I late?'

I made an effort not to be but I'm often late for everything. It's an inexcusable fact that I use to excuse myself.

Jean-Luc nods. '*Oui*, you are.'

'Shit, sorry,' I say and step through to the hallway where a blast of colour dazzles my eyes. A Hockney print in the hallway as tall as me.

'Let me take your coat,' he offers and I shrug myself out of it, follow him along a corridor with gold-framed musical posters and dancers to a kitchen which is the size of Nav's flat. It's all white; white cabinets and soft grey-white wooden flooring and a huge glass dining table. Twisted silver metal has been shaped into fish, which swim along the walls towards the French windows, and lead out to what looks like a boxy manicured urban garden outside. I blink. Are the fish actually swimming? Maybe I should have held off on the coke.

Jean-Luc smiles. 'Everyone, this is our tragic heroine Eliza, Cora Devaux!'

There are ten people sitting around the table and they simultaneously look up at me and I feel a thrill of pride because I am her – I am Eliza. I lift my hand in a wave and they all smile.

Jean-Luc gestures to a girl dressed in a woodland-green silk top adorned with gold-buttoned cuffs. 'Take a seat between Sophie and Zdravko, *oui*?' he says. 'She is Eliza's rival and Zdravko is Eliza's ex-boyfriend.'

I don't need to be told the story. It's about a messy love triangle – just like my real life.

I walk round and sit down.

'Not sure we should be sitting together,' Sophie says. She's cute, has a button nose and curls the colour of brown sugar. 'Given what happens between us in the play.'

'But everyone likes the villain,' I say. 'Don't worry.'

She laughs. 'But I think that's you?'

'You're right,' I say. 'It is.'

'Jean-Luc told us how amazing your audition was,' she says.

'I've studied *Mirror, Mirror* for a very long time. I had a dance mentor who played Eliza years ago. She was obsessed with it.'

'Really?' Sophie says. 'That's awesome. I'd never heard of it before my agent put me up for it. Who was your mentor?'

'She was once a prima ballerina for Zurich,' I say. 'Her name was Patricia Bergen, but I doubt you would have heard of her.'

Sophie shakes her head. 'No?'

'She had to retire early because of an injury,' I say. 'Her sister was actually more famous. She married Patricia's dance partner. Who also happened to be Patricia's husband.'

'Ouch,' Sophie says.

'Double whammy.' I laugh. 'She was mad about that for a loooong time. She probably still is.'

I see Miss Patricia in my mind's eye – prim, early forties, petite and blue-eyed, with dimples in her cheeks. She always wore her hair in a slick bun and clacked around in pretty court shoes. She became a Mary Poppins to our family when Margo and I were two and our mother was pregnant with Annie. Mother was anxious for more help because we were about to jet away to Brazil for a couple of years for our father's work, and Miss Patricia passed the test of folding our clothes with military precision, making shortbread, singing songs. Far from her old life as a dancer. Until we were thirteen and sent to boarding school in the UK, Patricia travelled the world with us and taught us all how to diamond jump, how to spot, how to arch, how to *feel* a piece of drama, and how to translate words to our bodies. Most of my technique was – and still is – thanks to Miss Patricia's discipline.

'I'm bricking it over this play to be honest,' Gisele says across the table. 'And I'm only the understudy!'

'Let's get pissed.' I wink at her.

'That sounds like a very good idea,' Zdravko says from my other side.

I turn to face him. He's tall and graceful, and even under the white shirt he's wearing, I can tell his body is honed to the highest level of what ballet asks for. His face is striking with sharp angles and hooded brown eyes.

'You have a beautiful name,' I say.

'Thank you,' he says. 'It is Slovenian. But it is not so beautiful when I try and spell it on the phone.' He smiles, two big goofy front teeth that gives his angular face surprising warmth.

'So you're my terrible ex?'

'Or am I?' a voice asks from opposite. A black man from across the table grins at me. 'I'm Cal, his narrator.'

'I love how confusing this is,' I say. 'Two people for one part.'

Like Margo and me, I think. We should have been one person.

Jean-Luc stands at the head of the table, has bottles lifted in each hand. 'Indeed,' he says. 'A play of doubles and hidden meanings and truths. You and Rosa, Sophie and Ivana, the rival. And Zdravko and Cal, the dastardly ex-boyfriend. And all our beautiful understudies, *oui*? And myself and Joanna. And so it begins and I'm incredibly excited for it. This dinner marks the first night of the three months we'll be working together. We have reviewers coming for a couple of our rehearsals. Photos. Early marketing from *Dance*, *In Step*, *Filmmaker Magazine*.'

'That's . . . unusual?' Cal says.

'That's amazing!' Ivana exclaims at the same time.

'It is both unusual and amazing. But this play is special, *non*?' Jean-Luc says. 'I've put in capital for it because I believe that it deserves recognition and a build-up. Joanna knows a lot of journalists – Hazel O'Mara, Kaito Kobayashi. And it is important to create early buzz around a project. But, *ecoutez*, listen. It is a demanding schedule, *d'accord*? If you're on schedule, it's nine in the morning until five at night and, by next week, I want lines learnt and dancers ready.'

'A toast to our new family,' Joanna says. 'And to this brilliant play.'

A new beginning. I raise my glass for a toast and glassware clinks around the room. Am I going to be able to do this?

'Of course you are!' Sophie says next to me and I realise I've spoken aloud.

I smile at her. 'We'd better not screw it up, right?'

Dinner is produced seemingly out of the air, brought in by three men in black suits. Truffle-oil pasta, sea bream with potatoes and steaming spring greens.

'Here,' Zdravko says and he hands me a bowl of broccoli. I can smell that it's sautéed in garlic. 'The best test for us as dance partners is garlic.'

For the next few hours we play games around the table and get to know each other better. Cute narcissistic monologues, truths and lies.

'I once French kissed a camel,' Cal says.

'Lie, Cal,' Gisele says, laughs.

'Well, it's half a lie because I did kiss one,' Cal says. 'But I didn't use tongues. It was for an advert and it was fucking gross and the money wasn't even good.'

'When I was little I got my head stuck in the railings at the Tower of London and my aunt had to ring the fire brigade,' Mia, Sophie's understudy, says.

'I hope that's true,' Rosa says.

'True,' Mia laughs.

The evening goes on and becomes everything I love about being in this industry – casual name-dropping, ill-informed and lazy statements about arts and culture, politics and literature, and gossip. Lashings of it. It gets to ten o'clock, then eleven, and I watch as people get more drunk, more sloppy, start slurring, leering but I'm used to drinking a lot. The coke has helped me stay awake. I see everything – I always see everything. Annie's face in the dark.

I jolt out of myself. Why am I thinking of Annie, of that night? Because of the play? For the first time I wonder if it was the right thing to have chased this role but no, I have to do this. Destiny and all that.

'Your turn,' Jean-Luc says, the first thing he's said in a long time and its only when the room goes quiet that I realise he's talking to me.

'My turn, what?'

'A truth about yourself,' Cal says.

'I can't think of anything,' I shrug.

'Everyone has a story,' he says.

'I was almost paralysed,' I say. 'From the neck down.'

I don't even know why I've started to share this story when I have reels of them, lies mostly, catalogued for situations exactly like this, but I bend my head and sweep away my hair from the back of my neck. I can hear them all gasp as they look at the knotted white scar that spans three inches of it.

'Shit,' Rosa breathes.

'What happened?' Zdravko asks.

'An accident,' I say. 'When I was younger.'

The room has gone quiet. They want to know more, how it happened, but I'm silent. Why did I say it when I've all but brick-walled it away?

'That looks like a horrific injury,' Jean-Luc says. 'This is why you want to dance so much, *oui*?'

'Yeah,' I say. 'Because I didn't know if I'd ever be able to chase my dream. But I did. I'm here.'

But it's more than that of course. It's my private revenge.

'I'll toast that!' Sophie raises her glass and the others follow suit. Our glasses all clink over the white linen and I give them my best smile and the weight of my truth lifts from their eyes and the game goes on.

The evening at Jean-Luc's ends after midnight but I'm not going home yet. No, I have an obligation to fulfil. 'Part two' with Guy Harris.

I push the door open to the nightclub where he said he'd be and immediately my eyes are assaulted by blue and purple neon against black walls. It's a pulsating bruise of a room but we both like clubs like this; thudding vibrations through my chest as I follow the snaking corridor and push the door open through to the main bar. A heady cocktail of sweat, booze and bodily fluid hits me full in the face because it's *that* kind of a club. There are dirty glass chandeliers and black walls and a smell of coconut oil. Mirrors line every wall, even the bar.

A few lone younger men and many more old ones scatter the bar and the girls employed by the club skip among them, and around the small sticky stage where they dance lazily around greased poles. They are all adorned with lace and tassels, glitter and sequins, belts and whips, and are all slender and toned with huge breasts, but their defining piece of covering is that they're all wearing black gothic masks. I wonder if they give the girls comfort so they can pretend to be someone else for the night, their identities protected even when their bodies aren't. They hang around necks, and plant whispers in ears, drape themselves over knees and kiss cheeks and pour themselves champagne and smile and laugh when they're supposed to. I know how to play that part too.

Guy walks towards me with a cocktail in each hand. 'You had a good night at Jean-Luc's?'

I take the drink offered to me. 'I should be buying these. You won me that role – even if you did tell them I'm unreliable.'

'I don't want my reputation on the line, Cora. I had to tell them you've got a fancy for flight but I also told them that you're probably the most passionate dancer I know.'

'In and out of bed.'

He grins. 'I'll drink to that.'

We drink together.

'But you won that part on your own merit,' he says. 'Just don't fuck it up.'

'I won't. Come dance with me.'

I should be resting, should be sleeping, but for the next two hours we dance together. I lead him easily, turn in and out of his body like a leaf in the wind. I'm better than any of the girls on that stage and everyone knows it. Guy's dark eyes are like black saucers and he smiles. He's smooth and strong and although I can't hear it, I can see the laughter on his face and I think I'm laughing too but I don't feel like laughing. I need more to drink. I'm surrounded by people, am wrapped up in Guy's arms but I feel oddly alone. I'm thinking of the part, of the words.

Mine was a life of a thousand possibilities but you took the one meant for me.

I put my lips close to Guy's ear. 'Let's go,' I say and then I bite it gently.

As I pull away from him, I look over his shoulder and catch eyes with a woman across the room. She stands by the bar, wearing jeans and a T-shirt and her hair is dark with soft curls.

'Annie?'

'What?'

I race forward, nearly crash into one of the waitresses with a tray of drinks.

'Hey!' she squeals as we spin to avoid each other. 'Watch it!'

'Sorry,' I say and I go to run on to the bar but the woman is gone. I look around for her, into the club's shadowy corners but she's disappeared.

'What was that?' Guy says as I return. 'You almost took that waitress' eye out!'

'I thought – I thought there was someone I used to know. By the bar.'

'Who?' he says.

I pause. 'Never mind, it wasn't her.'

Because it can't be her, of course. Why did I think that could be possible? I'm hallucinating – there are too many chemicals flooding my brain. Annie is not here, will never be standing by that bar. I start to laugh, spooked by my own game playing, and I must sound weird because Guy puts his hand on my arm and actually looks concerned.

'Are you OK?' he asks.

'Couldn't be better.' I pull his face towards me, flick my tongue into his mouth.

Annie, my shining star. How I loved her. How I suffocated her with my love.

SEVEN

MARGO

The entirety of Annie's existence is a blurred tangle of memories. I remember little things about her, like that she picked up bugs and beetles on walks, that she loved watching the gymnasts when the Olympics came round, that she had dark hair which she cut the fringe of when she was ten and it regrew upwards for months and we called her – though not unkindly – 'Troll', like the nineties dolls with colourful sticking-up hair. But the fact is that even if I wanted to, I can't remember the big things – I can't remember how Annie died, where she was, where *I* was.

Why have I never searched for the answers to these questions? I know that in the year after the accident, when Cora and I were eighteen, we stayed in our parents' house in Switzerland, but it became like a tomb. Grief hung like shrouds in every corner and we all moved around each other in silence. After months of unrelenting mourning, Cora decided she wanted to leave and return to the UK, so I – of course – went with her. One night, we just left that house and I can't even remember saying goodbye to our parents. I only remember that we sat on a train from Paris to London and Cora made me swear that dragging ourselves back to the past wasn't helpful in any way. We would build something of ourselves in the city. And so we did and somehow the years have passed and I realise that nine years is such a long time to lock someone away in a corner of a mind.

It's been two days since I saw the writing on the back of that photograph, and during the forty-eight hours, I've been on my laptop writing Annie's name in every search engine I can find but there's nothing written anywhere to give me any clue as to what happened. She used to have social media platforms but they've disappeared, and as a child she was once in local papers for awards she'd won at dance, art, drama, but none of those seem to exist. My head is banging with the effort of my searching, amplified by the lack of pills. It would have been sensible to try to rest, but I've decided to come to Granny's again. I've put the picture down to being one that Annie had that has somehow worked its way here from years ago, but I'd be lying if I told myself it hadn't upset me and I want to see if Granny has other pictures, and, more importantly, answers.

'I put the apples there.'

Granny, who looks cross, folds her arms across her chest and then stares at the table.

'Sorry?' I say.

'The apples should be in the bowl like always.'

She stares accusingly at the space where I assume the fruit bowl must be in her head. She never has fruit because she forgets about it and it rots.

'Will you buy me some?'

I exhale. She's disorientated, and having a bad day, but I want to probe her. 'Has Cora been to see you?' I say. 'Was it her that left the photos for me?'

She frowns. 'Maybe she brought me apples?'

I grit my teeth. I thought we'd agreed that Cora wouldn't visit unless it's Granny's birthday or another special occasion where we can go together. I like to keep an eye on my sister because she always confuses Granny; she's too loud and too jumpy, like a puppy.

'Has she left anything else?' I say.

'I get lots of letters,' Granny says sniffily. 'People write to me, you know. I still know people who aren't dead! Oh! Did I tell you about Julie?'

I try to hide my mounting frustration. 'Yes.'

'She wants your number,' Granny says. 'Not Julie because Julie's dead, and don't you forget it. Your *sister* wants it.'

I frown. 'But she's got my number,' I say and then I sigh.

Unless Cora has lost her phone again and got a new number because she's forever dropping handsets in gutters, down toilets, or losing them in apartments where she's spent a night but never has any intention of going back.

'Oh, heavens, I don't know what you're talking about. I'm just a messenger.' Granny huffs, holding out a pen. 'I need your number and your address, please, dove.'

I nod but I won't leave either with her because I've made that mistake before and Granny has ended up calling me over and over, tying up both our phone lines for hours. I had to change my number. There's no way I'd be giving her Emmeline and David's home number or their address for that matter.

I suddenly wish I was back at the Kensington house. Now the children are back at school my working days are busy; I need to organise their school bags and sort the lunches for the week and iron the sports kits. I need to rearrange the weekly riding lessons for Marie, pay for Jonny's drum lessons, sign up to swimming again for the both of them and then update the huge planner calendar on the kitchen wall so the family can organise itself efficiently and effectively.

'Will she come for my birthday?' asks Granny. 'Tell her I want to see her.'

'OK,' I say, resigned.

Cora is the fun one, the wild one, and that appeals to Granny's new-found love – deliberate or not – of being spontaneous. I'm envious of how easily she flits through life, not dealing with any of this or any other real responsibility. I bet she's never called a plumber for Granny.

I look out of the window. The view is forever unchanged, the communal garden is small and needs more attention than it's been given, and is populated by stone statues of foxes and cats, gnomes and a copper fairy. There's a bird table that dribbles water down its lip, a feeder which has cemented peanuts at the bottom. I'm so unbelievably tired. I have another twelve days until the pills arrive from the US and can help me manage the crippling feeling of desperation that I've always had living my life. I feel sick constantly.

'We spoke about that man of yours,' Granny says.

I rub my eyes. 'What man? I don't have one.'

'You did!' she says. 'The boy with the lovely eyes. Green eyes. Richard? Ralph? Oh, you would never stop talking about him!'

I freeze, pinned, because I know who she's talking about.

'No—' I start.

'Raff!' Granny is triumphant.

I feel a coldness sweep over my body though there are no windows open – it's come from within me. Raff Alon was never mine. He belonged to Cora.

'Why was she talking about Raff?' I ask.

'I think she's trying to find him.'

My heart is hammering. 'Why?'

'I don't know, dove,' she says. 'Ask her! You need to *correlate* your visits. My birthday, remember? It's tradition that I see you all then, isn't it?'

Granny fishes a tissue from a pocket in her knitted beige cardigan, blows her nose. The veins on her hands are prominent, like rivers under her skin.

'Are you going to get me some more apples?' she says. 'Be a love and go to the corner shop for some? And stop scratching your hands.'

I look at the back of my hand, at the skin that is angry and raw from my nails scratching at it. I haven't even noticed I've done it. I do this often; live through some sort of tunnel vision where I watch someone else work my hands, my body. At the realisation that I've done it, my hand starts to sting with pain.

'My hand cream is on the windowsill,' Granny says. 'Use that – but sparingly because I'm running low, dove, all right?'

'Right.'

I lift my jacket from the back of the chair, swing my bag to my shoulder and open the door into the corridor. It's far too hot out here – they keep it hot for the old people – but it seems to be moving in waves, close and then away from me. I reach the front door, feel the cold air hit my face. I haven't thought about Raff Alon for years. Since when? School? I shake my head; I don't need to be thinking about him, but then stop suddenly, blinded by a flash of clarity. Raff, Cora and me. The echo of our voices in a room where the air was heavy and musty. The night we lost Annie.

My heart is thumping and I suddenly can't breathe properly. Where was that room? Where was Annie? I don't go to the shop; I get into the car and I drive away from Granny's flat. She'll forget I was even there anyway.

My head feels jumbled, underwater, but along with the familiar swell of an oncoming panic attack in my chest, is a stirring of memory. I had blindly accepted that I'd never remember what happened to Annie because for years I sat and tried to connect the dots but never could. Now I know Raff was there, I try to think what else could help me, and then I remember I have my school trunk here.

I have two hours before Emmeline, David and the children are due back from Suffolk. I put a casserole in the slow cooker, quickly tidy the kitchen and then I go upstairs. In the closet, under shoeboxes and scarves, and the dress-up box that Marie likes so much, I reach to haul out the black trunk. It's come with me to the three houses that I've nannied for. My childhood is in here, and yet I've never opened it before now. I think that I've been afraid to and perhaps that fear could somehow be related to what happened to Annie. I kneel before it, anxious of what I might find within it, and then I lift the lid.

My school kilt is laid out on the top, washed and with each pleat crisply ironed and I pick it up to hold it up against myself. At sixteen I was tiny, a twenty-four inch waist, and all these years later I'm the same size. I remember that I loved this school uniform. White shirt and green-and-black kilt, black blazer, black tights. I wore it with pride; wore sensible shoes and didn't roll the skirt at the knee like all the other girls did. I was always so good, so responsible. Always so worried about being told off. I was excited when our mother and father first showed us the school brochure with its impressive red-brick building and tree-lined avenue on the front cover. Inside were children in their uniforms with their violins, their sports trophies and their academic achievements smiling out from the pages and I could see myself right there with them. I wanted secret midnight feasts and notes passed in prep with friends and leisure time spent in the town. I wanted the bright future promised to me in gloss finish. When we bought the green-and-black kilt and the white shirt, I was ready. I was so happy to be away from home, ready for a fresh start but the happiness was desperately short-lived because I was bullied relentlessly and mercilessly. My towel was taken when I showered, my homework was flushed down the toilet, my teddy was stolen and then returned to my bed a week later with his head removed. Girls whispered about me and though I learnt to zone out of the moments that they bent their heads and giggled, I grew increasingly lonely with each passing year.

For Cora and Annie school was an altogether different place because they never experienced things as I did. Cora found social interaction effortless – she was witty and sparkling and therefore was left out of any unkind behaviour that was thrown the way of people like me. She was everyone's kind of beautiful and I didn't understand how it could be so different for the two of us because we were two sides of the same coin, weren't we? Annie basked in Cora's shadow – the children in her class admired and respected Cora and therefore Annie. As the years went on, I began to think of how odd I must be. Everyone else was coping in this strange, militant place, which could only mean one thing – that I wasn't normal – and I folded myself more and more away. I started to stoop, my parents told me off for slouching when we'd see them for holidays in whichever far-flung place they were in the world, and I started to move slower so that I could feel invisible.

Sometimes Cora would notice my discomfort and would squeeze my hand. Other times she'd simply look the other way and let me cope alone and I knew why – she blamed me for being there because boarding school was never part of her plan. She had been due to go to Tring, a renowned dance school, but I had stopped her; I had made her come with me to an ordinary school and I had clipped her wings. Sometimes, when I was bullied, I could see that she felt it was worthy punishment.

I put the kilt on the floor next to me. It has blanketed the orderly files and school books below and one by one I lift them out. In another life, perhaps I'd spend hours poring over them; the academic essays I saved, the eighteenth-century history text books, the collections of poetry books, but there is nothing here to help me remember Annie.

Except one thing that I nearly miss. In the corner, below a school scarf, is a photograph album, red and bulky, and I recognise it as one my parents had on their shelves in the mountain house, so I must have taken it from Switzerland. I wonder if my parents have ever noticed, or whether, like me, they haven't dared look at any memories of life 'before'. I open the first page, see a faded picture of Cora and me on a pink quilt with Annie, newborn and tiny, lying between us. I turn the page, see one of Annie when she was one and we were three, all eating ice creams on the beach.

I feel shame that I haven't looked at any of this for so long.

I turn a few more pages; there is Annie licking Cora's arm like a cat, there is me and Cora smiling at Annie who's laughing on a swing, there is our mother with all of us on her lap. All of these photos that I can see here plainly but which I have no recollection of. Looking at them isn't triggering anything of what happened. I shut it, put it inside, and then my eyes rest on the final school yearbook.

If talking to Granny about Raff made me think about that night, then looking at a photo of him might give me more answers. I flip to the end pages, to the photos of us all – seventeen years old and with the world ahead of us. I know exactly where Raff's photograph is – first page, fourth row, third from the left. I sit on my heels, breathe in his face. He was handsome then, I imagine him to be even more so now. He's Slavic descended, thin and angular with those brilliant green eyes. He was tall and lean and therefore an excellent athlete, but he was more than a sports accolade for the school's reputation; he was smart too. Everyone in that school was smart, of course, but he also possessed emotional intelligence and it made him seductive.

He descended from a wealthy New York Jewish family who, like my parents with us, had put him to board in England when they moved around the world for work. He fast learnt how to hold onto that honeyed American drawl and use it to his advantage. He could talk himself out of prep at school, could explain himself out of being out of the school premises after curfew, could spin himself around any little finger. He spun himself around mine completely.

I put the yearbook inside, take out a paper crane that's been underneath. I hold it in the palm of my hand. It's light and soft from years of unfolding and folding up again like a flower. I open the petals of paper and read the words he wrote in blue biro from long ago.

Sweetheart, let's lay under this embellished sky,
Under the way and atop the scent of flowers,
Cosy up to me like I'm the bonfire of your childhood
*   years,*
Kiss me on this endless night for hours.

I touch my fingertips to my chest. After all this time his words have the power to undo me. Yet nothing more about Annie's death has come to my mind by looking at his photo. I wonder if I should try and find him, as Cora is doing. Why hasn't she told me that she's looking for him? What could she want with contacting him after all these years and after all that we've promised one another about the past?

I open my laptop and type his family's accountancy company in the browser. I'm surprised to see that there's no mention of him there – only his younger brother is listed alongside his father as a director. I try again in a new browser, just his name in the search bar, and see that there are hundreds of Raff Alons and they all have links to the murky world of social media that I've avoided.

'Hello? Margo?'

I snap the lid closed. Emmeline and David and the twins are back and I've been up here for hours without noticing the dark closing in.

'Coming,' I say.

I put my hand to my forehead, realise I'm clammy with sweat and I yank one of the drawers from the cabinet, pop some of the pharmacy-bought pills into my mouth.

I'll make an appointment with the doctor to get some beta blockers before my anxiety takes a stronger hold of me.

I am safe here, I tell myself, in this present moment, in the life I've built. I don't need to go looking into the past because no good can come of it. But I find I glance back at the laptop anyway.

EIGHT

CORA

'Dancers,' Joanna calls. 'Come and grab some towels and water. We'll finish for today.'

I'm grateful that this rehearsal has finished because I'm in pain. Jean-Luc told us not to push ourselves on this rehearsal – after all, it's only been a rough run – but I have. I've been strong and focused because I don't want to let anyone question my position in this role but now my legs are shaking.

'It is rough,' Jean-Luc says as we sling towels around our necks. The narrators stretch their legs out of their stillness. 'And there's a lot to work on but it is fucking incredible, *non*?'

We all smile at each other.

Even if it hadn't been for the dinner at Jean-Luc's, the element of interaction that dance brings has already pulled us together. Dance is all about connection – it breaks down inhibitions and for me, it's candid happiness. It's been four days of rehearsals for the whole cast and even though we've only marked out the first two scenes, they show glittering promise as to how the whole dance is going to look. It's not how I danced it all those years ago – it's better. It's bolder and sexier and I'm thinking about it twenty-four-seven, itching to dance when I'm still because every moment I spend not dancing is a moment wasted.

'I think we have got something really special on our hands,' Jean-Luc says and he looks straight at me and I feel myself radiate under his praise. 'Get some rest. Next rehearsal is tomorrow. Whole cast again, *oui*?'

He busies himself with talking to Joanna and I feel myself grimace. I tell myself the pain is because I didn't eat enough for lunch before I came – I slapped peanut butter on a slice of toast and ate on the run here – but it's more than that. I'm not practicing enough. I need to cram more dance classes, need to go to the gym for some strength training and I'd like to schedule private sessions with Zdravko because I rarely practice lifts and I've not had the opportunity in a long time to work with a dance partner. My last partner was Danny, six months ago. He and I were in a two-week show together and he stayed with me most nights. On the morning after the final performance, when I was in the shower, he found a photo album under my bed. He was flicking the pages as I came back into the room in my towel and he looked up at me, smiled innocently and pointed at a picture.

'Who's that?' he asked.

It was a picture of Annie and I. I was seven and Annie was five and I had dressed her up in a pink tiara and bunny ears and I was kissing her cheek and she was laughing. Oh God, she was such a cute kid.

I didn't even speak when I saw Danny with that photo. I screamed and I lunged forward, my towel dropping to the floor so that I was naked. I snatched the album from him and threw it so hard that its spine broke with the impact as it hit the wall and he looked at me like a frightened animal and shrank back on the bed – all six feet three of him – with his hands up defensively like I was going to hit him. Maybe I would have done if Nav hadn't rushed in.

'What's he done?' Nav said, assumed the worst because I was naked and shaking uncontrollably. He didn't see the album, didn't wait for an answer from Danny. He grabbed him by his arm and threw him out of the flat and I never saw him after that.

'You OK?' Gisele says, drinking from her water bottle. 'You look a bit pale.'

My face must have been contorted by the pain in my legs. 'I'm fine,' I say, stand straight and smile.

'It's a stressful piece, isn't it?' she says. 'It's going to be a crazy rehearsal schedule.'

'I can handle it.' I regret my tone because she raises her eyebrows.

'I wasn't saying you couldn't.'

'Quick drink in the pub?' Cal asks, coming towards us.

'Great,' Gisele says.

'Not for me,' I say. 'I've got to be somewhere.'

I don't want to be here but here I am. It's night now, dark.

She is in a row of fifty and I think how strange it is that a place can be so full and so empty all at the same time. I can see that the wands of grass over the grave are kept short, neat, but there are no flowers laid because I never come with flowers; she'd not appreciate them anyway.

I skirt wet leaves to sit on the bench twenty yards down from her, under trees that smell of pine needles, and I light a cigarette. Above me the moon is bright, like the smoke burning in my throat, and I sigh. I read once that the moon is slowly moving away from the Earth and about how that would affect us all. Without the moon the nights would be much darker, the tides would change, a day on earth would last around six to twelve hours. Without the moon the tilt of our earth's axis would vary over time and we'd get wild weather.

I think of Annie and how she came away from us and how, like the moon, she also altered the entire rhythm of my being. I see her in my mind's eye, seven years old and lying down in a fresh fall of snow in our garden back in Switzerland and making angel wings. She should have been in bed but she had always been mischievous like me. We were so alike, Annie and I. Margo was always left out.

Choose me.

'What are you doing?' I'd asked, leaning out past the sill.

'It's so cold!' Annie had squealed, looking up at me and laughing.

''Course it is, idiot!' I'd said. 'Get out of there, you'll get caught.'

'No, I won't.'

'What's going on?' Margo had stood behind me and looked down to see Annie giggling in the snow. 'Annie! Get back in bed! Miss Patricia will see you!'

'Patricia's asleep in her chair in the sitting room,' she'd said. 'I can see her from here. Come down!'

I'd chuckled and closed the window. 'Come on,' I'd said to Margo who'd stood looking apprehensive.

'We shouldn't, Cora!'

But I'd smiled at her, grabbed her hand, and we'd snuck down the stairs, creeping past the sitting room where Miss Patricia was slumped and snoring on her chair with her book skewed on the floor and Swan Lake playing on the radio.

I'd opened the back door and out into the snow we went, in our nightdresses with our feet shoved in wellies. I'd seen that it had covered the trampoline and the slate roof of the house, and had slipped into all the crevices of the sleeping tree branches.

'We're going to get into trouble!' Margo had whispered as we reached Annie.

I'd pulled her down so that we'd gasped together as our backs hit the snow next to Annie and I'd lifted her arm with mine – up and down so that we'd made wings together. I'd looked over at her and she was looking at me and smiling like I hadn't seen her smile in so long.

'Heads up!'

A snowball came up and out of the dark and smacked down on Margo's face and she'd sat up, spluttered and gasped, and Annie and I howled with laughter.

'Sorry,' Annie had said.

'You're not,' Margo said.

'You're right.' Annie had grinned but she'd reached to squeeze Margo's arm in kindness before lying back down again. 'Look at the moon.'

We'd all looked up at it, fat and round in the sky, casting its glow on our faces.

'We three will always be together,' Annie said. 'Right?'

I'd wanted to pull that bright moon down for her. 'Promise,' I'd said because I didn't know – how could I? – that I couldn't promise something so huge.

I stare at the moon now, a sliver of white against the black.

'I'm doing this for you, Annie,' I whisper. 'I'm making something of myself, finally. Otherwise, what would have been the point of it all? Going through what we did?'

There's no answer, of course. I look at the grave. Sometimes I feel that being here closes the gulf between us, but I know the essence of her is a whole other world away.

'I brought the script,' I say.

I balance my phone on the arm of the bench, so that the torchlight shines onto the pages. I'm wearing blue cashmere fingerless gloves but the night is cold and my hands are slow to turn the pages, slower to write my notes with the pencil stub I've brought.

'This is the right thing to do, isn't it? I had to do this play.'

For a brief moment it's as if I can hear the way she laughed but I know that it's the wind in the trees above me.

'What if there was a spot turn here instead of the line before? More dramatic? I think it works better. Miss Patricia would think so.'

I scratch a marking on the page.

'You would have loved to see me do this, wouldn't you?'

I suck on the cigarette. My phone buzzes and I tilt my head to read the screen. My calendar has reminded me of Granny's birthday on Sunday and I'll go, of course, because it's tradition.

NINE

MARGO

The doctor appears dubious in prescribing me beta blockers.

'Why do you think these are the answer?' she says, scrolling the computer screen.

'I'm very tired,' I say. 'And I'm . . . not functional.'

The doctor studies me. My hair is blonde and thick, my eyes luminous and made-up, my body toned. I don't look like a woman whose life is on the constant brink of collapse. Perhaps I should have come here in loungewear and with my hair unwashed.

'I feel very anxious,' I repeat. 'And sick.'

'Why so suddenly, do you think?' she asks.

I can't tell her that it's because I've been taking illegally strong benzodiazepines and that I've had withdrawals from them for three weeks.

'I worry a lot about doing the right thing,' I say. 'I need a pick-me-up, short-term, so I can work some things out.'

'Work things out?'

She's a private doctor which is a perk of signing with an elite nanny agency, but today I wish for an overworked and stressed GP who might just hurry a prescription through.

I shake my head. 'I just need the pills. Please. If that's OK. Please?'

I can hear myself in my ears – shameless pleading.

The doctor laces her fingers. 'Would you like to spend some time talking to me about how you're feeling?' she asks.

'No,' I say. 'That won't be necessary.'

It would also take too long, I think, to reel off exactly what my brain goes through day to day, how it tries to navigate an ever-moving, shape-shifting fear of the unknown. Especially now as I'm plunging into a time in my life that I'd previously thought inaccessible.

'I can sign you off work,' she says. 'For a couple of weeks to allow you some rest?'

The very thought makes my throat constrict. 'That's not possible,' I say. 'The agency will replace me.'

Then I could be replaced permanently and I can't lose the twins.

'You're a nanny, correct?'

'Yes.'

'And you live-in. So tell me how you take some time off to gather yourself?'

'I have my own room in the house,' I say. 'I can hide out there sometimes. I can rest. It's not like boarding school.'

'Boarding school?'

At boarding school I was so desperate for silence. I used to find bizarre places to hide: in bathtubs, behind classroom doors, in the sports centre locker room after prep. I barely slept for the five years I shared a dormitory with some of the girls in my year, and the sleep deprivation made me nervous, paranoid. There was a study done in 1964 on a seventeen-year-old called Randy Gardner who stayed awake for eleven days as part of a psychological experiment. After two days he was unable to repeat simple sentences, after three he was reported to be morose and uncoordinated, and after five he started hallucinating. I wonder if a lot of my schooldays were spent vague and hallucinating because there were days, weeks even, that I could barely remember what we were doing in class. I forgot projects that we were halfway through, forgot books we were reading.

'But you need to rest,' the doctor interrupts my thoughts. 'You've told me that you're bordering on exhaustion and we don't want you to spiral into a breakdown.' She looks at her computer. 'I can see from your records this is something that you're prone to. You've also experienced blackouts.'

I swallow. 'Yes, I've had panic attacks before.'

'What about trying some cognitive therapy?' the doctor says. 'Stress is tiring.'

'Yes. And Annie. What happened to her when she . . .'

I pitch forward, put my head in my hands. I feel so light-headed and want to be sick.

'Do you talk to friends and family about your sister?'

I frown. 'What?' I say.

'It must have been very traumatic,' she says.

'I haven't had a trauma!'

'But you said you had lost your little sister?' she says.

'Did I say that?'

'You said it just now,' the doctor says.

I must have whispered it. 'Yes,' I say. 'Yes, she died.'

'Do you talk to anyone about what happened?' she asks. 'If it's too difficult for family to talk about it, perhaps some good friends?'

'I – not really,' I say.

She opens a drawer in her desk. 'I'm comfortable writing you out a short prescription to help manage your anxiety, but it's not a long-term solution,' she says. 'So I would also like to give you this practitioner's number. He's a private counsellor. I think you'd benefit from some counselling.'

She passes me a card and I look at it; a simple white card with black writing – Mr Hawkins, psychotherapist.

'A therapist?' I say. 'Do you think I need to be fixed?'

'I think you need to talk.'

I wake up in the middle of the night with my hair stuck to the back of my neck. Something has woken me and I realise, from the light glaring from the bedside cabinet, that it's my phone. I have an email notification – my pills have been shipped five days earlier than the original delay message and the relief of this almost overwhelms me.

I lie back down, realise that my sheets are damp from sweat, and that before the phone woke me, I had been dreaming. Soupy pixels of it cloud my eyes as I stare into the dark – a blurred face in a cavernous room that I can't make sense of, and Annie was there and Cora and Raff. I can't tell if my head is taking me to the place Annie died, or if I'm just confusing myself.

I can feel my heart thudding in the silence of the house. I look to the door, which is closed, so why do I feel watched?

Scared? There are no monsters here; the children are safe. But is that true? Are they safe? I'm forever convinced something will happen to the children in the middle of the night and I'll feel solely responsible, even if David and Emmeline are here.

I get up, open my bedroom door and steal out into the landing, glancing momentarily down the corridor at the yawning dark. For the last few weeks, I've thought I heard someone behind me and then I realise it's my own footsteps because no one is here; no one ever is. I'm paranoid. I walk to Marie's room, peer inside to see her wrapped up in her hot-air balloon duvet, her dark curls fanned out on the pillow and a small foot out of the covers. I lean in her doorway, listen to her breathe before I move along the corridor to Jonny's room. Rockets and stars dance along the walls, cars and teddies litter the floors. His matching hot-air balloon duvet is on the floor and I slip inside the room, pick it up and drape it back over him. He shifts and I kiss his forehead, smell that beautiful scent of childhood that they both share – grass stains and innocence. I wonder how long it'll be until they lose the latter.

I walk down to the basement. I can iron when I'm tired but awake. I need to get ahead of myself on the piles anyway – somehow they've risen like mountains – and it's a therapeutic activity. The room is calm. The walls are painted a brilliant white and have pictures on them of flowers. There's a bowl of pot pourri even though the room already smells of clean linen.

I lift one of Marie's pinafore dresses to my face to feel its texture – smooth against my cheek – and then I start to iron it. All their clothes are expensive, soft and well-cut. I finger the cuffs and the collars of Emmeline's blouses and the hems of her dresses, take my time over the sharp creases of David's trousers and wonder what that dream meant. An enormous and open room, wide like a screaming mouth. Details of it ping into my head – there was a huge chandelier, and there were lights that caught the gold of the dress Cora was wearing. It was the same dress as the one in the photograph. What's real about this dream and what isn't?

I feel on the brink of something important resurfacing and I'm trying so hard to recall fact from fiction that my bottom lip begins to tingle because I'm biting it. Why am I feeling all this now? I was fine until . . . I pause. I was fine until I stopped taking the drugs. My pills have kept me from feeling anxious, and have kept me functional, but perhaps they have also kept my brain foggy to the past. Is memory loss a side effect of taking them? I feel sick with the possibility.

My ears are hit with an ear-piercing shriek. Someone is in the room screaming.

'Annie?' I say.

I whirl around, panicked, but Annie isn't here.

'Cora?'

There's no one here but the screaming is deafening and I'm blinded with confusion. Who is screaming? One of the children? But no, it's above me, all around me, *inside* of me. My heart starts to slam in my chest, and I shut my eyes tight, feel terrified because this must be because of the pills – I shouldn't have come off them so abruptly. It's loud, so loud, and I start screaming too to drown it out until I feel fingers suddenly tightening on one of my arms. Someone is shaking me and I open my eyes, see David naked but for his boxer shorts in front of me. He grabs at my hand and it's like I'm watching him from above as he pries open my fingers. I watch him take the iron out of my hand. It's welded to one of his shirts; it's black and singed. I've burnt his shirt and that's what the screaming is – it's the fire alarm.

'Margo! What are you doing!' he yells and he puts the iron down, wrenches the plug from the socket before racing upstairs again. In a moment, the fire alarm stops, but it continues to ring in my ears. The smell of the burnt shirt is overwhelming and I run the basement sink full of water, submerging it. Upstairs I can hear the children crying from the shock of being jolted from sleep.

'I'm sorry,' I say to no one and everyone at the same time.

The doctor is right; I need to talk to someone about what happened that night and I'll start with Cora.

TEN

CORA

'All right?' I say as I slide myself into Margo's cream Fiat.

It's been valeted; she always keeps it pristine like everything in her life.

'Did you buy Granny a present?' I say as she pulls away from the kerb.

'Yes,' she says. 'Did you?'

I turn around to the back seat, see a bag of carefully wrapped presents and bunch of flowers.

'Yup,' I say.

'No, those are from me,' she says.

'Come on now. I didn't have time.'

'Why didn't you?'

I ignore her, lean further backwards so that the seatbelt jars. 'Ooo, you brought a picnic too?'

'A cream tea,' she says. 'Nothing much.'

'And champagne?'

'You know how Granny likes it.'

'It'll send her to sleep.'

'We can steal the silver.'

I look at her in surprise and laugh and she smiles too for a brief second, and then shuts it down again. It's always been this way with Margo – she produces a rare glimmer of something wonderful, and then fades into herself again.

I put my trainers on the dashboard, tuck my knees up to my chest. Going to Granny's for her birthday is a tradition born from early childhood. Mother would take Margo and Annie and I from wherever we were in the world, and we would jet to the UK to celebrate with her. In those few days Granny would lavish us with love and presents, kiss our heads and stuff us with chocolate while our mother went around the country and visited all the friends she'd been forced to leave behind in following our father around the world. We didn't care about her absence – we'd play tag with Granny in the garden, paint her pictures of animals and flowers and dance for her.

I change the radio station to drum and bass.

'It's a bit loud, Cora,' Margo says after two minutes.

'Yeah,' I say. 'It's expression, Margo. Art.'

'Your *art* is giving me a headache.'

'Soz,' I say, but don't turn it down.

She turns it down. 'Why didn't you tell me you were going to visit Granny?'

'Do I have to tell you everything?'

'When did you go?' she asks.

I shrug. The truth is that sometimes I like to go to Granny's to intercept any letters that are sent our way because it wouldn't do for Margo to see them. She's already anxious as hell and our parents' letters are toxic. 'Can't remember. Why?'

'Did you leave me some pictures when you went there?' she asks.

'No,' I say, but I hope she doesn't sense my growing unease. 'Did she tell you I did? Do we need to add a shiny new stamp to our Granny Dementia Bingo Board?'

'Cora, don't be insensitive.'

'What were the photos?'

She pauses. 'Just some I hadn't seen before.'

'Well, you know what Granny's like,' I say. 'She unearths shit all the time. Her flat is like the Tardis.'

'There was one of you.'

'Was I cute?'

'There was writing on the back of it. Annie's writing.'

My heart skips but I don't react. 'So it's an old photo then, what's the big deal?'

'That's what I thought,' she says. 'It just . . . unnerved me. Seeing Annie's writing made me feel . . . odd.'

'And you're already a weirdo,' I say. 'So we don't want double helpings. Forget it.'

'Yes. But I've also been having these dreams . . .'

'Of what?'

'A big room.'

I roll my eyes. 'Wow. *Profound.* Don't mind me zoning out here, OK?'

We're silent for a moment until I notice that the car begins to drift and I grab at the steering wheel.

'Mind the kerb, woman!'

'Sorry,' she says.

'Jesus!' I say. 'Did you have a heavy night last night?'

'No, I – I was just cleaning for a long time last night.'

'Goals,' I say dryly.

'I feel a bit confused about things,' she says. 'And a bit sick. I've got a terrible headache.'

'Are you going to kill off some old people with your germs? Maybe breathe on that grumpy old bastard with the little balcony. We could set Granny up in there when he's carted off.'

'Oh my God, Cora,' she says and she rubs at the back of her neck with one hand. 'It's not a virus. It doesn't matter, I'll be fine. Tell me how you are?'

There was a time where I'd tell her about the shows I was cast in, would bask in her elation and admiration because who doesn't love to be admired? But how could I tell her about *Mirror, Mirror*? This obsession is mine alone and would ruin everything.

'Fine, fine,' I say. 'You know. Same old. Dancing, having sex and a good time.'

'Right,' she says and her lips pinch into a hard thin line just as they always do when she hears something she deems unsavoury.

I lean forward, turn the volume dial up to full again and she drives. We're both fine with silence because, being a twin, we can usually feel everything that needs to be felt through unspoken words. Today, however, there seems to be a barrier. I look at her from the corner of my eye. She looks nice; her hair is lightly curled, she's wearing make-up

87

and a cute button-down turquoise shirt over black jeans. Who does she dress up for, I wonder. There's no one in her life to give her meaning. Is it cleaning and cooking and tidying up other people's crap that gives her purpose? She exists, hides, shadow-like in someone else's life. Someone wealthy with an immaculate house and immaculate children. She never invites me round to these houses, maybe she's worried I'd steal something – she'd be right to worry.

I yawn and go through the dance moves for *Mirror, Mirror* in my head. It's becoming like a mantra, committing each scene to memory over and over even though I know I could dance it for real with my eyes closed.

The car stops and I pitch forward.

'Margo! For Christ's sake!'

'What?' she says.

'Why did you brake so hard?'

'I didn't,' she says. 'You've been asleep.'

'Shit,' I say.

I look at the building that we've pulled up at, crumbly red bricks that make up a jaded squat square block.

'Look,' she says. 'They've got flowers out the front today. That's nice.'

'Maybe someone's died and these are the ones out of the church?'

'Oh, Cora,' she says but she smiles – I can always make her laugh. 'Did you know Julie died? Granny's friend from down the corridor?'

'Shame,' I say, unsympathetically.

'I know,' she says.

I step towards the entrance leaving Margo to carry the bag of presents and the picnic that I'll claim to Granny to be my idea. The air smells heavy – like old knitted cardigans and buttery biscuits.

Margo looks to the book on the front desk. 'We have to sign in, remember?'

'You sign us in,' I say because the noticeboard has caught my attention. 'Listen to this – bridge competition next Wednesday. Mini-golf outing next Saturday. Jumble sale tomorrow. Granny has quite the social calendar.'

'Don't be mean,' Margo says and picks up the pen and signs us in.

'What a life, eh? Sit and eat cake and wait to die.'

'Cora!'

'I bet all sorts goes on in this place,' I say.

All the rooms here have pictures of flowers on them so that the residents don't get confused which room is theirs. Granny was appointed a lavender sprig but the lady who had the rose died two years ago and Granny campaigned to have it reassigned to her because Rose is her name. We stop at the door with the rose motif on the front and knock.

'Come in!' says a fluttery voice from inside.

Margo pushes the door open.

'Dove,' Granny says.

'Happy birthday, Granny!' I barrel forward, whisk the flowers from Margo and thrust them out to Granny.

'Oh!' Granny says. 'How wonderful to see you! You brought roses for Rose! Well! What a lucky girl I am!'

'Eighty-seven young,' I say.

'Eighty-six,' Margo corrects.

I sweep the present bag from Margo's fingers, swing them forward.

'And these are for you too, Granny,' I say.

Margo opens her mouth and closes it again.

'Oh love! Come to the lounge and help me unwrap them.'

'I love your pink sofas,' I say, because I've always loved them.

'Had them since 1989, my girl,' Granny beams. 'The old ones are the best.'

'Shall I put the kettle on?' Margo says, sounds redundant.

'Please, dove,' Granny nods in agreement.

Margo disappears and Granny opens the presents like a little child. I smile at her tinkling laugh as she unwraps each gift.

'Shortbread!' she cries. 'A new book! New hand cream, thank you for remembering! Writing notelets!'

I'll give her this – Margo knows how to keep an old lady happy. To be fair, she knows how to keep everyone happy and that's why she's so good at her job. I'll bet she folds the kids' pyjamas over hot-water bottles when it's cold.

'Just be a minute,' I call to Granny and I skip to the kitchen to find Margo standing and staring out of the window. 'You missed Granny opening everything.'

'Yes,' Margo says. 'It's OK.'

'You didn't get very far.' I flick the kettle on, put the mugs on a tray.

'Sorry,' she apologises.

She takes the scones and jam and cream out of the little bag and arranges them on a big plate.

'Cream tea!' Granny says when we go in. 'You've spoiled me.' She places her hands around my face, kisses me on the cheek with a prickly top lip. 'And I love the hand cream.'

'White Company, Granny,' I say. '*Très* expensive.'

'And no new biscuit tin like you threatened,' Granny says. Margo smiles. 'No, Granny.'

'And champagne! Well! Did I ever tell you about the first time I drank champagne?'

Margo and I shake our heads but we've heard the story a thousand times over the course of our lives and could probably repeat it back to Granny; better, in fact, because now Granny seems to forget some of the details.

'It was the night I met your grandpa,' she says.

I look at Margo in the mirror behind Granny's head and put a finger to my head like a gun, pull the trigger. She shakes her head at me like a school matron and I grin.

'1956 it was,' Granny says lifting a scone to her lips.

It was 1958 but we smile at her encouragingly.

'And I didn't like his glasses,' she continues. 'Big round things, like milk-bottle tops. Black.'

They were tortoiseshell glasses; I've got a picture of them at that dance in my purse but I don't correct her and nor does Margo.

'An engineer, he was!' she says. 'Never without his tool-kit for an emergency. You've got that now, haven't you, Margo? In your car. We ladies have to look after ourselves, don't we? Change a tyre.'

91

'Yes, Granny,' Margo says obediently and then offers a plate. 'Have a scone?'

We sit through her war stories, her courtship and marriage to our grandfather, and then we sit through her having her children and having her grandchildren – only the three of us – and we make more tea, eat more scones, drink the champagne until Granny starts on a micro-nap and Margo cleans the kitchen, puts Granny's washing on, irons some of her blouses. I scout about the flat, pick up tarnished framed photos from windowsills, finger the lace doilies, open the pantry and eat Granny's Lindt chocolates, until I spot something interesting.

'Granny, I found another bottle!' I say.

'Another bottle?' Granny says, startling awake.

'Bubbly! Shall we open it?'

'Do we need to?' I hear Margo say.

'Yes!' I say.

'I should clear some things,' Granny says looking around the room, which is now spotless.

'Oh, don't worry, Granny. I've already cleaned the kitchen,' I say.

Margo comes in, looks at me sharply and I shrug. I like to take credit for her niceties mostly because it irritates her so much.

'And I've put some nice dinner for you in the fridge,' I add.

Margo did that too – she probably cooked it last night and wrapped it in tinfoil this morning with the same care she gives everything in her life. I see her roll her eyes.

'And you've opened your presents,' I say. 'So now we deserve more drink.'

Granny pats my hand. 'You're not driving?'

'Not me,' I say, delightedly.

Margo looks to Granny. 'Are any of your friends from the other apartments coming by this afternoon?' she asks.

'Oh, Sybil will pop over. And Julie.'

Margo frowns. 'I thought Julie had passed away?'

Granny looks horrified. 'Of course she hasn't!' She pauses, purses her lips. 'Has she?'

'I think so, Granny,' Margo says and she squeezes Granny's hands reassuringly.

'Dead and cold in the ground,' I say bluntly, folding an origami crane out of an old shopping list on the sideboard while Margo glowers at me.

'Stop it,' she whispers. 'She doesn't remember.'

'Clearly,' I say.

'Not Julie then,' Granny says with a sad shrug. 'But Sybil, yes.'

I put the crane on Granny's mantelpiece and then cork the champagne and pour out fresh glasses. Granny lifts it with a trembling hand – this is her third glass – and I think, by the look on Margo's face, she's thinking about confiscating it because she's boring.

'Granny, you must be sitting on a gold mine here,' I say, looking around. 'Bet you've got some cool vintage clothes.' I look to Margo. 'You know where all Granny's old dress-up shit is?'

Margo sighs. 'Yes.'

'Rose?' a voice calls.

Sybil has appeared at the door with some limp flowers and a box of chocolates for Granny.

'Syb!' Granny says. 'Come in! You wait and hear what my granddaughter is proposing we spend the afternoon doing!'

'We're going to have a catwalk, Sybil,' I say.

I skip to help Margo retrieve the box of Granny's moth-balled clothes and half an hour later and we're all dripping in pearls and gloves and stiff tweed and hats. The champagne is flowing and Granny and Sybil are clutching each other's shoulders, reminiscing about dance halls while I dance to some 1950s music I've found on my phone. Margo looks on, lost.

'Do you want to see some photos?' Granny says.

'Of the dances?' I say.

'Actually, no, Granny,' Margo says. 'We'd better be leaving.'

'Don't be a dick,' I say as Granny bends to tug out an album from a shelf. 'Granny wants to show them.'

'I've seen them all a hundred times,' she says. 'And don't call me a dick. It's so crude.'

'But I haven't seen them,' I say. 'And you *can* be a massive schlong.'

'You confuse Granny,' she hisses.

I ignore her, sit on the arm of Granny's chair and stroke her thinning hair with a velvet-gloved hand.

'Look!' Granny says and flips a page over as photographs fall out.

'Oh, that's nice,' Sybil coos.

'Cute!' I say, bending down to retrieve them. I glance up at Margo. 'Ha! Look!'

There's one of the two of us standing by a church on holiday, both wearing shorts and blouses. I'm holding the Norfolk walking guide.

'We look awful,' I laugh. 'We should burn this one, Granny.'

Margo moves to start clearing the champagne glasses, but then she stops, looking to something that's dropped to the floor and is poking out from under the sofa. I catch her alarm and look to it too.

'What's this?' I say.

'Oh!' Granny says in a voice that's changed. Her smile has gone, replaced by an expression that's lucid, sharp. 'It's not a photograph.'

'Let me see it,' I say and whip it up from the floor.

It's a small booklet with a lily on the front cover, and I immediately know what it is.

'The memorial service,' Granny whispers. She looks up at us. 'I didn't want to keep it. But I *had* to keep it. Does that make sense to you?'

Margo and I glance at each other and wordlessly remove the gloves on our hands because we both know that dress-up now feels frivolous.

'My brain,' Granny says. 'I had to remember she'd gone. Sometimes . . .'

'I understand,' I say and I slip the booklet into my pocket.

Silence fugs the room.

'Should I – should I go, Rose?' asks Sybil.

'No, Sybil,' I say. 'You stay and keep Granny company. We'll put a film on for you both?'

Margo looks to Granny. 'Is that what you want? Are you OK?'

Granny strokes the photo album which now lies like a tome in her lap. 'Yes,' she says. 'Sorry. I didn't know it was there. I mean . . . I did. But . . .'

Margo takes the remote from the mantelpiece, looks at me. 'We should go,' she says quietly.

I ease the album from Granny's knees as Granny stares ahead at the television screen coming to life.

'*Casablanca*? *Gone with the Wind*?' Margo asks Granny.

'Frankly, my dear,' I say, 'I don't think she'll give a damn.'

Margo drives home slowly and I wish she'd go faster because I want to be somewhere else, anywhere else but here. It feels like hours before she pulls up to the kerb and I'm about to jump out when I realise the car door is locked.

'Open it, Margo,' I say.

She turns to me. 'Do you think about her?' she asks me. 'Annie?'

I'm silent.

'Cora? Do you?'

Her eyes are filled with something like desperation.

I sigh, look out of the window. 'Of course I do. What's brought this on? The memorial service booklet?'

'I've been thinking about her a lot recently.'

I close my eyes. 'I think of all the times she insisted on going out dressed as a fairy when she was little,' I say. 'I think of the way she packed her toy crocodile in that ridiculous orange suitcase when we went on holiday and there was never any room for anything else. I think of the way she loved the snow and the moon. I think of the way she laughed.'

I look back at Margo, see her nodding silently.

'It kills me not to see her.'

'And Raff?' she says. 'Do you think about him?'

I feel my body tense up. 'Why would you ask me about him?'

'Granny said you'd been talking about him.'

'Granny's mad as a box of frogs,' I say.

'Are you trying to find him?'

'Are you kidding?' I say. 'Absolutely not. Don't invite the past back in. That's what we decided, wasn't it?'

She starts to scratch at the back of her hand. 'I know . . . but when Granny talked about him, it made me think about what happened that night with Annie and I can't – I can't remember it, Cora, and I should be able to, shouldn't I? Raff was there, wasn't he? Where were we? Why can't I find anything out online about her?'

'We're not having this conversation,' I say. 'You've done well for yourself. You've built a life of luxury where you don't need to dwell on what happened, so why are you?'

'Is that what you do?' she asks. 'Have you forgotten too?'

'I do whatever gets me the fuck through the day,' I say. 'The pills help me forget all the things I need to. The ones

I recommended to you – from America. You take them, right?'

'They help me too,' she says. 'They help me sleep, but I don't think I *should* be taking them. Maybe they're why I haven't thought about Annie when I should have been. I should have more memory of her, shouldn't I? I'm thinking of making an appointment with a therapist, you know? Someone to help me remember. My doctor has recommended someone.'

I scoff. 'Good luck unpacking your persona.'

She looks wounded. 'What do you mean?'

'You're complicated,' I say. 'You've always been complicated even when things have been simple.'

I see her shoulders slump. I lean across her, push the lock button and then I get out of the car, slamming the door shut.

I'm angry and I'm worried. If Margo starts talking to a therapist, she might unlock something that she shouldn't. I've kept her drugged the last nine years of her life – on the edge of sanity – for her safety.

And for mine.

ELEVEN

MARGO

All day my head has been blowing at the embers of memory. Annie's funeral is beginning to move to the forefront of my mind, whereas before I had no clarity of it and this is progress, albeit a difficult time to process.

I can't seem to see the people properly, or the vicar who led the service, but I can now recall vividly my father's watery eyes, and that his black tie was skewed but no one wanted to correct it for him. I remember that no one seemed to want to touch our family because we were so fragile. All anyone dared give us were soft handshakes, soft embraces and butterfly kisses on our cheeks.

We sang her favourite hymns, a cousin we didn't know read a poem and, although I did listen to it at the time, all I can recall hearing now is the sound the wind made on the church panes – like a gentle constant sighing. It was October when we buried her but I remember thinking that wasn't right because it wasn't her season. She was summer.

We walked out to the churchyard to her graveside and the wind flurried up skirts and dresses and jackets. We stood silent at the grave and the breeze twisted my hair about my face and I was glad of it because it hid my tears.

'There you are,' a voice had said softly behind me. Granny with her eyes closed and her face tilted up to the sky. 'Up with the moon and the stars now.'

I look at the clock. It's half past four in the afternoon, and the children are back from school and are watching television. Emmeline is working in her study, David is coming home late, dinner is on, and I have an hour until I need to lay the table. I go upstairs, get my laptop out. The mystery of what happened to Annie feels like a splinter that I need to pull and expose myself to its damage. I need to find Raff, because if Cora can't give me answers to what happened that night, perhaps he can. I'm going to have to delve into the hundreds of Twitter and Instagram and Facebook profiles. I decide to start with Twitter, begin to scroll and read the biographies of those that don't have a profile pictures obvious enough for me to discount them, but after an hour I begin to worry he's not even on here. Has he done what I've done and hidden himself away?

I keep clicking, an addict for a hit, even when my eyes start to blur and my fingers ache with the repetition. And then I think that maybe he'd never call himself Raff Alon. Perhaps he'd call himself what he once told me he would if ever he became a famous poet. He had been joking but I write it in anyway – Rafael Harebell.

There's a hit and only one, an avatar of a silhouetted man in a fedora hat and with a bio that is just one word – *Writer*.

My heart thrums at the joy that he has used this name, that I've found him, and then the spark dies again. This might not be him, I remind myself. But how could it be anyone else?

I click onto the account and start to read the snippets of poems, short stories, haiku.

Tangle me in roots
Lose me to the woodland floor
Let me breathe again.

Breathe, Margo.

A fragile heart of glass is shattered and becomes mosaic. It has fractures that bend the truth of smiles. Fragile heart, listen. I will take care of you.

I don't know for how long I sit on the bed and let these words saturate my soul. These poems sound like him. There are four events scheduled on the banner of his home page; Cambridge, Ely, Norwich and London and I zoom into the last event. It's in three days, on Thursday at a bookstore called Tales of the City in Marylebone.

A wave of nausea rolls over me – if this is him, what would I do if I were to see him again? I clutch at my throat, inhale the air in the room that feels close and humid although it's neither of those things.

'Margo?'

Marie is at the door frame and I get up like she's set me alight.

'Hi, dove,' I say. 'Are you OK?'

'Something smells in the kitchen,' she says.

I frown and then look to the clock on my wall, realise that I've been up here for nearly two hours. I run down the stairs to the kitchen to the smell of burnt meat and take the pot from the oven. I lift the lid, stir the now-claggy contents, see that the bottom is charred.

'Where's your mum?' I say.

'She's on the phone to Grandma in the conservatory.'

I open the windows, thankful that Emmeline isn't here to inhale the aftermath of my distraction, before I scrape the food and plunge the offensive pot into hot soapy water and open all the windows. I need to start dinner again and fast. I peel and slice potatoes thinly to make a gratin, get cream and butter and cheese out of the fridge and thyme from the windowsill. Something quick and indulgent and something I know that Emmeline adores. I'll fry gammon to go with it, make a fresh green salad with a lemon and chili dressing. I need lots of flavours to mask the smell that hangs in the air. Marie looks on as I speed around the kitchen.

'Can you tell your mum that dinner is slightly late?' I say. 'And not to come into the—'

'Margo?'

I spin to the door. 'Hi, Emmeline,' I say, brightly.

'Are you making gratin?' she says.

'Yes.'

She flops down on one of the kitchen wooden chairs.

'Perfect,' she says. 'Why are all the windows open?'

'Oh,' I say. 'Just to clear the air.'

The three days pass in a blur of lost shoes, picking up discarded toys from inside the washing machine and other various random places, hoovering and cooking. Through it all are bouts of threatening nausea, soreness of my eyes, and unrelenting tiredness, which cloud the progress I want to make in lining up my memories of Annie and of that night. I'm certain that room I dreamt about is relevant somehow.

I look up at the store window with the huge black letters on the glass front spelling Tales of the City.

The store is shouldered in between two larger brick buildings, which make it look small but welcoming. Through the glass I see shelves of beautiful books, table displays and spinners and in any other situation this shop would beckon me and I'd run inside like it was a long-lost friend.

I've dressed mutely today in a long-sleeved black top, glasses, black jeans and a dark grey poncho and I've tied my hair loosely at the nape of my neck. I want to blend into the background because I'm not entirely sure what I'm going to do if it's actually him. Would I come to the front and demand answers or would I wait and gather myself to ask questions later?

'Do come in,' says a voice and I startle.

A reed-thin man in his fifties is standing at the door, putting out a sign that reads *Poetry Reading Today!*

'Are you after anything in particular?' he asks. 'A gift?'

'I think . . .' I tail off. 'I'm here to . . .'

'Are you here for the poetry?' the bookseller asks, smiling.

My fingers are at the back of my hand and I see the bookseller's eyes drop because I've started scratching again. I let my arms swing down to my sides.

'I was in the area, just browsing.'

'A bookshop is the perfect way to spend a Thursday,' he says. 'Or any day!'

He gestures inside. I swallow down the flickering nerves that are scratching the back of my throat and follow him inside. I'm hit by the smell of a polished wooden floor, the smell of pages. Books are stacked in towers, arranged haphazardly on shelves.

There are a couple of people already inside who stop their conversation, turn and smile at me. I inhale, worried, as I register their faces but his isn't one of them. Thank God.

'Your store is really beautiful.'

'Forgive the shambles,' he says.

I finger the spines of the books nearest me and then my eyes rest on a table set up at the back of the store with fifteen or so chairs in front of it.

'Is that for the poetry reading?' I ask.

'That's right,' the bookseller says. 'There are ten poets who have worked on an anthology and they're all from around the globe. I've been lucky enough to have two of them in today because they're London based: isn't that wonderful?'

'Yes,' I say. My skin on my back of my hand feels hot and burning and I look down, realise I'm scratching at it again.

The bookseller turns to a small table with a coffee machine and cups and a milk jug atop it. 'Coffee?'

'No, thank you,' I reply.

He smiles. 'Feel free to take a look around the shop,' he says. 'We have about ten minutes before the readings start.'

I move away, thankful that the shop is beginning to fill with people so I can walk towards the back of it. I pass the table waiting for the poets – an exquisite oak desk with a pile of books on it, *The Anthology* and a pen ready for signatures, but if I know Raff, he'll have a pen of his own. I suppose all writers do – like wizards with wands.

I see some free-standing aisles of shelves behind the desk and go towards them. He won't see me if I'm behind these, will he? A swirl of memory flashes into my head. I've been in the wings of a theatre before, hiding like this, watching him.

'Raff!' I hear bookseller exclaim over the chatter of the shop. 'Come in!'

Something in my body feels like it's on fire. Breathe, breathe, don't lose yourself, Margo. I look out from behind the shelves and there he is. I was expecting to have a reaction to seeing him again but it's worse than I thought it would be. I'm paralysed, feel bile rising in my throat as I take him in. I grip tightly to the shelves in front of me. His same green eyes, that thick dark hair, but there are some differences too of course; he looks thinner, his cheekbones are knife sharp and he's wearing a shirt that's off-white, faded jeans with rips in them and a leather jacket. His clothing surprises me because I expected him to be a smarter, older version of that boy I knew at school, but he's transcended that boy and I don't know this man. My eyes drop to his left hand. I can't see any glint of a ring on his finger but that doesn't mean that he's not married, or in a relationship. I wonder if he has children.

'Mary is here already,' I hear the bookseller say. 'Couple more minutes and then we can get started.'

'Great, Martin, thank you,' Raff says.

His voice has a richer, deeper timbre. I watch him talk to a few people by the coffee machine. The chatter of the bookstore starts up again as people move towards the seats in front of the table and I hover nervously. Will people notice my feet under these shelves? There's a half-foot gap at least and anyone would think it odd for someone to be standing behind here and call attention to it. I wait an agonising five minutes until Raff and Mary seat themselves behind the desk and the bookseller stands to their right.

'Welcome everyone,' the bookseller says. 'This morning we're delighted to have some wonderful poets with us for a reading and for signing some books! Mary Kwok is on the panel for Nature Poetry Writing at Hay next year, and will also be attending the Lancaster Literary Festival as one of the poetry tutors. Raff has recorded his own audiobook of poetry, and will be doing a reading at the prestigious Chicago Library in the next few months alongside some of America's most renowned modern poets.'

From my position I can see by the curve of Raff's cheek that he's smiling out at his audience, that disarming smile, and it makes me feel faint. All the feelings that I haven't allowed to surface for so many years overwhelm me. The room is starting to spin. I tip forward to lean my hot forehead against cool book spines. I can't succumb to a blackout.

'Over to you then,' the bookseller says and he moves out of my eyeline.

'Thanks, Martin,' Raff acknowledges him. 'And thank you everyone for coming. Martin promised me there would be some cake at the end. Maybe you've come for that and not us at all, I don't know.'

People laugh because he's warm and open. This is the boy I knew.

'Raff will start,' Mary says. She's petite with long black hair and she's wearing a bright red dress. 'Because some of you hear enough of me with our book group meetings! And then after my reading, we'll take some questions.'

I have so many questions – unrelated – but the rest of the room is silent and waiting and so Raff begins to talk.

'This one is called "Murmurations",' he says and then pauses. '*How easy it is to overlook those winged feelings fluttering above my head. I need only look up to that marbled sky, see that in murmuration they spell out danger, but I'm infatuated by you. Instead I wear the rose-tinted glasses you bought me, and when you tell me that the wings make only red hearts for us, I will believe you.*'

The room is silenced by that beautiful voice.

'This one is called "In The Dark It Came".' Raff clears his throat. '*In the dark it came, the last goodbye. Invisible, silent. In the years since I write myself love letters and fill them with the starlit nights we shared, the fireball moons, the taste of your furious kisses. In the dark it came, stole our love.*"'

I close my eyes, listen to him talk, but my mind goes to when I first met him and to the first words he ever said to me when we were fourteen. It was a hot, blue-skied, cloud-scudded day in May and I had finished my homework and decided to walk to the wildflower meadow, something I often did before bedtime – alone of course. I stumbled, quite literally, on top of him in the long grass, and, for a moment, we were a mass of limbs and surprised gasps, before I realised who it was I'd tripped over.

'Oh my gosh, I'm so sorry,' I said, standing up. I wanted the ground to swallow me.

'Shit, I'm going to set the place on fire,' he said.

'What?'

'Ah, here it is!' He waved a cigarette aloft at me that had dropped from his fingers.

'I – I should go,' I said.

'Stay a while,' he said. 'Where else have you got to be?'

'Nowhere.'

'Well then,' he said. 'Sit.'

I hesitated, unsure, until he patted the grass next to him.

'What are you doing here?' I asked, sitting down.

'Waiting for beautiful women to fall over me and kick me in the face?' he grinned and took a drag on his cigarette.

The words registered – he'd called me beautiful – and hit me full in the heart.

'I'm sorry,' I said again. 'Did I hurt you?'

'Nah, you're all right.'

I saw a book beside him. 'What's that?'

'*The Book of Flowers*. I've got an essay due for English. Where better to study it, right? I fucking hate the prep room.'

'Does anyone know you're out here?' I asked.

''Course not.' He laughed. 'You?'

'No,' I said and didn't add that I doubted anyone would care for my whereabouts.

'Listen to this,' he said and rolled onto his side, facing me. '*Gather the early dewdrops of summer and wear them like a crown. Run through the wilderness so your feet are stuck with earth. Find him in the harebell and purple ragged robin, and you can make him your prince. Together you are invincible under cloud-scudded skies.*'

'It doesn't rhyme,' I said.

He filled my awkward silence with a peel of laughter that curled with the smoke of his cigarette.

'You're Margo,' he said.

'Yes.'

'I sit behind you in history,' he said. 'I'm Raff.'

'Yes.'

I knew who he was – everyone knew who Raff Alon was and exactly where he was in the room if you shared

109

a lesson with him. He had a laugh that bathed a room in sunshine.

'You wear your hair down,' he said.

'Yes,' I said, again, and then thought I should stop just saying yes like some sort of stupid robot.

'It's nice,' he smiled. 'Like spun gold so be careful of the Rumplestiltskins of the world.'

My heart thrummed. 'OK,' I said because I didn't know what else to say. Cora would have thought of something witty or flirtatious.

'What does Margo mean?' he asked.

No one had ever asked me that before and it took me aback.

'It means "pearl",' I said.

He looked up at the sky and whilst he did, I studied his face in profile. Strong and handsome with myrtle eyes. He was the most beautiful thing I'd ever seen.

'*I will line our memories up*,' he said. '*Polish them like pearls and then I will fill my pockets with them and wade into the black.*'

'Is that in the book?' I asked.

'No,' he said. 'I just made it up.'

'You're a poet?'

'I'm a fraud,' he laughed.

'I thought it was very good,' I said.

'You're too kind,' he said. 'Perhaps you're a good liar?'

I blushed.

'I'd need a fancy poet name,' he said.

'What's wrong with your name?'

'Is Alon very memorable?' he said. 'Not sure.' He looked down at the page of his open book. 'I could be Rafael Harebell.'

'It sort of rhymes.' I smiled.

He laughed, a loud bark, which settled on my heart like stardust.

'Do you like poetry?' he asked.

'I suppose I do.'

He dragged on his cigarette. 'Give me some of yours.'

'Some poetry? Oh no.'

'Why not?'

I looked at him, helplessly and with my heart hammering. 'I don't have – I can't think of something just on the spot like that.'

He waited a moment for me to prove I had anything that resembled confidence or a personality and then he stood and I knew I'd lost my chance.

'We better get out of here,' he said. 'Goodbye Margo-that-means-pearl.'

He smiled down at me, and whistled as he walked back towards the school buildings. I was left there rolling his name around my mouth – Raff Alon. In those snatched minutes with him, despite my acute embarrassment, I felt alight.

The sound of people clapping takes me out of my memory, and I see Mary closing a book, having finished her reading. Has the whole thing finished? I don't think I heard a word of her poetry.

The bookseller claps his hands. 'Let's have coffee and cake and sign some books, shall we?'

The room murmurs its agreement. Chairs scrape back on the wooden flooring, feet scuff and shuffle towards the back table, and I hear the sound of the coffee machine buzzing into action and the rattle of plates. Raff stands as I stay still, thinking now would be the time to make myself known to him. I could walk up to him and we could talk, I could try to finally make sense of what happened that night, but I don't move, my feet don't seem to let me. I'm a coward, I think. Frightened, anxious, stupid Margo – just as I've always been. I stay rigid behind the shelves, blood pulsating in my ears, and count off the minutes as the conversation murmurs in the background. I start to worry because I'll be needed at home soon.

'Bye, Martin,' Raff says.

I peer around the shelves to see him walk out of the shop and then I make a decision. I'm going to follow him.

I wonder if he'll take a bus, a train, if he's driven, but he's done none of these things. He walks up the high street and into Regent's Park and I follow, stay twenty yards behind him. His gait hasn't changed; he walks with purpose; straight-backed with his head up like a soldier and I'm bungled in comparison; I have to keep my mind focused on not tripping over my own feet. He still wears the same cologne – something fresh like the sea, or the woodland, something with pepper, black tea. I don't know what it is, but Cora would. I drink it up in the air as he pauses by the open-air theatre to reach inside his jacket, bending his head. A moment later a cloud of smoke engulfs him before he carries on through it and I carry on after him. In his wake I realise it's not a cigarette but a joint he's lit. He holds it pinched between his thumb and forefinger and I can see its glow as his arm moves by his side.

He walks west out of the park and I wonder if he lives in Maida Vale, in Swiss Cottage, St John's Wood. Has he got a house like Emmeline and David? He walks past the white-columned houses with their gold letterboxes and black-and-white chequerboard porch tiles and soon we've passed all the places I thought he would live. He flicks the butt of the joint carelessly on the kerb for a passing street cleaner. I wonder if he lives beyond, overlooking the green in Queen's Park because he's always loved green spaces; he and Cora would escape the school grounds and go to the fields and woodland beyond. I flush at the memory of following them on occasion. But he doesn't veer westwards, instead walks straight up Maida Vale Road towards Kilburn and I struggle to keep up with him in this mass of people. He walks past the Primark, the market stalls and betting shops, past an addiction rehabilitation centre, and a factory outlet store before he turns down a residential street. The front gardens here are unattended and there are cars parked, cramping both sides of the road. I watch as he takes a set of keys from his jacket pocket, lets himself inside one of the houses and closes its door behind him and I'm left in surprise. Is this his house? I don't know what I expected but it wasn't this. His parents lived half their year in Tel Aviv and the other half in Hampstead, but time has changed us.

I draw in a breath, step forwards to knock on the door, until I see a sudden movement in the window next to the door. It's a woman, blonde. I lean to see her but she's disappeared as quickly as she came. It's thrown me that there's someone else in the house, and more so that there was something familiar about her.

I sit on the duvet chair in my room and think about Raff. I'm scrolling through my phone, reading all the poems on his Twitter feed, giving myself up to his poetry. I think how much he changed me in just a few minutes in that field and treated me like I was worth something; a rare treasure that he'd found and was delighted with.

After that encounter in the meadow I was even more aware of him and so painfully conscious of myself and how I looked to him. In history classes I constantly worried if my hair was brushed neatly, if my shirt collar was pressed down as it should be, if I had a ladder in my tights, and then I would chastise myself because who would ever notice these things about me? Certainly not someone like him.

But a fortnight later, during silent reading, I felt my chair rock forward as he pushed it gently with his foot. Once, twice, three times.

'Pearl!' he hissed and I turned, flushed with furious embarrassment and excitement at his secret name for me. A girl next to him was looking at us and I felt her curious eyes on me as Raff passed me a folded piece of paper – an origami crane.

I turned back to my desk, awestruck at its delicate form.

'Open it,' he whispered.

My heart started to pound because I had never received a note before, and in the split second before I unfolded it, I was intoxicated at its promise. I opened it; alert that he was watching me do it and that that my fingers were clammy. The crane was tiny but scrawled on the paper was a poem written in biro.

Sweetheart, let's lay under this embellished sky,
Under the way and atop the scent of flowers,
Cosy up to me like I'm the bonfire of your childhood
    years,
Kiss me on this endless night for hours.

The rest of the room seemed to fade to white and my eyes could only see this piece of paper with these beautiful words in his slanted handwriting. A note, to me.

'Turn it over,' came his whisper.

I thought I might faint. Was it a date to meet him in the meadow again? No. It was three words that pierced my inflated stupid heart.

'*Ode to Cora.*'

'Will you put in a good word for me with your sister?'

The words in front of me blurred with a rush of tears to my eyes.

'Margo-that-means-pearl?' he said and he nudged my chair again. 'Yeah?'

115

I dipped my head in a nod. I couldn't turn around because he might have seen the heartbreak in my eyes. That was it then; I was forever the silver to Cora's gold. She deserved him, of course, because she radiated charisma like the sun, and I was everything, and also nothing, like her.

I feel my jaw clench. But *I* was at the reading in Marylebone and *I* have been the first to see him and not Cora.

There's a knock on my door.

'Hello?' I say.

David comes in and holds out a package to me. 'Hi Margo. This was delivered for you.'

'Oh,' I say and take it. 'Thank you so much.'

'Goodnight,' he says and closes the door again.

I stare at the package; I know what it is by its postmark. The pills have arrived from America but I don't move to open them. A week ago perhaps I would have torn at them, tipped them straight from the bottle into my mouth, but after all this time something has shifted. Physically I'm worse for being off them. Mentally, I'm stronger. I put them on a shelf, high where the kids won't reach them if they come into my room.

My phone beeps and I pick it up, opening the message app. Cora has sent me a series of texts.

Don't see a therapist. It's all a load of shit.
Come to me and we'll get drunk together. Reminisce about the good times – good times only. That's all you need. Some cathartic drinking, OK?

I put my phone down. Since when did my sister ever want to go out with me and reminisce the rosy scenes of our childhood? Clearly she doesn't want to even entertain the idea of what happened to Annie, or the night of her accident, and she doesn't want me to see the psychotherapist either.

I need to see Raff again; he might be the only person able to tell me about that night. I think I'll be doing Cora a favour not to mention it.

TWELVE

CORA

I wish that I hadn't gone to Granny's damn flat, hadn't had to see the whiteness of that service sheet. I don't want to think about the funeral, how I had to support Margo through it with whispered words of reassurance into her ears. Why did she ask me about Annie and about Raff? They belong to a yellow-brick road now overgrown and tangled with thorns.

She hasn't replied to the messages I've sent and I wonder if I need to go and see her. I know she's read them and it infuriates me that she has the audacity to ignore them.

'Not enjoying yourself?' Nav interrupts my thoughts.

He puts two cocktails on the table.

'No,' I say, 'I mean – yeah, sorry. I am.'

It's Thursday night and he's dragged me to a fetish club night in an old theatre where prop rooms and dressing rooms have been converted into torture and spanking rooms, where the main stage hosts a naked orgy of people writhing to classic nineties R & B. Bodies are vacuumed into leather, breasts spill from corsets, stiletto boots prowl for hearts to trample on and cocks are out for preening.

'You were miles gone. What were you thinking?' he says.

'I was thinking that I own that strap-on over there,' I say, nodding to a man a few meters across from us.

He chortles, takes a gulp of one of the cocktails. 'Wow, that's strong. Did you see the guy dressed as a unicorn with his wang covered in sparkles?'

'Seen it and won't ever unsee it,' I say.

'You haven't gone to the spanking room yet?'

'I'm not sure I'm in the mood.'

He frowns. 'You're always in the mood for that,' he says because his bedroom is next to mine.

'I've got things on my mind,' I say.

'Like what? The play?'

'Yeah. It's on loop in my head all the time.'

'Why did you chase that part so bad?' he asks.

'Mostly because of Miss Patricia,' I say. 'She was my old dance teacher. Our old nanny.'

He looks surprised. 'You guys had a nanny? Like, a live-in one?'

'Yeah,' I say.

'We've lived together nearly three years and you didn't tell me you were a little rich kid?'

'Believe it, babe,' I say. 'Boarding school, skiing, pony clubs, the works.'

'Jesus, what happened to you since then?' he laughs.

'I reinvented myself.'

'You sure did,' he says. 'Where's all your money gone? You live on beans and toast.'

'Let's just say I'm disinherited,' I say.

119

'Seriously?'

'And a bad cook.'

He raises his eyebrows. 'You know, it probably would have helped you open some doors if you had kept in with the rich crowd.'

'Well, I didn't,' I say.

'Idiot.'

'*Anyway*,' I say. 'Miss Patricia was first and foremost a dancer. She danced *Mirror, Mirror* when she was much younger and she taught it to us when we were little, before we even knew what the words were. And the words, Nav. It's like poetry. Speaks to my soul.'

He sips at his cocktail, makes a face again. 'Shit, this is going to blow my head off.'

'When I was eighteen at school, I suggested that we perform it for the last production before school finished,' I say. 'I knew agents would come to the show and I needed to dance my best dance and that was it.'

'So basically you're obsessed with it?'

'I *need* to do it,' I say. 'Because I didn't get to dance it all that night when I was eighteen, and I didn't get an agent and I didn't live the life I should have led.'

'Deeeeeeep,' he says.

'I didn't dance for a long time and it was because of Margo,' I say.

'Oh my days! Margo!' he says. 'When *do* I get to meet her? You tease me with her!'

I drink and the cocktail's sweetness fuzzes my tongue. 'I told you, our place is too dirty for her to feel comfortable.'

He grins. 'I find it so weird that you both live in London and you're so separate.'

I shrug. 'She works long hours. She lives in Kensington with a very wealthy family, like one's a professor and one's a barrister or something, I can't remember really.'

I'm vague with Nav but I know exactly where Margo is and who exactly her employers are. She lives with Emmeline and David Andrews and their twins in a white house, which rises four storeys. It has a heavy front door painted navy and with pot plants by the side of it that are never vandalised or stolen because that's not the sort of neighbourhood. I've seen her there but she's never seen me. Hell, I've followed her to the school and I've watched the kids skipping around her legs dressed in little white shirts and maroon jackets, black trousers for the boy and a pleated black-and-maroon skirt for the girl. I've seen how she has taken their matching maroon-and-black school bags from over her own shoulders and placed them on their small backs, all the while talking to them and they've turned and smiled at her until she's put her palms gently against the backs of their little heads to steer them ahead and into the school. I've watched her when she's picked them up again and she's bent down to those kids and kissed them on the cheeks like they're hers. She's loving, she's wonderful, she's everything I'm not. Sometimes I wonder if that's what she wants above everything else – twins of her own. Would one be good and the other bad?

'Kensington? That's not as cool as living with me,' Nav says.

'For sure,' I say. 'Your hovel is an undisputed palace.'

'Can we go and see her though? Maybe she can make us posh dinner.'

'No.'

'Why not?'

'Because she's a nanny, yeah?' I say. 'It's not *her* house. She can't invite people over.'

'Urgh, but she sounds so amazing! I imagine it would feel like meeting the Queen or something.'

I take another sip of the cocktail. 'You know what? Whenever Margo sees a coin with the queen facing downwards, she turns it back upwards as not to upset her Majesty or be taken away for treason.'

Nav laughs. 'Are you for real?'

'For real.'

'I'm actually in love with her,' he says. 'Did she ever want to be on the stage like you?'

'No.'

I don't tell him that Margo was a dancer like me. That when we were all tiny, she and Annie had gone to the same stage schools as I had, had trailed in the wake I'd forged for myself. I don't tell him that Margo was, in fact, technically better than me, especially in ballet, but when we'd gone to boarding school she'd forgone it because she knew that it was *my* thing. And she fucking owed it to me to let me have it, to surpass her.

'She didn't dance,' I say.

'She always wanted to look after brats like you were then?'

'She wanted to write. Or act. I don't know. Whatever she was reading – and that was always because she was such a book nerd – she'd pretend to be the characters. She'd be Aslan out of Narnia, and Huckleberry Finn. Such a weirdo.'

'Everyone does that stuff,' Nav says.

I arch an eyebrow. 'Carrie from *Carrie*?'

'Maybe not that one,' he says.

'When she was Aslan, she used to speak in this weird voice and go everywhere on all fours.'

'Method acting,' Nav says. 'I applaud it.'

'She couldn't act for shit. Even as Aslan.'

'Even with such support from the family?' he says sarcastically.

'She'd keep it up for days,' I say. 'And there was Bad Penny, who was out of some fairy tale or whatever, and was really angry at everyone. She played that part too. I made everyone at school call her Bad Penny for years.'

Nav explodes with laughter. 'Bad Penny? God, Cora, you're *such* a bitch.'

'Sue me.'

He drinks. 'You don't sound like you even like her much,' he says. 'Aren't twins supposed to do everything together?'

'You're thinking of Enid Blyton books.'

'But you've got the weird twin thing, right? When one of you hurts themselves, the other one feels it?'

I'm quiet a moment. 'There were some twin things actually,' I say. 'Like when she rung me when I'd cut myself on a kitchen knife by mistake one time, and when we were little she knew when I'd fallen off Brew, this absolute fucker of a horse I used to ride. She knew when I'd argued with my friend Sabine at school, when I was upset, or angry or happy, she'd text, she'd call, she'd *find* me. I couldn't ever be without her. It was like she was *living* me. Living me and not herself.'

'Fuck her for caring,' he grins.

'Shut up, Nav. It was weird – she knew all this stuff about me, but I never knew anything about her.'

'Because you're a narcissist?'

'That's one explanation,' I say.

'I think it's the *only* explanation,' he says.

'But we're not *meant* to be two halves that make one,' I say. 'We're individuals, each and every one of us. Independent from anyone else. It makes me mad that people don't think they're a whole by themselves, and Margo is like that. She's stifling and I was always assigned her fucking guardian.'

'Calm down, drama queen.'

I whack him, harder than I need to, but he doesn't get it. No one ever could.

When we were twelve we lived in Doha where our parents had been stationed for a year. We lived in a gated community, had a private swimming pool and access to an enormous communal playground. All of us kids played out in the streets together; games like marbles and hopscotch like we were something out of the seventies, and our parents approved of it because they felt it delayed the lancing of our innocence, and they could praise themselves on what a good job they'd done to protect us from the big wide world.

I remember the day Margo cut herself. Annie and I were in the pool on lilos, swaying with the rock of the water, when I heard the water slosh as Margo got into the pool. She was quiet a moment until she let out a scream that sliced through my head and I sat up immediately, wobbling on the inflatable crocodile, my lap plunged into cold water.

'What? What's happened, Margo?'

And then I saw it. A swirling of red into the blue, like paint in a water pot, which twisted towards me like a thing alive. I gasped, looked at Margo who was holding her wrist. I could see fat droplets of blood seeping through her fingers and landing in the water. She looked white, had already started shivering from shock, and I dived from the crocodile straight into the blood to her.

'What happened?' I cried.

'It doesn't hurt,' she said.

'Annie, get Patricia,' I said.

'No,' Margo said. 'Not Miss Patricia.'

Annie was sitting up on her lizard lilo, alarmed, her eyes wide with terror at the blood curling in vermilion ribbons.

'Mum isn't here,' I said. 'Or Dad. We need help, Margo.'

'It's OK though, I'm fine. I've just cut myself on something.'

'Is there glass in here?' I looked down at the pool floor where our legs bandied with the movement of water and then I looked to Annie. 'Don't get off your lilo, paddle over to the side and then get out, OK?'

'OK,' Annie nodded and she started to move towards the side of the pool.

I placed my own hand over Margo's, didn't think twice about the blood that would flood my own hands because we had shared a womb. Her blood was my blood, whether I liked it or not.

'Just hold it really tight, OK?'

Margo said nothing, let me guide her out and let me put a towel over her shoulders. I could hear Annie calling for Miss Patricia inside, saw her wet footprints on the paving stones start to evaporate.

'I saw some older boys here yesterday,' I said and I steered us over towards the steps of the pool. 'They must have broken a bottle or something, and I don't know, thrown it over maybe. Or maybe it's a loose sharp tile. Patricia will tell the pool people. Are you OK?'

She looked up at me, smiled weakly. 'I'm OK.'

'Can you get out? Because Patricia can't swim, remember?'

'Can't we stay in here?' she said and looked to the red thread of blood in the water. 'It looks so pretty.'

She was slipping into a strange state and so I put my arms under her body and I heaved her out and we lay on the side of the pool together, the heat from the stones keeping us warm.

'I did it,' she said into my ear. 'In the bedroom with Mum's razor.'

I looked at her in alarm. 'Your wrist?' I said. 'Why?'

'To see how it felt,' she said. 'And then . . . I wanted to show you. Here in the water. Just us in the water.'

'Margo,' I said. 'Did you do this because of . . . Tring?'

'No,' she said but she smiled and it felt sly.

Suddenly, I was angry. 'You're lying. You did this so I wouldn't go to dance school, didn't you?'

'No,' she said and her eyes switched and were anxious.

I got up and she reached for me. 'Don't go.'

'Miss Patricia is coming,' I said. 'Good luck explaining it to her.'

Later that night, when Margo and Annie were asleep in the bedroom upstairs, I told my parents about the razor. They were sat in the lounge with Miss Patricia, my father drinking his two fingers of Scotch, and my mother drinking iced rosé wine. Miss Patricia drank water because she only ever drank water in front of them.

None of them were shocked when I told them what Margo had admitted to me, they only looked sad. My mother knelt down next to me and looked into my eyes, and in the beat of silence before she spoke, I knew what she was going to ask.

'Can you be strong?' she said. 'Can you be the strongest person you can be?'

'No, Mum,' I began because I knew, I *knew* what she was going to say.

'We've decided not to let you audition for a place at Tring Performing Arts,' Father said abruptly and I remember my mother's face as he cut straight to the point as he tended to with most things.

'Samuel.' She breathed out his name like a sigh.

'You'll go to the boarding school in Windsor with Margo and Annie.'

'You can't do this to her,' Miss Patricia said, straight to my defence.

'Patricia,' my father said. 'This doesn't concern you.'

'It *does* concern me! I've watched her for years, *taught* her dance, and she's good, Sam. You have to let her go!'

'I have to do what's best for my family,' my father said. 'Don't live your life through my child.'

She stood then, shaking with rage. 'You don't understand her!' she hissed. 'What she could be!'

'Enough,' my mother whispered because she loved Miss Patricia, owed her so much in looking after us, but didn't want a bigger argument. Mother turned to me. 'Cora, Margo won't want to be on her own in a strange school, thousands of miles from us and a hundred miles from you at Tring and this – the razor thing – was her way of telling us all that she doesn't feel safe.'

'She'll have Annie!' I said.

'But Annie is two years below her,' Mother said. 'And you know that her connection with Annie is not the same as what you two have.'

'Mum . . .' Tears started to roll down my cheeks. 'Tring is all I've ever wanted.'

Miss Patricia tutted. 'Margo drags Cora down.'

She understood my pain; she had trained at the Royal Academy of Dance, had been a prima ballerina. She'd had it all before it had been stripped away from her and she didn't want the same for me.

'*Please*, Pat,' my mother said.

'We have to go to Venezuela when you all start school,' my father told me like I didn't already know. 'But we can't leave with Margo in this sort of state without knowing she'll be OK. There is an extremely good dance school near the boarding school. Your mother has made arrangements for you to join them.'

'You can still dance,' Mother said. 'I promise. This school tours for competitions, they put on shows every year and invite talent scouts and agents.'

'But it won't be the same!' I cried. 'Miss Patricia *knows* what she's talking about and you don't have a clue!'

'Don't you speak to us like that,' Father snapped.

Our mother put her hand to his arm but he shook her off.

'No, Amelia,' he said. 'I've made my decision.'

'You will ruin her one chance,' Miss Patricia said.

'She hasn't even done the audition!' my father said.

'You know this girl is a star and yet you have clipped her wings! You need to nurture a talent like this—'

'Enough!' Father shouted and when our father shouted, that was it. The final word.

I bit my lip. My twelve-year-old self struggled for the vocabulary to explain to them that Margo was an albatross around my neck, that I carried her emotionally on my back, and if we went to the same school I would buckle underneath her oppressive weight. I broke down in sobs and my father told me not to be so dramatic and to go to bed but instead I went to Annie's room, lay on her floor and stared into the darkness, seething with anger.

129

'I'm sorry,' I heard a voice say from Annie's door frame and it was her, Margo, because she had listened in on everything. 'I'm so sorry. I couldn't cope with the thought of being – of being without you.'

I pretended not to hear her. I was worried I would fly at her and tear at her face with my nails. Perhaps I should have done.

She lay down on the floor and curled up behind me and I was so beaten that I let her place her arms around my waist – just like we had done at the poolside – because love is so complicated, and so is pain.

Dancing *Mirror, Mirror* is my one ambition. It's my revenge on her. A play of rivalry and tricks because I do so love tricks.

'Shit, Cor,' Nav says. 'Look at that woman butt naked on roller skates.'

'I love her,' I say. 'And nine o'clock, man sandwich.'

'I adore this place,' he says.

'I'm going to take that guy home tonight,' I say, nodding over his shoulder.

Nav looks. 'Police uniform, eighties shades, ripped like a beast?'

I drink. 'Correct.'

THIRTEEN

MARGO

The school bell rings to signal an oncoming stampede of children. Marie and Jonny are two of the first out and they run together into the playground, weave between groups like they have sonar. I bend down and kiss them each on the head. These children give me stability, they are my strength. I take their bags on each shoulder and we start to leave the gates.

'Did you have a good day?' I ask.

They nod in unison.

'I thought we'd do something a bit different this afternoon,' I say. 'As you don't have after-school clubs and it's a Friday. The weather's OK for end of September, isn't it? Maybe we could walk to that place in Maida Vale for pancakes?'

They look at me, jaws dropping. 'Yes!'

'Tell me about your day,' I say as we walk up the road.

'We did phonics,' Marie says. 'Jonny made a spaceship.'

'That sounds like a lot of fun.'

'What did you do today? Marie asks.

'Nothing really, dove. Cleaning and cooking and filling in everyone's schedules on the calendar.'

And fretting about what I'm doing right now.

We walk through Hyde Park and up Edgware Road, skirt around market stalls and I inhale deeply because I've always liked this road – all its smells and flavoured smokes. I see droplets spotting on the pavement. I haven't brought an umbrella because I left the house flustered. The children will get wet, but they skip and jump between the beads of water on the ground before they bloom into one another and they're running now, laughing as the rain bounces off their heads. They remind me of Cora and I, and I adore their closeness, but pray for their sakes that they find their independence from each other and save themselves inevitable heartache – to be a twin is a poisoned chalice.

We reach the cafe, shelter inside and watch the rain through the glass windows as it pours from the sky. The children eat their pancakes and play I-Spy and I sip at a scalding coffee, watching a woman who's laughing and clutching at her man's jacket as he struggles with an umbrella. He pops it in time for me to miss their private kiss but I know that's what they're doing. She's standing on tiptoes and leaning into him, and he's holding her like only a lover could.

I remember being out in rain like this, I remember an umbrella. I was traipsing back indoors from the hockey pitch after Games, the last to be walking inside from the field – I was always last because I didn't want anyone to pay heed to the fact I never walked to the shower block with anyone else – and I was muddy and tired. I kept my head down against the rain but I felt someone was watching me and I lifted my eyes to see Raff twenty yards away by the rugby field holding a red umbrella. He'd been injured the week previously and was confined to the sidelines for a fortnight. He smiled at me, that lazy sexy smile I'd seen him use a handful of times on my sister, and I smiled back, delighted. But it was as if I's stolen his smile, because he stopped and looked away and I understood immediately that he had mistaken me for Cora. My usual bowed head had disguised me because of the rain – everyone had dipped their faces against it – and it had momentarily fooled him. I cast my eyes downward again, mortified because, to my shame, I realised that I had so wanted to experience that moment as Cora would have done. I wanted to have him smile at me that way, wave me over and shelter me under the umbrella and sling his other arm around my shoulder as he did with her. Why did I want that? Because I'd never had it with anyone? Or was it because I wanted to be like my sister?

People rarely mistook us at school but after that incident, I started to experiment with people who didn't know us. When I was sure Cora and her friends weren't anywhere near me, I found that I strutted down the corridors as she would have done. I smiled at the lower-year boys as she would have, with my chest out and lips pouted. Once, alone in the bathrooms before maths, I rolled my skirt up four times and slashed a bright lipstick onto my lips. Cora had left it in her washbag and I had taken it. I looked at my reflection for about a minute, astounded how different I looked, before I was interrupted by Sabine, Cora's best friend, walking out of one of the stalls. I froze with the lipstick hovering so close to my lip that I could feel my breath on my fingers.

'Oh,' Sabine said. 'Didn't know you were in here. We're going to be late.'

My rolled skirt was so dazzlingly short, a parody almost to how Cora and her friends wore theirs, that I was convinced that any second Sabine would notice and we'd lock eyes and she'd know it was me, but she barely looked at me. Without pause after shaking her hands of water, she hooked her arm through mine and waltzed me out of the bathrooms down the corridors. Through my black tights, I felt my skirt skimming my buttocks and I was terrified of being shouted at by teachers, was terrified of the feeling of air being where it shouldn't be, but the hallways were near empty because we were late for class.

'You know that Sal is going to run for Prefect next term?' Sabine said. 'She'd fuck up all the parties in East Block, I know it.'

I didn't know about any parties in East Block.

'And she wants shorts for Games,' she said. 'Which is fine but they're like boys' shorts. I want short shorts or nothing, right?'

I nodded, mute.

'Did you and Raff go out again last night after lights out?' she said. 'You've got to be careful, your luck is going to run out with who's on duty one night.'

We'd gone ten steps before I found my voice.

'Shit,' I said, in a slow and low-timbred voice, a voice that I didn't know I was capable of talking with – Cora's voice. 'Sab, I forgot my folders. I'll catch you up, OK?'

'Sure,' she said absently.

I unhooked myself from her and she carried on down the corridor. I ran back to the bathrooms and locked myself in the toilet, unrolled my skirt and wiped fiercely at my lips with tissue paper. I stayed there for a full five minutes, panting like a dog through terror and also exhilaration because I'd fooled her. She'd believed I was the shining, sparkling twin and not the dulled one. I looked at myself that night in the bathroom mirror when all the other girls were asleep in the dormitory and I put my fingers to the glass and I whispered a question to myself.

Who are you?

But the reply was, of course –

No one special.

I come back to the twins who have finished eating and stopped playing I-Spy.

'Come on,' I say. 'The sun is trying to come out.'

The droplets have eased, looking golden on the window pane. The twins jump down from their seats and start off out of the café before I've even picked up my bag. I follow them out of the doors.

'Why have we come this way, Margo?' Jonny asks, breaking my thoughts.

I've walked us up to Kilburn. I've walked them to his *house*. Raff's house.

'Shall we go home now?' Marie says.

'I just want to stay one moment,' I say. 'OK? There's someone I just want to see . . . someone who I just want to . . .'

I trail off. Why did I bring them with me? So I could hide away under the guise of being a parent if I saw him and bottled out? Did I want him to think they were my children and that I've made a success of my life, against all the odds people at school had decided to stack against me?

The children shrug, lean against the brick wall and play rock, paper, scissors, and I stay still, and watch his door. My head feels heavy, like my brain has swollen with the effort of keeping focused, but I'm rewarded another twenty minutes later when the door opens and out he steps in black jeans, scruffy white trainers and the same leather jacket he wore at the reading. A cigarette is between his fingers and he's digging into his back pocket for a lighter as he waits at the door. He is so bewitching that I feel rocket-speed pain bolt through my entire body. I could watch him but that's not why I'm here.

'Raff?' My voice is so quiet that I don't even think I've managed to say his name aloud but his body turns and his eyes meet mine.

His mouth slackens. 'Oh my God,' he says. 'Margo?'

The children turn, quiet, but my heart is thumping loudly – he recognises me. He knows it's *me*. I go to him, electrified by the warmth of his proximity and by his familiar, beautiful smell.

'Yes,' I say. 'It's me.'

I go forward to embrace him but he steps back.

'What are you doing here?' His tone is wary and cold. 'How did you find me?'

'I – I came to your reading,' I say. 'I found you . . . you used the name. Harebell.'

His expression flickers for a moment to one of recognition. 'Yes. But . . . I—'

'Can we talk?'

He looks at me like I'm a ghost before shaking his head. 'It's been *nine years*. You know the hell and back I've been through in all that time? I can't talk to you.'

I'm taken aback by his response. 'What? But Raff, please?'

But he doesn't answer me, directs his attention to the children who are staring at us. 'Are these your kids?'

'Yes.' I look at the children who frown at me. 'I mean, no.'

'Don't come back here,' he says and he goes back into his house, slams the door.

The three of us stand in silence before Marie moves close to me, and puts her hand in mine. 'Is that your boyfriend, Margo?'

I keep my eyes on his door. 'He was never mine.'

But as I say this, a memory assaults my senses. There's a zipping image of Raff in my eyes – his shirt is unbuttoned, and my fingers are running over his hot skin.

FOURTEEN

CORA

It's Wednesday and Hazel O'Mara from *The Stage* is sitting at the back of the studio on a chair with her long legs crossed and a notebook open on her lap. Her tortoiseshell glasses are propped atop her blonde beehive and a red and grey tweed suit encases her beautifully slender body. She's in her fifties, has led a colourful life on the stage and is now a top columnist for the magazine, infamous for giving honest and punchy reviews. For Jean-Luc to have invited her here on our fifth-ever rehearsal, a raw rehearsal, is a bold and confident statement and I'm nervous as hell.

The narrators are standing in a line to the left and are dressed in bold, bright colours. The three of us dancers match them and take up the rest of the space. Rosa and I are in gold, of course, the colour of sunshine, positivity and energy, but none of us are dressed in what we'll wear for the performance. That's a long way off being decided but I'm glad because everyone knows wearing performance clothes in rehearsal is bad luck.

'Hazel has kindly given us forty-five minutes of her time, *oui?*' Jean-Luc says. 'So let's show her what we have worked on. Theatre starts in darkness – which we don't have, obviously – so we imagine it. Spotlights on the narrators. *Debut*, Rosa.'

I glance at Hazel and then I exhale, try to blot her out. I also want to blot out Gisele who watches me intensely and makes me nervous.

It is winter and my tongue is cold. I cannot tell this story alone. Sit down and warm my hands. You were there, you remember. It could have been something wonderful, couldn't it?

'Spotlight on Cora,' Jean-Luc says quietly.

My cue. Face up, wide smile and outstretched arms with palms up and straight into a combined jazz tap routine. Thirty seconds where my feet are light and I work around the room. Click-click-click go my feet. Spin, heel, toe. I flit effortlessly between the moves, nerve roll, compass turn, body roll.

'Lovely,' Jean-Luc says. 'Move across towards Rosa after the riff, smile at her. You are one. You can interact.'

I nod, chasse towards Rosa and we smile at one another as she speaks.

Mine was a life of a thousand possibilities but you took the one meant for me.

I stop mid tap, arms drop. I look to Jean-Luc and Joanna, try not to look at Hazel but my eyes find her anyway. Her dark eyes are on me.

Rosa continues.

You became the all, ate me whole.

Spot and turn one, two, three, four times and then move backwards, arms outreaching.

'Into black,' Joanna says, for the benefit of Hazel.

I can hear Miss Patricia's voice in my head. *Concentrate, child.*

'*Bien,*' Jean-Luc continues. 'Drop your head on the third count when you're moving back. Carry on.'

I give it my everything and I'm painfully conscious of Hazel's pen flying through the pages of her notebook, of Jean-Luc's faith in me, and of keeping up with the other dancers who are technically better than I am. But the further we go into it, I begin to relax, feel the words running into my veins, and I see that her eyes spotlight me and then it's like I see nothing at all. I think of Miss Patricia and how she wove this play into my very soul. The words hang above my head like stars and I dance beneath them – this story holds power over me for so many reasons.

'What did you think, Hazel?' Jean-Luc asks as we finish.

We all turn to look at her, hopeful children to a messiah.

'I think I like it, Jean-Luc,' she replies.

'High praise indeed,' Jean-Luc beams. '*Merci.*'

'My photographer will come on your next rehearsal,' she says, closes her notebook. 'I want photos of a hold,' she says and then looks to Zdravko and me. 'These two.'

Jean-Luc snaps his folder of notes closed and stands from his chair. 'Check the schedule for your days in. I've texted it to you all.'

Me. A photograph of *me* in *The Stage.*

I take my time leaving the studio, pretend to sort my bag and call goodbye to everyone as they file out. When I'm certain of being alone, I get up to stretch some more and then stare around the empty studio. Doubtless there will be another class in here soon but for now the space is mine.

I stand up into first position and my eyes find themselves in the mirror. Focus. I spot and turn three times, round and around and around, head up, arms strong, leg muscles screaming.

Perhaps it's not your fault? Perhaps it's mine? Perhaps I would never have kept him tangled in silk sheets in my bed. Perhaps he would have always cut through them to get to you.

I should be dizzy but I feel alive. This, this is the moment I've been waiting for all my life. I'm now on the cusp of something big and wonderful that marks the start of my life as a dancer. It should have happened years ago but it's finally arrived and I can't fuck it up. I grand jeté to the other side of the room and chaine back again, spinning into a flurry of cabrioles and brises, delicate but demanding jumps. There's no routine here, only steps and jumps, energy and passion and all the things Annie loved about dance.

I stop, hear my breath in my ears. Annie? Did I say her name? I scold myself. Since Margo brought her up in the car, and *Raff* up too, my head has started to drift in directions I don't want it to. I push them from my head. There's no space for them here.

'Hello,' I hear a voice say behind me.

I jump, see Gisele in the mirror.

'You dance so beautifully.'

'You scared me,' I say. 'I thought I was the only one here.'

'I was just talking to Hazel,' she says.

'You know her?'

She smiles. 'Only a bit,' she says. 'Good to keep in with the journos though, isn't it?'

I suck my teeth. I've never been in with the journalists, only with casting directors in hotel rooms. 'Yeah,' I say. 'I guess it is.'

'You are an actress too, aren't you? Have you auditioned for stage before?'

'An actress?' I say. 'No, I'm only a dancer—'

'Perhaps not trained,' she says. 'But you act in your dance. It's really good.'

'Thanks.'

'I think you could really be something,' she says. 'I know Hazel thinks so.'

I stare at her. 'You think?'

'I know,' she says. 'She told me.'

'Thanks,'

'I'll leave you to it.'

I wait until I can hear her footsteps fade and still there is no class outside so I continue dancing, slower now, and sensuous. Raff liked me dancing like this. Urgh, stop, Cora, I think. Stop thinking about him.

But he would want to see me dance this. He would want to see me again, I know. He loved watching me dance, was wild about jazz and tap but especially ballet because I loved ballet out of all the other disciplines and he loved the passion I had for it.

He would sit on the floor of the local stage school studio and read his books whilst other girls were dancing, and only stop and look up when I came on stage. When he watched me, I felt like I could be anything, do anything. It was pure unrestrained joy to be studied by those green eyes. On big performance nights he would come and find me in the dressing rooms with flowers and, regardless of whether we were alone or in a room full of other dancers, he used to find the sweet spot of my neck, lick at the vein running down and bite at it to send me convulsing with delight. I liked it better when there were people watching him do it because in the mirror I could see their envy and bask in the heat of it.

For years he wrote me poetry and promised me the world. Raff and I were like mirrors to one another and happily blinded each other by our young, egotistical ideals of love. It was easy as kids, I think now, in the safety of that boarding-school environment, to soar together and for our love to be unbridled. He'd parade me to his friends like a trophy and I did the same with him because he was handsome and people adored him. We'd hold hands down the corridors, kiss under the avenue of trees between the maths and science buildings, and at night he'd climb the fire escape to my dorm and we'd fool around under the covers whilst the other girls were asleep or pretending to be. We'd sit at break time on the playing fields, my head on his lap, and he'd outline plots for novels he was going to write. I remember being sixteen and lying together in the darkness under a blanket of cloud.

'I've started a novel,' he whispered to me.

'Oh?' I said.

'It's about you, babe,' he said. 'And me.'

'Will you show me?' I asked.

'Not yet.'

'What's my role in it?' I asked.

'The love of my life,' he said. 'Of course.'

I'd smiled into the sky above us because he would always love me and I would always love him.

And then came that play. *This* play – *Mirror, Mirror*. I go over and over that night – the way the wind billowed through the window, how the piano rolled across the floorboards. How we screamed in fear as the door trembled on its hinges. There was nowhere to run.

I leave the studio, desperate for the cool of the air outside. The words from the play have filled my head and I can't escape them.

Mine was a life of a thousand possibilities but you took the one meant for me.

Mine, Margo's, Annie's. What roads might we have taken if not for that night?

I bike down the main road, go to cross the junction and then – like magic – I see her through the glass of a restaurant window, sitting and talking to someone that I can't see but know instinctively that it's a man.

'Mum?' I breathe.

144

I start pedalling, am going too fast and I'm not sure I can cross now but she might disappear, maybe she's reflected from somewhere behind me. She looks older – of course – but is it her? My eyes are dry and blurring because I need to blink them but I don't want to take my eyes off her. A car beeps me, a walker shouts, and shit, I'm going too fast. I squeeze on the brakes and lean to compensate for my speed when I see a rush of a blue car bonnet. My vision flips and I hear car tyres squeal and a crunch of gravel on the road and then the wind is knocked from my body.

'Oh!' I hear a woman gasp.

I see a blur of legs, hear a thud of trainers. I realise my head is on one side and that my face is cold on the concrete ground.

'Shit, are you OK?'

There are hands on my shoulder and my back.

'Hello? Do you need an ambulance?'

I heave myself up to sitting. A woman and a man are kneeling next to me, hands on me, human connection. I feel sick. My leather jacket is sticking to me somewhere. Something feels wrong.

'Are you all right?'

'I'm sorry,' the man says. 'I didn't see you!'

'My fault,' I say, because it was. I blink, my vision is off and I'm shaking.

'You're in shock,' says the woman.

'Is that your name? Amelia?'

I've said our mother's name. I look to the restaurant but the woman has disappeared.

'Shall I get you some tea from a café, Amelia?' the woman asks.

'I'm OK.'

'Your side,' the woman says. 'Are you hurt there?'

'No,' I say but am I? My fingers are gripping my left side and I didn't even realise.

'Can you stand?'

'I'll help you up,' the man says. 'Can I put my hands on your arms to help lift you?'

I shake my head. 'I can do it.' I get up, wince. I look down. My jacket rode up in the fall and I've scraped myself on the tarmac. There are three claw-like marks on my ribcage and they're bleeding.

'You should get those seen to,' says the woman, watching me tug my jacket down. She picks up my bag, which is lying by the side of the bike. 'You could have grit in them.'

'Shall we call you a taxi and you can go home with your bike?' the man asks. 'I'm worried you might have concussion. Shall we call someone?'

I nod. 'Yeah, thanks, a taxi.'

The woman touches my arm. 'Do you want that tea?'

'I had some water in my bag.' I look at my rucksack but I can't see my water bottle, it must have rolled out when I fell, and this tiny thing makes me want to cry.

'Sit down by that wall,' the woman says, 'and I'll be right back.'

'I'll stay with her,' says the man, putting his phone to his ear. 'I'm sorry again.'

'I crossed the junction when I shouldn't have done,' I say. 'My head was somewhere else.'

I hear him request a big car so I can fit my bike inside. 'Where do you need to go?' he asks. 'Home?'

The woman then returns with a disposable cup for me.

'I put sugar in it for the shock.'

The concern in their voices makes me want to cling to them.

'Thank you.'

I take a sip and it tastes like syrup, like Baileys, my father's favourite drink. I suddenly want my parents, both of them. I miss my mother's smile, which was rarely used, but when it was, it felt like honey.

They sit with me for a few minutes whilst I drink my tea and the taxi arrives.

'Here we go,' the man says and I can hear the relief in his voice. 'Let me put your bike in.'

'Thank you,' I say again.

They put me into the car and shut the door. Once they're out of sight, I press my hand against my side and howl with pain.

'Mum,' I whisper. 'I wish it had been you.'

Stupid child, a voice rasps in my head. Miss Patricia, my biggest supporter but also my biggest critic.

FIFTEEN

MARGO

It's Friday and I've dropped the children at school. Normally I would be heading home to start on scheduling the weekend meals but instead I'm ringing the buzzer of the dark blue door on Russell Street. I almost forgot I made this appointment to see the psychotherapist my GP recommended. I don't even really know if this is the right thing to do, but Cora doesn't seem to want to help me in remembering Annie, Granny can't help, my parents won't because I broke off all contact with them and it seems that I've already blown things with Raff.

A voice comes through over the speaker.

'Hawkins Psychotherapy Practice?' It's a soft and male voice, and crackled by distortion.

'It's – I'm Margo,' I say. 'Margo Malone.'

'Margo,' he says. 'Yes. Please come in.'

The buzzer clicks and I step inside the house, welcomed immediately by dark green walls and warm wooden flooring, tall lush green plants and bookshelves. This hallway feels so serene, like I'm breathing new air. I inhale. Mr Hawkins comes to greet me from a room to the right – I assume his office – with a coffee cup in hand. I put him at mid-fifties; he's lean and poised and wearing a blue jumper with tan elbow patches and black-rimmed glasses.

'Thank you for seeing me,' I say.

'You're most welcome,' he smiles. 'It's lovely to meet you. Please come through.'

He motions to his room. It's a cosy space painted in ocean blue with a grey sofa on one side and a big chair and desk on the other. Between them is a coffee table with a jug of water, glasses, a box of tissues, and a big glass vase of fresh flowers, in a dazzling golden-yellow.

He takes a seat on a chair and motions for me to sit on the sofa.

'This is lovely,' I say.

He smiles. There's a big clock on the wall behind his head with a frame embellished with wood carvings. Leaves and acorns and a snake, and I like these details. They give me something to focus on because I don't want to look at the flowers.

'Thank you,' he says. 'I love this space. Would you prefer it if I moved these flowers? Are you allergic?'

I blink. Why had I been staring at them?

'Oh no, sorry,' I shift on the sofa. 'They're fine.'

'I love yellow,' he says.

'Do you live here as well as work here?' I ask politely for something to say.

'I live very close,' he says, neither confirming nor denying. He places his coffee on a navy-blue coaster on the coffee table between us. 'Why have you come to see me today?'

'My GP recommended I talk to you.'

'OK,' he says. 'And why is that?'

I swallow. 'Something . . . something happened to me a long time ago that I have trouble remembering. I've had some memories come back to me but . . . everything seems like fog. I've got nothing solid.'

He picks up a pen and notebook from the desk next to him and begins to write. I notice that the front cover of the book is marbled, like a child's school art project and the colours are purples and blues. It looks like the cosmos and I wonder if Mr Hawkins thinks minds are like little universes and that's why he chose it.

'What is it about your past that you're wanting to think more clearly about?'

'My sister, Annie,' I say. 'She died when she was sixteen. I'm – I *was* – two years older than her. I was eighteen when she died.'

'I'm sorry to hear that,' he says, gently.

'I can't piece together what happened to her and I want to but it's like my brain won't let me.'

He nods. 'The trauma of losing a loved one is never easy to talk about. Death will upset our balance.'

My throat feels dry. I point to the jug of water. 'May I?' I say.

'Of course.'

I pour a glass, drink it all.

'Would you like to talk about her?'

'No,' I say, quickly. 'I mean – I sort of came here *to* talk about her but . . . I don't feel ready to yet. Is that silly?'

'Not silly in the slightest,' he says. 'Quite understandable. We can talk about her in your own time. Is there anything you would feel comfortable in talking about? Do you work?'

'I want to talk about the children,' I say.

'You have children?'

'No,' I say. 'I look after children. I'm a nanny. That's my job.'

'That's nice,' he smiles. 'Have you always wanted to be a nanny?'

'I like to keep people safe,' I say. 'That's what a nanny does.'

'Yes.'

'But I worry about them,' I say. 'I worry that I'm not doing enough for them.'

'Jobs can be very stressful even when we enjoy them. Especially when they involve direct care of another person.'

'I imagine it's stressful doing what *you* do, Mr Hawkins.'

'It's rewarding and terrible in equal measure, Margo,' he says. 'Thank you for asking. It does tire me too.'

'I'm making mistakes,' I say. 'It's the tiredness. And it's because I'm thinking about . . . I'm thinking about Annie. She's filling all my thoughts. I'm getting forgetful.'

'It's human to make mistakes.'

'But there are consequences to mistakes. I don't want to lose my job. Those children are precious to me.'

He uncrosses and recrosses his legs and I think of him like he's a long-legged bird. Perhaps a stork or a heron. 'Tell me what you love about the children.'

'They're innocent,' I say. 'That's precious.'

'Childhood can be a very special time,' he says writing in his notebook. 'Did you enjoy yours? With your sister, Annie?'

'We moved around the world because my father was in the oil trade. We didn't really see a lot of my parents but we lived in some lovely places.'

'That sounds special,' he says. 'Would you tell me about your best childhood memory in one of those places?'

'They all blur. But the best ones were the ones where she was always with me. Cora.'

Mr Hawkins frowns. 'Cora? Was she a relative? A friend?'

'She's my twin.'

'Lovely!' he says. 'I've never spoken to a twin before. Are you close?'

I shake my head. 'She and I don't talk too much since Annie died. She doesn't like that I'm coming here.'

'She knows you want to talk about Annie?'

'Yes,' I say.

'And she can't talk about her?'

'No.'

'Why is that?'

'It's too painful,' I say. 'I took pills for anxiety after Annie's death. I never came off them until recently. I think Cora just chose to forget and then *did*?'

He looks thoughtful. 'And what about your parents?' he asks. 'Do they talk about Annie?'

'They're far away now, in Switzerland. I left a long time ago and I don't contact them. They don't contact us.'

'How does that make you feel, not having family to talk to about something so big?'

'My parents have always been strangers,' I say.

'But your twin – Cora – she now also feels like one?'

'Yes. I think that's my fault though.'

'Why do you say that?'

Choose me.

'I – I don't know.'

I hold my head in my hands, look down. There's a ruby-coloured Persian rug beneath my feet and it swirls restlessly like blood.

'I love those flowers,' I say but I don't – I hate them. I hate the gold of them.

I should be cleaning the bathrooms and then the children's playroom, but I can't move from the duvet chair. My head seems to be aching not only from withdrawal but from the session with Mr Hawkins. Did we have a good childhood? I can't remember.

'Margo?'

My eyes snap open and I see Emmeline at my door frame but she's tilted. I realise that my head is on the arm of the chair and I'm curled into a tight little ball. Have I been asleep? I don't think so because I've been thinking about Annie and of Cora, of sunshine gold and of huge empty rooms.

'Where are the kids?' Emmeline says.

I sit up, stare at the clock that reads almost five.

Emmeline's eyes widen. 'Are they still at the school?'

'I—'

But she's spun away and I can hear her running down the stairs, keys being grabbed from the drawer and then the front door slamming. She's gone to get them herself. What did I say only hours ago to Mr Hawkins? I love those children more than anything and I've failed them.

I can hear my pulse thrum in my ears in the silence as I race to the kitchen, start dinner for the children and prepare a meal for Emmeline and David. I will go out and buy them an expensive white wine to say sorry and I'll buy Emmeline more flowers. I'll buy the children some gifts. How must they feel to have been abandoned by me? A sob rises in my throat. I left them, how could I have done that?

A fish pie goes in the oven just as Emmeline's key turns in the lock and I have the children's tea on the table as they walk in. I smile at them when they enter the kitchen but Emmeline looks so angry that my smile dies on my lips.

'I made you spaghetti and meatballs,' I say.

'Ooo!' the children say.

'I'm so sorry I wasn't there.'

Marie shrugs. 'That's OK.'

'We had biscuits in Miss Gray's office,' Jonny says and smiles.

I glance at Emmeline whose mouth twists in displeasure above their heads as they sit down and pick up their forks.

'Margo and I are going to chat,' she says and she gestures silently for me to go to the hallway.

I follow her as she shuts the kitchen door so that the children won't hear us.

'Emmeline—'

'What's going on with you, Margo?' she asks.

'I'm so sorry.'

'Are you unwell? You've been very off-kilter lately.'

I blink and then blink again. My eyes are so dry. 'I'm not feeling 100 per cent,' I say.

'Do you need some time off? Should I call the agency? We can cope with a switch for a while.'

My heart is crashing against my ribs like the tide.

'No,' I say. 'I don't want that. I'll be fine.'

She's being kind and I don't know if I can cope with her kindness. She needs to be angry with me because I've disappointed her.

'I'll be better.'

She nods. 'I need you in the present. My sister is ill and I can't run around picking up mistakes you're making, understand? Go upstairs and take the evening to yourself, OK?'

She's dismissing me. Can I say goodnight to the children, I wonder? Should I still do their bath time? I love bath and bedtime. What if Emmeline decides I'm not fit for purpose any more? What would I do then?

I go to my room, glance at the pills in their package, unopened. Should I take one, get myself back to normal? I don't. Instead I open the window and stare out into the

155

pretty garden below, and my eyes catch the wilted sun-flowers that the children and I planted at the beginning of the summer. They were golden yellow and beautiful, just like the flowers in Mr Hawkins' office, just like Cora's dress in the photograph.

A memory punctures my brain like the sting of a needle. The night that Annie died, Cora was dancing in that gold dress and I realise that the huge room I've been dreaming about is a *theatre*. What were we doing there? Was Cora in a show? What was the room I remembered that smelt musty? I should feel elated that I've remembered some-thing, but I feel my tongue shrivel. If the photograph is from that night then it *can't* be an old one that Granny just unearthed because how would Annie have signed it? Someone else has written it and sent it to Granny pretend-ing to be Annie.

My fingers are clammy as I dial Cora. Her phone, pre-dictably, goes to voicemail.

'Can you call me back?' I say. 'The photo of you that Granny gave me . . . the one Annie wrote on . . . it's not an old one, so it can't be Annie, can it? I'm – I'm worried, Cora. Something doesn't feel right.'

SIXTEEN

CORA

I'm shocked awake by an image of Annie in my eyes. Her terrified face in the blackness. At the thought of it, my fingers grip the pillow as if I'm falling. I need to get up, shower away the thoughts of her, and of our mother. Margo has got to me with all her talk about the past.

I move carefully out of bed so as not to aggravate my side. It's been a couple of days since I fell from the bike but, fuck me, it feels like I've been speared between the ribs. I go to the bathroom and put the shower on full. Margo is the one who always liked hot water, not me, and sometimes I wonder if she ever self-harmed when we were younger by scalding herself. At school she'd emerge from the bathrooms red-raw and flushed and I used to call it her orgasm blush to get a laugh from the other girls.

'Booya!'

I spin around to see Nav's fogged frame standing in the bathroom. 'Fuck, Nav! Didn't I lock the door?'

'No, and you've been in here ages,' he says.

'I've been in here for about five seconds!'

'You need to work on your relationship with time,' he says and he strides forwards and opens the cabinet, takes his industrial-sized hair mousse and scoops enough to hold a horse tail vertical. 'What are you still doing here, lady-friend? Thought you had rehearsal?'

'Yeah,' I say. 'Yeah, I'm leaving right now.'

'I swear I buy you an alarm clock every birthday. What do you need to get you up in the mornings?'

'Shut your face.'

I turn the shower off, grab at the towel I've draped over the glass door.

'I saw that empty bottle of vodka downstairs,' he says. 'Did you have a guest?'

'You know when I have guests,' I say with a wink.

'Then I guess you were just very thirsty. Have you got hairpins?'

'In my bedside cabinet.'

He gets up and I hear him rifling through my cabinet drawers.

'Why do you lose so many?' I call as step out of the shower.

'They've run off with the socks and all formed a cult.'

I can hear him opening and shutting the drawers, grunting like a caveman and after a couple of minutes, I roll my eyes. 'Let me look,' I say and go in.

He's standing, holding two little red booklets. 'Why have you got two passports?'

'One's an old one,' I say.

He opens one of them. 'Ha! Cora! Look at you!'

I swipe at it. 'Oh shut up, I was sixteen! Bet you looked a fucking picnic at that age.'

'You're wearing a choker! Tell me you were wearing double denim too?'

'It wasn't the nineties.'

'No?' He grins and then he opens the other passport. 'God, you've aged in this one,' he laughs.

'Dick,' I say but I'm up and reaching out for it, stretching, but he snaps it out of my grasp.

'Why does this one say Margo Malone?' He looks at me, confused. 'You have your sister's passport?' He flicks pages. 'This is a sticker from when we went to Greece last summer! You went on holiday on her passport? She knows you've got this, right?'

'Of course she does.' I snatch it back. 'It's her Swiss passport. She'll have her UK one. I couldn't find mine, so I booked the tickets under her name.'

'Felon,' he laughs.

'Don't be absurd,' I say but it's true. I know all her PINs, know how to imitate her when it suits me. Truth be told I have a lot of her things and she has a lot of mine and that's what happens when you're a twin; the lines get blurred. You forget what was once theirs and yours and although you're two distinct people, you can fit within each other. A dancer and her shadow.

He tosses the other passport at me and I fumble and drop everything and my towel on the floor.

'Shit,' he says with his eyes on the marks on my side. 'What have you done to yourself?'

'I fell off my bike,' I say.

'Oh my God, did you actually *steri-strip* yourself?'

'Is that what I did?' I say, amused. 'I drank a lot of vodka to numb the pain.'

'Explains the bottle,' he says. 'But that'll get infected, you daft cow. I'll get you some iodine.'

He disappears, leaves me getting dressed. I glance at the clock on my wall.

'Fuck, I'm so late!'

'I know,' he calls. 'Story of your life. But you can't rehearse today, not a cat in hell's chance.'

I can still hear him looking for iodine when I slam the front door shut.

I push the dance studio door open and Jean-Luc scowls at me.

'I'm sorry,' I say and then I stop dead.

There's a photographer in the room – Hazel O'Mara's photographer from *The Stage*. I've forgotten he was coming. He was coming for *me* and yet he's taking pictures of Gisele and Zdravko.

'You are an hour late,' Jean-Luc says quietly and I can hear anger in his voice. 'It's past midday. This is Rob from *The Stage*. He has to leave in twenty minutes.'

'I'm so sorry,' I say again. 'Family emergency.'

I throw my trainers and my bag to the side of the room and join them, try not to catch the eyes of any of the others because they all look pissed too. Except, of course, Gisele who is looking pretty content to be photographed as Eliza.

160

'We'll do the arrow lift on the third scene,' Joanna says. 'Cora, get into position.'

Gisele moves aside and I leap up into Zdravko's arms. As soon as I do, my side screams, but I can hear the photographer working his camera and so I arrange my face into character as best I can.

'It's a little "staged",' Rob says after a minute. 'Can we run through from the beginning of the scene so I have the emotion? Cora, you don't look too comfortable.'

I'm fucking not.

'You are right, Rob,' Jean-Luc agrees. 'We'll go from the beginning so you can warm up into it, Cora.'

'OK,' I say. 'Thank you.'

'Everyone *concentrate*,' Jean-Luc says.

We can all hear that the last word is italicised and that it's directed at me. Come on, I say to myself, fucking do this. This is your shot at dancing this play how you always thought you would. Your body is a weapon.

Rosa and I open the scene with my jazz tap routine and I'm precise and strong but I can feel beads of feverish sweat forming on my hairline. I want to wipe them away but I can't mess this up. I see Jean-Luc starts to relax as I continue and I hear the camera clicking.

'Good, Cora,' Joanna says.

You became the all, ate me whole.

Zdravko lifts me up by the waist so that I'm sitting on his shoulder and I raise my arms to the ceiling, the lights, head lifted before he lets me down to the ground and I spin away from him. Shit, my skin feels like it's coming off my side. I leap back towards Zdravko and he catches me in his arms so that my legs are arrow straight and my feet are pointed, high over his shoulder and my body is poised diagonally downwards, like a bow he's about to shoot.

Click-click-click again goes the camera.

'Lovely,' I hear someone say. Rob? Jean-Luc? I can't hear over the throbbing in my side. Zdravko's fingers are digging into the raw flesh from the accident and I'm white hot with pain.

Perhaps it's not your fault? Perhaps it's mine? Perhaps I would never have kept him tangled in silk sheets in my bed. Perhaps he would have always cut through them to get to you.

I feel Zdravko tighten his grip on my waist to keep the hold.

'Focus,' Jean-Luc hisses with warning.

He was everything and you took him.

I remember Miss Patricia spitting these words in my ear. This play meant so much more to her than it did to me. Until now. Now maybe I feel as passionately as she did when she danced it. This is my moment.

Except. Except I can feel something slipping, twisting, and then everything goes into slow motion – my legs unlock and I'm falling, smacking to the ground.

Joanna is up from her chair. 'Are you all right?'

I sit up. 'What happened?'

'You fell,' Zdravko says. 'I don't know how you did it. I'm sorry if my hold was wrong—'

'You just went slack in the air,' Gisele says and I throw my eyes towards her like daggers.

'What on earth, Cora?' Jean-Luc is talking to me but looking at Rob who's lowered his camera.

'Are you OK?' Joanna has her hand on my shoulder. 'Do you need to sit down?'

'No,' I say. 'I'm fine, I'm sorry.'

'You've got blood on your vest.' Cal says.

'It's *fine*,' I snarl and then I smile sweetly at Rob. 'I'll go and grab another top.'

I jog to the side of the studio and throw on a dark top over my vest. I want to be sick.

'Are you all right to carry on?' Joanna says, flicking her eyes in Jean-Luc's direction.

'Yes,' I say. 'I nicked myself the other day – it's nothing, really.'

But there's an atmosphere now and I'm the one who's created it.

'Honestly, I'm OK.'

I walk back over with focused steps but my fresh top is already sticking to the wound and I'm worried the blood will start to show through this one too. Then they'll have to stop rehearsal, they'll ask me to lift my top to see what's wrong and then what? They'll insist that I'll need proper treatment and insist that I won't be able to do lifts until it's healed. Would they kick me out of the play? The show is young enough that I'd be instantly replaced. I grit my teeth and we start again and I settle into the dance but I'm worried, and livid with myself.

'I should go,' Rob says after ten minutes. 'Thanks for your time.'

'Did you get what you needed?' Jean-Luc asks and we can all hear the tone of anxiety in his voice.

'I got some good shots,' Rob says. 'I know Haze wanted the lift with Cora and Zdravko but I'm not sure I got a strong enough one. We'll let you know, yeah?'

'*D'accord.*' Jean-Luc's tone is flat and I swallow down shame.

We all watch Rob leave the studio.

'I hope for your sake it was strong enough, *oui*?' Jean-Luc says to me when the door closes.

The rest of the day is agony. I pretend that my side is fine but it's not. I'm dizzy with pain, can hear the blood pulsating in my ears. Zdravko's agility and strength are making up for my lack of both. It's obvious that he's forced to compensate for me and Jean-Luc is no longer smiling but stares with eyes narrowed and arms folded.

'I'm sorry,' I say when we break and Jean-Luc calls us both over.

'You need to practice the lifts outside of rehearsal,' Jean-Luc says. 'It is not fair for Zdravko to have to counterbalance you because he'll get hurt and it looks clumsy.'

I gulp down water. 'No. I mean, yes I'll practice.'

'I didn't think you'd be weak at lifts,' Jean-Luc says bluntly.

His words sting. 'I'll not be a weakness.'

I decide to stay in the studio for another hour after everyone else leaves. I should be resting, wrapping my side with a bandage to let it begin to heal but embarrassment is keeping my body flooded with adrenaline. I punish myself with gruelling patterns; toe taps, heel taps, single-time steps to quadruple-time steps, cramp rolls and single wings and then I'm into it.

Choose me.

I have to keep my part. I was chosen, born for this.

I take the routine too hard, too strong, too fast. I'm spinning and I'm angry at myself and I land heavily, wrongly, and my ankle turns. My cry ricochets around the studio and I hold my foot until I'm numb all over with cold and shaking. I'm unravelling.

I have a new voicemail on my phone. Margo. For fuck's sake. I press answer, and sigh, think that I'll just be listening to her spout her usual rubbish. But this one is different.

'Can you call me back?' her voice says. 'The photo of you that Granny gave me . . . the one Annie wrote on . . . it's not an old one, and it can't be Annie, and I'm – I'm worried, Cora. Something doesn't feel right.'

She sounds scared, but that's not what worries me. She sounds *sharp*. Alert. I call her back but she doesn't answer and this in itself is odd because Margo always answers when I call.

'Shit,' I say. 'Shit, shit.'

SEVENTEEN

MARGO

It's Monday and I've been waiting on the pavement opposite Raff's Kilburn house for the last two hours after dropping the children at school. It could be that I've already missed him going out early but still I wait, hovering like some spectre with my coat hood up to protect myself against the cold morning sun. The wind swirls an empty crisp packet up from the side of the road.

His front door swings open and I look to it, hungry to see him, but it's not Raff who has come out but a well-dressed woman in navy jeans and black patent high heels and an olive-green beret. I recognise her as the woman who was in the window. She's of a similar height and build to me, whippet thin with blonde hair, light brown eyes and high cheekbones.

I gasp. It's *Cora*.

I step forward, am about to call to her, but am stopped as Raff follows her out of the door and kisses her on the mouth. I watch as he snakes his arm around her to hold her tightly around the waist – as he always did – and then they part company. She starts down the street towards me, and as she nears, I can see that it's *not* Cora after all but a woman who looks exceptionally similar. I watch as she turns her head to wave back at him and I see that her neck is elongated and exposed to me and I think that she could be a dancer. I touch my own neck self-consciously, turn away from her and bend my head to pretend to look in my bag as she passes.

Raff has started down the road the opposite way, cigarette smoke blooming into the air behind him, and I follow. He walks to Queen's Park, through the gates, past mothers with children playing in fallen leaves, and runners skinned in Lycra. He goes to the coffee hut, orders a drink and pastry and I wait behind him as he exchanges pleasantries with the server before walking to an empty bench.

'Raff?' I say.

He jumps at my voice and his face sets to an expression of anger when our eyes meet. 'Why are you following me, Margo?'

'I only want to talk.'

'I've got nothing to say,' he says and he diverts from the bench, starts to walk quickly away.

It's effort for me to keep up but I hurry to fall into step beside him.

'Leave me alone,' he says gruffly. 'I swear to God. I can't see you, OK?'

'Please, Raff,' I plead. 'Just wait a minute—'

'You don't get to walk into my life like this, you must understand that?'

'I need you to tell me how Annie died,' I say at the same time.

He stares at me, all the anger in his eyes changing to horror. 'What?'

'Annie died,' I say.

'Oh my God,' he says. 'Oh my God. Annie *died*?'

'Can we talk?'

He runs a hand over the stubble on his chin. 'I—'

'Please,' I say.

He gestures to the bench that he was going to sit at before I called to him, and we perch awkwardly beside each other.

'Fuck, I'm so sorry,' he says. 'Annie *died*?'

'Yes. How can you not know that?'

I feel panicked – if Raff didn't know that Annie died, then how can he help me piece all this together?

'They moved you,' he says. 'Your parents moved you to Switzerland, to the hospital, without telling any of us. We tried to contact you all . . .'

He stares at the sky. It's a dove-belly grey, clouds threatening rain.

'Where have you been all this time?'

'Here,' I say. 'We – I moved back to the UK.'

'And Cora?'

'She's in Switzerland,' I say.

The lie has spilt from my mouth before I've even thought about formulating it and I'm surprised at myself because I didn't have myself down as a liar. I could correct it, tell him that Cora's stage name is Devaux and tell him where to find her, and reunite them, but the truth stays static on my tongue. I promised Cora I wouldn't delve into the past but there's also something else that's keeping me from telling him about her and it's my own selfishness. I don't want him to look for her.

'She must be devastated about Annie,' he says. 'I need her number. Did she change it? I called it over and over and it just rang out. God, I tried for *years*.'

'She doesn't want to talk about the past.'

'But this changes everything,' he says.

'Not for her.'

'I'd like to see her, Margo. Please? Don't you understand? How could I not reach out to her knowing this about Annie?'

'She's moved on with her life,' I say. 'She took Annie's death so hard. She was closest to her, you know that.'

He holds his head in his hands. 'She should have told me,' he moans. 'She should have made contact. I'm angry, Margo, I'm so angry with her for leaving me in silence like that. Not knowing for fucking years if you were all OK. You know Sabine and I went out to Switzerland to try and find you all? But your parents had sold your house in Bern and you'd just vanished without telling any of us. Cora's *punished* me, you know?'

'We were grieving,' I say. 'It wasn't about you.'

'Why are you here?'

'Because I don't know what happened that night. And you're my only hope to find out. We were at the theatre, weren't we? Was it the one near the school? It must have been.'

Behind his lips I see his tongue lick at the tops of his gums.

'It all started,' he says, 'when you wore that gold dress.'

I stare at him. 'What?'

But his phone is ringing and he pulls it from his jacket pocket.

'It's my landlord,' he says. He picks up the coffee next to him on the bench slats and stands. 'I have to get this . . .'

I stand abruptly too, knock into his coffee. It spills onto his hand and he sucks in breath. His phone bleats and he goes to answer it but I reach for his arm.

'Sorry, but can you . . . I wore the dress? Cora's performance dress?'

'I can give you back your memory of that night,' he says. 'What I have of it. But I can't do that right now; you must understand? I need more time to process this – seeing you. I've built my life on the understanding of never seeing you again, any of you, and now here you are.'

'But—' I say but he shakes his head.

'I dream about her dancing,' he says, scribbles on a scrap of paper produced from the back pocket of his jeans. 'I dream about her most nights. You remember how you and I would watch all the rehearsals she did for *Mirror, Mirror*?'

His phone stops ringing.

'*Mirror, Mirror*,' I echo him.

'That was the play that was supposed to launch her career,' he says. 'And then . . . Here's my number.' He holds it out for me to take. 'Call me so I have yours.'

I take it, go to reach for him – I want him to stay, want him to explain. 'Wait, please,' I say. 'The theatre . . .'

'It's on all our hands,' he says. 'What happened that night is on all of our hands.'

And then he walks away. I call his phone, hear it ringing as he goes.

EIGHTEEN

CORA

'This is an unexpected surprise!' Granny says when she opens the door.

It's Thursday and I've not been called for rehearsal today. And thank God because a) Margo is creeping me out with her voicemails and b) my foot is as painful, if not more so, than my side at the moment and there's no fucking way I'd be able to make all those turns on it. This morning in the shower I noticed an ugly purple line running down an inch from my toe and I'm worried I've fractured it. I'm worried about a lot of things.

'Didn't I just see you?' Granny says.

'I came for your birthday.'

She looks muddled. 'Yes,' she says. 'Did you bring any apples?'

I frown. 'What? Listen, can I come in? I need to ask you about a couple of things—'

'Of course, dove,' she says as I step through. 'Why are you holding yourself funny?'

'I hurt myself,' I say. 'My ribs. But it's OK.'

'Let me see.'

'No—'

'Let me see,' she says, more firmly, and I lift my top to reveal my side. She gasps. 'Have you put TCP on that?'

'No: shit, that'll sting,' I say.

'Language,' she chastises.

'I haven't got long,' I say. 'It's a flying visit, right, but I wanted to ask—'

But she leaves the room. I can hear her in the bathroom, the clink and chinks of bottles in the cabinets. I walk over to the door frame.

'Granny?'

'Sit down at the table,' she says authoritatively and navigates me back to the kitchen. 'Why don't you take proper care of yourself?'

'I do. Mostly.'

She tips the TCP upside down onto a cotton pad. 'Stay still,' she says and she dabs it to my side. I hiss with pain. 'Oh, you were always getting hurt when you were younger. So clumsy.'

'Is it possible to be a clumsy dancer?'

'You're evidence of it,' she says and her face is furrowed in concentration as she dresses the wound. 'Talented but clumsy.'

'I'll bear that in mind for my headstone,' I say.

She tisks. 'Miss Patricia was always stitching you up, wasn't she?'

'Yeah,' I say. 'With a needle like a sword.'

'Remember when you cut yourself in that pool in Doha? Your mam told me about it on the phone. Gave her such a shock, it did!'

'That was Margo,' I mutter. 'Stupid cow.'

'What? Speak up.'

'Nothing,' I say.

'Miss Patricia had to take you all to hospital for that, do you remember?' Granny says. 'But all the other times, oh that woman could stitch you all up.' She laughs. 'Such a support to your parents and to you girls.'

I nod. 'Humm. Oww, Granny! Jesus!'

'And she was a stunning lady,' Granny adds, ignoring my protest and dabbing at my side. 'Wasn't she? She must have been something really special before her accident on stage.'

'Yup,' I say, gritting my teeth.

'Well, you were all good at dancing,' Granny says. 'Those stage schools you went to when you were abroad, amazing they were.'

'Not Tring though, were they?' I say. 'I could have been something big, Granny.'

'Tring?'

The TCP seems to burn a hole right through me. 'Fuck me! That hurts, Granny!'

'*Language*,' she says. 'She's going to visit me soon.'

'Who?'

'Miss Patricia,' she says.

She applies cream and then sticks a gauze haphazardly across my side. Tiny lights explode behind my eyes.

'She's visiting you?' I say.

'Yes, she wrote to me out of the blue about six months ago,' she says. 'We had a bit of a row, you remember, but I never believed it. And nor should your mother have.'

'She did though. Both of them did.'

'I shouldn't have brought it all up,' Granny says. 'Sorry. Anyway, she's in Hampshire now.'

I pause, thinking. 'Has Patricia sent you anything? Photos or something? Has she sent *Margo* anything? Margo said you gave her some photos recently.'

'But that's all in the past now, isn't it,' Granny carries on, ignoring me. 'And do you know, Patricia's decided to start a dance school! How marvellous at her age! Sixty-five!'

I look down to look at the gauze, and press my fingers to it. The pain causes me to suck at the air through my teeth. 'For kids?' I manage.

'That's right, dove,' she says. 'And she's also thinking of doing some nannying again. She told me she misses little ones.'

I think I might pass out from the pain. 'You got a sherry, Granny?'

'You know where it is,' she says. 'Help yourself.'

I go to the tiny cupboard above the draining board, take the tiny bottle. The neck of it is sticky with residue and I don't bother with a glass but drink it neat, and the stickiness transfers onto my lips. It's as I put it back that I see a Jiffy bag peeking out from the toaster on the dresser addressed to Margo and its writing looks familiar.

'What's this, Granny?'

'What's what?' she says.

I walk over to the bag to snatch it up and tear it open. I lift out transparent white tissue paper to reveal a small leather-bound book and I inhale sharply. This is mine – a book of dance given to me by Miss Patricia when I was seven. There's a strip of purple satin, a bookmark, and I open it where it's resting, at a page of a ballet dancer, and there's a tiny card nestled inside. I pluck it out and open it.

I thought you should have this. Axx

I yelp and throw the book across the room and it lands with a soft clunk, upside down by the wall in the hallway.

'Are you all right?' Granny has looked up at me, alarmed, and I look to her and then to the book again. 'Oh, you found the package?' she says. 'Take it, will you? Honestly I'm becoming a postal service. I'll have to start charging.'

'A postal service?'

'From Annie,' she says and she smiles at me.

'No, Granny,' I whisper. 'No, that's not possible. Was this from Miss Patricia? Has she been here already?'

'No,' Granny says. 'It's from *Annie*. Isn't it lovely that she's started to write to you after all this time?'

'No,' I say. 'It's fucking *nuts*.'

'Please stop swearing.'

'Granny,' I say. 'I've got to go.'

'But you've only just arrived,' she says, forlornly. 'The kettle is whistling for our tea.'

'This is our fourth cup,' I reply. 'Really you should be cutting down on your caffeine intake. I've been here since midday.'

'You have?' she says and looks confused at my lie. 'My fourth cup already?'

I stand up, kiss her forehead. 'I love you.'

'I love you,' she says and smiles up at me. 'Look after yourself, all right?'

I grab my bag, my coat and I bang the door shut behind me, run down the corridor and flip the pages of the guest book, all the way from the beginning of the year. On the left are a list of names and on the right who they're visiting, but when it comes to Granny there is no one here but Margo and I and a list of medical staff from the hospital.

On Friday morning I watch Margo as she takes the children to school, drops clothes at the dry cleaners, and then I follow her home. From where I'm standing on the pavement I can see straight into the open-plan kitchen window, see that it's flooded with early afternoon light. The room stretches from the front to back of the house but I can't see her in there.

I'm safe to pick up her key.

I've watched her enough times when she's been absent minded with her key, watched how she's bent down to one of the tiny rocks that acts as a key safe. I've seen her pick out the numbers – I've been *that* close to her but she's never noticed me. I unlock the door and slip through her house like some sort of a snake and am met with the large hallway with an elegant staircase opposite and two open doors to the left and right of it; the kitchen and the living room. Where is Margo? Will she come out and stop me?

'Hello?' I call softly.

Is she cleaning somewhere? Making beds? Poring over a cookbook in her room? Perhaps she's in the basement.

I cross the hallway, put a hand to the polished banisters, glance to the living room. There are the two stud-backed sofas and a high-backed winged armchair next to a high bookshelf. I can see the living room leads out to a conservatory where there are more plush sofas, tall lamps with Tiffany crystal lampshades and high plants. There are French doors leading to their lawn outside – I know where the key to those is too.

I climb the staircase to the first floor, pass the family bathroom, spare rooms and up to a second floor. Kids' rooms and more bathrooms, which I take a cursory glance inside in case she's scrubbing a bath or hiding in one. I can smell cedar wood scented candles, can see the gleaming tiles that are iridescent mosaic and match throughout the whole house. I notice the sets of towels and they're all fluffy, all ironed. This is what my sister does – she makes a nice home. She cares for others and most importantly, she's safe here. Or so she thinks.

I go up further, past pictures mounted on landing walls of the dark-haired twins beaming out of frames, until I turn down a smaller corridor.

I open a door and her familiar scent spills out; hand sanitiser and washing powder.

'Are you here?' I call.

But she's not here so I go inside. The room is flooded with light, white and stark, but feels like it's full of sharp edges. Margo's bed is as neatly made as ever: a white cotton duvet and pillow set with no motif because she's so dull. I sit down on the friendly looking plush chair in one corner, take in her space, and then I stand again, start to open her drawers to look for whatever she might have taken from Granny's house.

'What the fuck are these pants?' I say, lifting grey cotton briefs and dropping them back inside. 'Come *on*, Margo.'

I hear a noise and I freeze, look to the door but the sound exposes itself as the rumbling of a lorry somewhere outside on the street. I open the closet, see rails of neatly hung white blouses and cardigans, pressed dark trousers and mid-length sensible skirts. Nothing is out of order.

'Let me see what else you might have here. What the fuck has that woman been sending you?'

I go to close the door of the closet again when, in the mirror's reflection, I see an envelope on her bedside cabinet with a photo peeking through. I go to it, open it, see the picture she told me about when we drove to Granny's, and then again in her voicemail. A photo of me in the gold dress. My stomach lurches. I didn't ask her what the photo was when she mentioned it. If she makes the connection that it's from the night of the accident then I'm in serious shit.

I look at it, and then turn it over.

I know you will like this one. Axx

Exactly like the book. Jesus wept. I need time to figure this all out, plan what I'm going to do. I pocket it, turn to leave.

'Oh, Margo, I didn't hear you come in.'

I snap straight, spin around to see the mother – Emmeline – standing at the doorframe.

'Hello,' I say.

'Will you run to the shop for me before you go out?' she says.

I smile tightly. 'Sure.'

'There's a list on the kitchen table,' she says. 'I'm going to finish up on a paper, OK?'

'Yep. Great.'

I walk down the stairs, hear Emmeline shut a door upstairs, and then I start running. My heart is hammering like a bird in my chest as I open the front door and leave the house.

NINETEEN

MARGO

It's Saturday night and I lie in bed and inhale deeply to still a rising panic inside my chest, try to summon any memories of the play Raff mentioned, *Mirror, Mirror,* to the forefront of my head. I've searched everywhere online I can think of to connect Annie's name to the play and to the theatre near the school, but there is nothing. Everywhere I look I'm met with walls. Perhaps her death had nothing to do with the theatre. Perhaps we had all already left it? But then Raff said it started with the gold dress. I wonder if all this time I've got it wrong – is it *me* in the photograph that was at Granny's? Did *I* dance the play and not Cora and somehow that lead to Annie's accident? But no, it can't be because Cora was the dancer and the star and I was the nothing.

I used to love watching her dance, and rehearsals often more than the finished performance. She was wilder then, unconstrained. When everyone else had gone home, Cora would stay late practising her shows with only Raff and I for company. Something jolts me to sit up, blinking in the

181

darkness. In my mind's eyes, I can see the darkness of the theatre but I can *hear* voices. Raff and Cora. They were alone on the stage – or they thought they had been – but I had been there too, previously spending time in one of the dressing rooms preparing a pair of her ballet shoes. I used to wile away hours helping her break them in; cutting the shank away so she could bend the soles how she wanted; cutting away the satin around the toes for her to make them less slippery when she was en pointe; sitting with a needle and sewing on ribbon and burning down the frayed edges with a lighter. I had come down ready to call for her that I was going to go back to school, when I stopped dead in the wings of the theatre because I saw them together, their silhouettes centre stage locked in an embrace.

'Do me here,' she'd said and his laughter rang out around the empty stalls.

'In the dark, leading lady?' he said. 'But you're usually a lights-on kinda girl.'

She giggled. 'Tonight you can explore me in the dark.' She wrapped her bare legs around his torso. 'The dark could swallow us whole! I can swallow you whole.'

He laughed again and they kissed loudly.

'*A smile to light the ocean floor,*' I heard him say. '*Put me to bed there, let me lie behind those lips.*'

'And you can fill my mouth with dirty thoughts.'

I should have left – could have left easily; behind the stage and out of the stage door – but I was rooted to where

I was behind the heavy black curtains of the wings. For an hour, or maybe it was more, I heard them do all sorts of things to each other, heard fast breath, moaning, and I was fascinated, appalled, but above all, excited. I saw him lay her down and undress her, and although I had seen my sister naked countless times, the way he talked about her body stupefied me. It was like she had become a canvas for him to paint on with lustful eyes and a panting tongue. He spoke to her simultaneously like she was an angel out of the sky and a red-light district prostitute and I wondered, was this love? Their bodies rolled and writhed on the cold wooden planks of the stage, where countless performances had been put on, but, for this one, I was the only spectator. At times I closed my eyes so *I* could be her, Cora, and I knew that when I got back to school and lay in my bed I would replay the whole thing, changing only who Raff's leading lady was.

'This play speaks to me, Raff,' Cora said in the darkness when they'd finished.

They lay together in the dark – naked and glistening with sweat.

'Yeah, you told me,' he said. 'Your old mentor taught it to you.'

'It's bigger than that,' she said. 'It's about obsession and rivalry and *her* rivalry and obsession with *you* is fucking exhausting.'

'You know I'd never be with Pearl,' he said, casually.

'Don't call her that,' Cora said.

'Why not?'

'I don't like it.'

'You know you're my queen,' he said, laughing.

'It's not just the rivalry between me and Margo though,' Cora said.

'What then?'

'It reminds me of Margo and Annie when we were younger.'

In the wings, I frowned, not understanding.

'Meaning what?' he said.

She shook her head. 'It doesn't matter.'

I saw him reach for her for comfort, but she flicked a switch from within herself. From a moment of vulnerability – and my sister never liked to show vulnerability – she flashed him a dazzling smile.

'Take my photograph,' she said after a while.

'You're such an arrogant bitch.'

'Just how you like it,' she laughed. 'I look better through a lens.'

'You look good always.'

I heard him rustle for the bag he'd cast aside, heard the click of a camera.

My eyes snap open in the darkness and I switch the bedside lamp on. It was Raff who took the photo of Cora for the play, *Mirror, Mirror*, so did *he* send it to me? His reaction to Annie's death appeared so genuine, but now I don't know what to believe.

I reach for the photograph on the bedside cabinet, desperate to study it, but it's gone.

'Have you been in my room?'

Marie blinks up at me. It's three in the morning and I am looming over her in the dark.

'There's an envelope missing from my bedside table,' I whisper with urgency. 'Please tell me now if you've taken it. I won't be angry.'

She rubs at her eyes. 'I haven't been in your room.'

I turn on my heel, go to Jonny's room and I hear Marie coming behind me as I open her brother's door.

'Listen, Jonny, please,' I say as I shake him gently. 'You've got to tell me.'

He wakes, props up on his elbows. His hair is sticking up on one side. 'What's happened?' he says.

'We haven't been in your room, Margo,' Marie says, behind me.

'Well *someone* has, Marie,' I say, feel my voice rise in panic.

I tell myself to stay calm – David and Emmeline are up another floor but I can't wake them.

'And it's often you playing dressing up,' I say. 'Be a good girl, why were you playing around with my things?'

'I haven't been in there,' Marie says.

'What have you done with it?'

'I don't know what it is?' she says.

'Can we go to sleep?' Jonny says.

'No,' I say and I grab Marie by the shoulders and press down on them.

'Ouch!' she says.

'Stop it! Stop being silly! Tell me!'

'Margo!' Jonny says. 'You're hurting Marie!'

I take my hands from her shoulders at once and she shrugs them up to her neck.

'You hurt Marie,' Jonny says protectively.

I bite my lip. 'Oh Marie, I'm sorry, dove. I didn't mean to. I'm so sorry.'

She and Jonny exchange a look.

'I think she's ill,' Jonny says to Marie like I'm not part of the conversation. 'We hear her come in late, don't we, and do the washing at funny times.'

'Sometimes I run out of time in the days,' I say.

'Maybe it would be nice if you had some friends,' Marie says.

I open my arms to have her cuddle up to me. 'I'm sorry for hurting you, darling.'

'That's OK,' she says into my ear. 'But why did you do that funny thing with your eyes?'

'What funny thing?'

'Your eyes,' Jonny nods. 'They went shaky.'

'They – went shaky?' I say.

'Your eyes wobbled.'

'I don't know what that means.'

'It's OK,' Marie says and she kisses me on the cheek. She gets into bed with Jonny and they snuggle into each other. I used to do that with Cora before she realised she could kick me away. Her rejection of me was always hardest in the pitch-black of night when I wanted her most.

I touch Marie's kiss with my fingertips and then I run to the bathroom. I close the lid of the toilet, sit on it and start scratching at the back of my hand, at the backs of my thighs, at my neck. My skin feels like it's on fire.

TWENTY

CORA

The graveyard is cold this early in the morning but I was pulled here. Sometimes I need to remind myself that her grave marks a new beginning for me – a rebirth. I need to keep going. I can't let Margo distract me from realising the one thing I've always wanted.

I look at the script.

'You'd like this bit,' I say aloud. 'You always loved a grand jeté. And this jazz combination? One step, turn, two and three kicks, shoe shine! Apple jacks! You'd go crazy for that too.'

It's Monday. I have rehearsals soon, and before that Zdravko and I have to put in an hour of lifts. I'll have to leave soon so that I can warm up properly without doing myself any more serious damage. I've been taping ice packs to my side and praying that the pain there and in my foot would have died down but it's still absolute torment to move, let alone dance, and my head aches with what I found at Granny's, and at Margo's Kensington house.

'We're heading for a fucking apocalypse,' I say to the grave. I light a cigarette. I should stop smoking. Dancers should never smoke. 'What do you think? Do you believe in ghosts?'

And then I laugh until I'm howling with hysteria and, shit, my side hurts when I laugh like this. I think that if anyone passed by, they would think me insane. But something *has* shifted in the dynamic of mine and Margo's relationship. I have always been the dominant one, can usually hush her when she gets upset, but she hasn't even responded to my call yet.

I take my phone from my bag, text her again.

I need to see you.

I'm about to put the phone back in but I let my finger hover over the web browser. I haven't signed into my old email address for years. I didn't want to be contactable after what happened to Annie. I almost deleted this account because I didn't want to see emails from anyone who would anchor me to the past. I swore to myself I wouldn't look at it again but today I log in with my password – Ann!3 – and the inbox springs open. The notification number blazes out at me. I have over five thousand emails but it's mostly all spam. I click to the end page and to the emails dated a few weeks after the night at the theatre.

Cora, we're so sorry about what happened. We love you, we miss you! Can you give us your address so we can send you some things? Visit you? Sab and Helga xxxxxxxxx

Can you call me, Cora? Did you get my voicemail, my texts? Are you OK? What's going on? I can't get through to your family. Raff is going spare. Sab xxx

I love you, Cor. Sab xxx

Sabine, my best friend. Reading her words is like stepping into a familiar pair of shoes, but I delete the messages one by one because what good are they to me now? I left her along with the rest of them. As I delete them more filter downwards to take their place and then I see it. Raff's name on an email dated a month after the night.

Cora, I don't know if you're OK?? I'm worried. I don't know how to contact you. I couldn't see you in the hospital, obviously. They told me that your family moved you all back to Switzerland. I don't know what to say, don't know why I'm emailing you other than to say I love you. I'm sorry beyond words for everything. Please email me, call me. Your family has locked down on everyone. I understand their need for privacy after something so bad but this can't be goodbye forever, can it? After all we promised each other? I love you, I'm yours xxx

My fingers are shaking and I realise I'm dropping ash on my thighs. It's hot on the material of my leggings but I don't care, I hope it burns through to my skin because I need to feel a physical pain to distract from my emotional one. Perhaps it would be easier to live like Margo has done; in ignorant bliss, but that's not possible because I remember everything.

I need to spin a story.

I look at the message I've sent Margo. She's not read it, the cow. I'm going to have to skip my rehearsal with Zdravko.

She walks with her eyes cast down, doesn't even notice me until she's on top of me.

'Shall we talk?' I say.

She looks up, startled. Her face looks like it can't decide on surprise, anxiety or joy at seeing me. Perhaps it's all three at the same time.

'What are you doing here?' she says. 'It's eight-forty in the morning!'

'We need to talk,' I say. 'And you need to look at your messages.'

'Did you message me?'

'Don't play games.' I sigh.

I don't wait for her to answer. I march her to a café on the corner of the road, which has dark wood flooring and blown-glass bulbs hanging from a high ceiling, and we take a seat right at the back. Two teenage girls are sitting at a table behind us in school uniform, drinking coke from cans and obviously bunking morning registration, and I smile at them. Margo can see them too, reflected in the mirror on the back wall.

'Oh, Cora,' she says. 'Your top looks – have you hurt yourself?'

I look down to see the ugly mar of red blood has seeped through the white of my vest again. Shit, I can't hold my fucking body together. I thought Granny had sorted me out but her care is obviously as shaky as her mind.

'No, I'm fine.'

'But it looks like—'

'I said it's fine,' I snap.

A waiter comes up to our table. 'What can I get you?' he asks.

Margo stares down at a menu.

'I'll have a kale smoothie and your biggest croissant,' I say and then look to Margo who doesn't order but instead plays with the menu in her hands. I notice her skin in red. She's all anxious and shitty again.

'Is that all?' the waiter says.

I look to Margo who shakes her head. 'Yeah, ta.'

We wait to talk until he brings it all over and then I slurp on the smoothie, which is both gross and delicious.

'It's come to my attention,' I say, 'that you're delving into territory that might tip you over the edge.'

Margo scratches at the skin on her hand and at the back of her neck.

'You got my voicemail,' she says. 'About the photo? About Annie's writing?'

'Yes. Stop scratching.'

She looks down at her hand. 'Sorry.' She looks over my head into the mirror. 'Those girls behind me keep looking at us,' she says after a moment.

'No, they're not.'

'They're whispering and then giggling,' she says. 'I think they must be talking about me. Is there something stuck on the back of my dress? Is my hair looking bad?'

'Chill out,' I say. 'Jesus.'

'People have always talked about me.'

'That's your paranoid disposition,' I say. I lean back, fold my arms. 'Let's talk about your panicky voicemail then, shall we? Talk to me about the photo.'

'It was you in a gold dress outside a theatre. You were dancing in a play called *Mirror, Mirror,* and it was the night Annie died. On the back was Annie's writing.'

Christ alive, she's made all the connections. My confidence is knocked sideways. I swallow, buy myself a moment to think. 'Or someone who has writing very *like* Annie's,' I say. 'How was the photograph signed? Did it say Annie on it?'

She frowns. 'Well, no. It was signed with an *A,'* she says. 'Like she always did—'

Thank fuck. 'But who also used to sign off like that?' I say, galvanised. '*Amelia*. Mother wanted you to have it. That's all.'

She looks surprised. 'Mum . . . ?'

'Mystery solved, Sherlock.'

I watch her face as this sinks in. As much as I don't want Margo to think about our parents – our mother especially – she needs to buy it.

'No,' she says. 'It looked like Annie's.'

'All our writing was similar,' I say. 'I copied Mother's writing, Annie copied mine.'

I see the cogs in her head whirring. 'That's true, your writing was all so similar.'

'Boom,' I say. 'There we go. Case closed. Wow, this croissant is as big as my head.'

'But even if that's true—' she begins.

'Which it must be,' I interject. 'Because it sure as hell isn't Annie's, is it?'

'Even if it's true, it's made me think about the night. And I want to put it all together. Annie deserves to be thought about and that means accepting what happened then. I'm ready to think about it. Accept it.'

The pain in my side seems to swell. I need to rescue this situation. I lean over the table and I'm so close to her that I can see myself reflected in her eyes.

'But *I* don't want it put together,' I say. 'I want it *lost*. We left Switzerland for a reason, Margo. To disappear. You've got to bury it all with her, with Annie. Nothing is bringing her back. You understand?'

'Sometimes it's good to remember things. What happened that night, Cora? Why won't you talk about it? Sometimes we *should* remember things we'd rather forget.'

I smirk. 'Your therapist told you that, did he?'

'I've only seen him once,' she says.

I try a different tack. 'You like your job, right?'

'Yes?'

'So don't jeopardise it. Lie low and leave the past alone. I'm saying this for you, for your health. You're on the pills to stop your panic attacks and you can *live*, Margo! You can be happy. You're happy, aren't you?'

'I—'

'You don't want to say goodbye to your twins, do you?'

She's quiet now. 'No,' she says finally.

'Good,' I say. 'Now, is there anything else you should be telling me?'

She shakes her head, slowly at first, and then fast like a child.

I narrow my eyes at her. 'You'd tell me, wouldn't you?' I say.

'Yes,' she says.

We fall into silence but I'm trying to calculate her; I've never worked so hard in my life to figure her out.

'Are those girls still looking at me?' she says.

I look over at the girls behind us.

'Hey, girls!'

They are looking now and I smile at them before jabbing up my middle finger and mouthing 'fuck you'. They look initially alarmed and then they laugh again but it's tinged with a nervousness because I have that impact on people.

'Cora!'

'We should call out people who make us feel like shit,' I say and in a rare moment of tenderness, I reach across the table and I take her hand. 'You have to trust me, OK?'

She looks at me, nods slowly.

'I love you,' I say. 'And I'm going make things right for us.'

TWENTY-ONE

MARGO

The conversation with my sister in the cafe earlier this morning rings in my ears. Was it really our mother who sent the photograph of Cora? Why would she want to get in contact after all these years of silence? I feel so muddled when it comes to how I feel about our parents and I look to the glass vase in front of me for calm. It contains an arrangement of fuchsia and red orchids, freesias and muscari and I think I should remember this for when I next order flowers for Emmeline's dining table, or when I next mess something up.

Mr Hawkins comes in with a coffee for himself and a tea for me, placing them on the low table. Today he's wearing another jumper with tan elbow patches and for some reason this detail makes me feel safe here with him. I think that the world could be spinning into chaos outside this room and he'd still be sitting here with the ornate clock on the wall, the vase of flowers, and with tan elbow patches on his jumpers.

'Thank you for seeing me again,' he says. 'Where would you like to start today?'

'I don't know. Do I have to choose?'

'How about your family? We touched briefly last time on them and I'm wondering if you'd care to tell me a bit more about your early life?'

'It was good,' I say, bluntly.

'You said that you feel your parents are strangers to you. Are you able to tell me more about why you said that?'

'Sometimes they worked abroad even when we *were* abroad. Sometimes they went on holidays without us for weeks at a time when we were home from boarding school. I wonder if they had us because they thought it was the thing to do. I think I felt more of an inconvenience to them.'

Mr Hawkins, says nothing, just waits for me to keep talking. I wonder for a moment if I want to keep talking. I don't know if I want to think about our parents. The smell of lemons – my mother – seems to inhabit my nose even though there are no lemons here and she definitely isn't either.

I pause, thinking. 'I remember I was often in trouble,' I say. 'I was the bad side of the coin, I'm afraid.'

I watch him scratch in his notebook and it makes me want to scratch at my hands.

'Can you tell me what you mean by that phrase, Margo?' he asks.

'Cora was the good one. And I was the bad one. That's how it was.'

'What is it that you did that you think was "bad"?'

'Sometimes I would tear up the house,' I whisper. 'In the night I would go down to the kitchen or the playroom and

I'd completely rip them apart. Sorry, I don't know why I told you that.'

'This is a space where anything can be voiced, Margo.'

'It wasn't me though,' I say. 'Well, it was, but I was sleepwalking. I did that when I was anxious.'

'Do you still?'

'No,' I say. 'But only because I was taking the medication I told you about . . .'

I think of the pills, still unopened in their package. I think about what Cora said. The pills have kept me sane, kept me happy. But have I ever really been?

'Were there consequences when the rooms were messed up?' Mr Hawkins asks.

'I always cleaned up any mess,' I say. 'Even if I didn't know if I'd done it. My parents never knew and that was good because my father was so strict. Sometimes my sisters helped me.' I pause. 'We all said maybe it was Penny.'

'Penny?'

'She was from a book, I think. We all used to blame Penny because then I wouldn't feel bad. Does that sound stupid?'

'No,' he says. 'It's what children do. They pretend. And they act out things in play to deal with things in real life.'

I sigh. 'I don't know what the truth was . . . Sometimes I still wake up in the morning and go down early, before the twins are awake – I live-in with them, you see – and I check I haven't messed the house up.'

'And have you ever ripped their kitchen apart?' he asks.

'No.'

'There we are.'

He writes more in his book, and I wonder what he's writing. He uncrosses and recrosses his legs on the other side. 'Tell me about your relationship with Cora.'

I smile but feel it faltering on my lips. 'I said before that our relationship became quite different after Annie died,' I say. 'We're rather separate now and that makes me sad. After the funeral, I don't know, she pulled away from me.' I suck my lips into my mouth. 'And it hurt.'

'Tell me how it hurt,' he says.

'I gave her everything,' I say. 'I thought I did. All my love and my energy, but when Annie died, it was like part of Cora had died with her. There were nights I'd lie in bed and wish I'd been Annie.'

'Why?' he asks.

Choose me.

'Because Cora had always loved her the most,' I whisper. 'She – she chose her.'

'What do you mean by that?' he asks.

But a swirling cloud has blanketed the reason to why I have said this because I don't know what these words mean. I know they're significant somehow. Or perhaps I am just confusing the memory of watching Cora and Raff make love on stage.

'When we were young, I was always the outsider,' I say. 'I wanted to be loved and cherished and I wasn't . . . As soon as Annie was born, Cora loved her more than me, and it made me so sad. I was so . . . angry.'

My heart is thumping in cold realisation – I didn't love Annie, I *hated* her. How can I have forgotten such an intense emotion for Annie? It was true that Cora had more in common with her, but did my sadness at this preference manifest itself so vehemently that I could have hated my own flesh and blood?

I remember now, with striking lucidity, that for years I pretended with all my might that Annie and I were as close as she and Cora. I gave Annie my favourite toys, I read her books, I took her hand when we crossed the roads. I made her laugh by putting on the one funny voice I could do, I gave her my best clothes when I grew out of them. Later she laughed at my clothes and went to Cora's wardrobe instead, used Cora's make-up and painted her nails like Cora did hers. She and Cora pored over dance magazines, put on dance shows for our parents and made them clap with delight whilst I sat in the corner and watched them over the tops of the books I held in front of my face like masks. I don't know when it was that Annie suddenly found me lacking.

I read books about sibling rivalry so I could try to teach myself how to be less jealous and possessive of Cora, and become more forgiving and generous of Annie. I read the testimonials on how the books had changed people's lives but wept with frustration because at the end of every single book, I still felt this unquenchable rage towards Annie. I thought she wouldn't even notice my lack of affection towards her because she had unconditional love from my parents and from Cora but eventually she did notice and used my jealously towards her and deflected it back at me. She and Cora whispered, ran away from me, excluded me from games.

I blink and look around. I'm still in Mr Hawkins' room. My eyes settle once again on the vase. The afternoon light shines through the glass and the table is dappled by refraction.

'Margo?' Are you OK?'

'I think something is being hidden from me,' I say. 'It's like, even though Annie's gone, the two of them are keeping things from me.' I sigh. 'Cora thinks I should stay safe and not ask questions and I don't know how to make her communicate with me. There's something about that night . . . and – and my mother sent me . . .'

I stop talking. I'm so confused.

'Perhaps Cora would be willing to come and see us both here?' he says. 'Perhaps she would help shed some light about what happened to Annie?'

'She wouldn't come,' I say.

'Why do you think that?'

'Because I've hurt her too badly,' I say.

He looks confused and of course he is, because I'm confused too.

'Why did you hurt Cora?' he says. 'Or do you mean that you hurt Annie?'

My throat feels like it's closing up. 'Is there water, Mr Hawkins?'

He gets up. 'I apologise,' he says, goes over to a cabinet behind his chair. 'I usually have some out.'

He opens the door to it and inside I can see neatly stacked water bottles and also a decanter. He takes out some water and a glass, hands it to me.

'Thank you,' I say.

'Please, continue.'

I sip at the water. 'I – I can't remember what I was saying.' I look at him. 'It's like I'm waiting for the end, whatever the end might be,' I say. 'No one is *helping* me. Why aren't they helping me to find out what happened?'

'Perhaps your loved ones believe they are keeping you in the dark with good reason?' he says.

'That's what Cora says,' I say. 'But I want to make an *active* decision in this, do you understand, Mr Hawkins? Can you help me? Could you hypnotise me, maybe?'

'I can offer to refer you for a few sessions to alleviate anxiety but clinical hypnotherapy isn't what you see on the television. It's a state of relaxation where you think more clearly.'

'That's what I want.'

'OK,' he says. 'I'll make a note of it for you.' He pauses. 'You're doing so well in talking to me, Margo. I feel there's a lot we haven't gone into. Really. A lot.'

I look at the clock above his head. 'I should go now, Mr Hawkins. I have to pick up the children.'

'Let's see each other again, shall we?' he says. 'I think I can help you remember if that's truly what you want.'

'It's what I *need,* Mr Hawkins. I feel like I'm going mad.'

The children are asleep in bed. They're exhausted because I took them into central London after school where I let them choose a toy each from Hamleys at my expense. I've been really spoiling them since Saturday when I woke them, frightened them, *accused* them, but they don't seem to have held a grudge against me, and for that I'm thankful and marvel at the capacity for forgiveness that a child seems to possess.

I find driving in central London extremely stressful, and all I want to do is lie down and try to sleep, but I've left the house to meet Raff. I texted him when I left Mr Hawkins', and he replied immediately to say he could see me tonight but that I had to come to him. I really don't like going out at night – the darkness scares me – but here I am.

Raff opens the door and I watch as he leans against the banister and grabs a faded tan leather shoulder bag. He's wearing glasses, rounded black frames that make him seem boyish again though he never wore glasses as a teenager.

'Are we going out?' I say.

'Yeah,' he says, closes the door behind him quickly. 'My girlfriend is in . . . We'll go to the pub.'

'OK,' I say.

I don't like Kilburn's noise. People are shouting across the road, horns are blaring, there is loud music spilling out from shops and an echo of a brawl further down the street. We walk two hundred yards until Raff stops outside a red-brick building – a pub that once could have looked regal but is let down by peeling paint and scrubby graffiti along the wall.

'Here,' he says.

Inside, it's dim – there are lights on the walls but the glass globes that surround them are unclean. I can make out the red swirl of an old carpet and the dusty oak timbers that run the length of the pub. There are a few people at the bar, some talking, others sitting alone. Two men are setting up guitars and there's an amp in one corner. Immediately I feel exhausted by them and their as-yet unplayed music.

'What are you having?' Raff asks.

'Sorry?'

'A drink?'

'Soda and lime, please,' I say.

There's a young woman behind the bar who wears her hair in a tangle of scribbles and a low-cut gypsy-style top. I can see the beginnings of a dark tattoo on the flesh of her breast.

'It's a dragon,' she says and I look up at her, embarrassed that she has caught me staring at her but she grins. 'I call him Bob.'

'A pint of the Green King and a soda lime, please, Michelle,' Raff says.

'Sure,' she says.

She pours the drinks and we wait in silence. I watch Raff as he plays with the buckle of his bag. He seems nervous, or perhaps I'm deflecting my anxiety on him. We walk to a table near the back of the pub and I don't really want to sit on the bench because I don't know what's been spilt on it but Raff is looking at me with an expectant smile on his face and so I perch uncomfortably on the edge of the cushion. There is a man that I hadn't spotted opposite us with a mangy-looking dog at his feet and they're both staring at me. I cast my eyes downwards.

'You OK?' Raff says.

'Yes,' I say. 'Is that man looking at us?'

'Where?'

'Over there.'

He looks. 'No. But why should you care if he was?'

'I don't like people talking about me.'

'He's not talking about you,' he laughs. 'Besides, even if he was, who's he going to be talking about you to? His dog?'

'I don't like it,' I say.

'Shall we move?'

'Yes please.'

We get up, shift a few tables down near the men with the guitars who are having a pint and talking about songs. I don't want to sit here either but Raff will think I'm strange to move again. I need to bring up the photograph, the fact that he took it, but he speaks before I do.

'It's nice to see you,' he says.

'You too,' I say.

He pauses, I see him considering me. 'Are you lonely, Margo?'

His questions throws me off guard but his perception of me is exactly right. 'Yes,' I say.

'I'm lonely too,' he says. 'Funny, isn't it? That you can be surrounded by people and still feel so utterly alone? I share a bed with Leonie, for fuck's sake. But you know what? I don't know her. And I don't know any of my neighbours. I don't know what the guy's name is who sells me cigarettes every second day at the corner shop. I *should* know these things.'

'Why should you?'

'I want to feel connected,' he says. 'I'm disconnected from everyone now. I don't talk to any of our old friends, not my family either after . . . I was supposed to take over my father's business and couldn't do it.'

I almost tell him that I tried to find him online there. 'You didn't want to?'

'No, not after . . . I lost myself.'

'But you're writing,' I say. 'That's what you always wanted to do.'

'Yeah, but I feel disconnected even from that. The truth is that I haven't been able to put my pen to paper like I did when I was . . .' He looks straight into my eyes. 'Like I did when I was with Cora. I'm a failure at the one thing I thought I was good at.'

'No, Raff—'

'Don't tell me my poems are any good,' he says. 'Please.'

'They are.'

'Tell me something about you,' he says. 'Tell me what you've been doing all this time?'

'I'm a nanny,' I say.

'Like Patricia.'

He bounces his leg under the table and it's a distraction. It seems to be a nervous tic; I've come to recognise them because I have so many of my own – clawing at the skin on my hands, fiddling with my hair – but the Raff I knew was always calm, assured – his life of privilege allowed it. I don't know who this Raff is.

'Do you enjoy it?' he asks. 'Being a nanny?'

'It's nice to have a family,' I say. 'Emmeline and David and the children. We live in Kensington. I can do routine because that's not stressful. I know where I have to be and when. A routine is safe.'

'But in a few years you'll have to move on again, right?'

His words pierce me. 'Yes. But I hope not for a long time. I love them.'

'I can imagine that'll be hard if you love them,' he says. 'But you've obviously done it with other families?'

He's right – I've been a nanny for two other families but Jonny and Marie are special because they're twins.

'What about words?' he says. 'Do you write? You liked words, I remember.'

My heart soars that he remembers that, but I shake my head. 'I don't write.'

'You should make time for writing. It's like therapy. And cheaper. Trust me, I know.'

I'm surprised by this confession. The Raff I knew at school scoffed when it reached our ears that our old maths teacher had had a nervous breakdown and had started seeing a psychotherapist.

'You see a therapist?' I ask.

'Did,' he says. 'I found it a bit useless.'

'Cora says they're useless too.'

He's quiet a moment and I think that I shouldn't have mentioned her.

'It was more me than them, I think,' he says. 'I didn't want to let anyone in and then . . .' He looks at me intently. 'Then you walk into my life after nearly a decade.'

I stay silent.

Raff opens his bag. 'I thought you should see this,' he says. 'I blew it up so you could see it better than on a phone screen.'

He puts a photograph on the table and I look at it and then recoil back into the booth. It's of a room, with a freestanding metal rail for costumes to be hung, and a small white wooden dressing table with an oval mirror above it against a wall. In the corner is a tired-looking piano with its lid shut, and behind, a window. It smelt musty. It echoed with voices.

'Do you recognise this?' he says. 'It was the music room on the top floor of the theatre. Cora was using it as a dressing room.'

'This is a photo taken from that night? When Cora danced that play, *Mirror, Mirror?*'

'Yes,' he says. 'I took it before she went on stage. You remember this room?'

'I . . .' I trail off. 'No. I don't?'

He drinks and I study it again but the reaction I had when I first looked at it – something like fear – has faded into nothing.

'You took a photograph of Cora that night in that gold dress by the wall of the theatre, didn't you?' I ask. 'There was one of her outside.'

'Yes,' he says. 'I took a lot of photos that night, Margo.'

'I have that picture,' I say. 'Or . . . I did. I've lost it. How did it get to me?'

He's staring at me so intensely that I begin to sweat. 'I lost my camera after everything happened.'

'My mum wrote on the back of it and sent it to me. I thought it was from Annie . . . but it's not, of course. Did you give your camera to our parents?'

He frowns at me. 'I just told you, I don't know what happened to it. And I told you that I haven't ever see your parents after that night. They literally shut you all up – physically, emotionally.'

I hold my head in my hands. 'I'm only trying to put things together. You know things I don't, Raff.'

'And *you* know things that *I* don't,' he says. 'Look closer at the photograph of the room, Margo.'

I look, lick my lips. 'What am I supposed to be looking at?'

He pauses. 'You really don't know?' he says.

'That's why I'm *here,*' I say. 'Because I don't know.'

He sweeps the photo back into his bag and I look at him in surprise. 'What are you doing?'

'You should be speaking to Cora about what happened,' he says.

'She doesn't want to talk about it,' I say. 'She doesn't want to talk to *me*. No one seems to. I thought you were going to help me?'

He drinks his pint while watching the men next to us pick up their guitars. 'I loved her so much, Margo. I loved the bones off of her. Seeing you is like seeing her, but you're not her.'

'I'm sorry,' I say and feel like it's not the first time I've apologised for not being her. I've spent my whole life apologising to myself for not being like Cora.

'Folks,' one of the singers says. 'It's time we play you a ditty.'

He's Irish, skinny with a paunch and a farmer's flat cap. He starts up a riff and the other man taps his foot to the rhythm, joins in and the first man whoops and they descend into a frenzied shanty. It's loud, energetic, crashes through me.

'Can we go?' I say. 'Talk some more where it's quieter?'

'No,' Raff says. 'You know what we should do? We should dance.'

'Dance?'

'You went to stage school when you were little,' he says. 'Before boarding school. Cora told me you all went. She told me that you were good. That you could have been great.'

She told him that?

'I'm not,' I say.

He smiles, stands up and offers his hand to me and this unfolding scene feels like something straight out of my childhood dreams, but I feel worried. I feel like there's something dark etched on the tip of his tongue that he doesn't want to reveal.

'Dancing is about letting yourself go,' he says. 'That's what Cora always told me.'

There's a little space in front of the musicians, big enough for us to stand pressed against each other and that's what happens.

I nod. 'Yes,' I say. 'I was never very good at that.'

'Letting go?'

'It feels . . . out of control.'

He laughs, puts one of his hands on my back and the other in mine.

'Clear that table, Charlie,' the man in the flat cap shouts over his guitar and the other man drags a table so there's more room for us.

'It's OK—' I start but the men reply by playing harder.

'Dance,' Raff says and he turns me and I spin out and then back into his body with an awkward thud.

'Oh!' I exclaim.

He does it again but I'm ready this time and I wheel with him, fast and smooth. He moves me into a cha-cha routine and I go with him and I wonder how our bodies know how to move together. I'm reminded of the expression that dancing is for the soul and if this is true, is this why Cora loves it? Is it why I'm spinning with my arms up over my head, fast, pirouetting like I was younger again, like a dancer.

'I could close my eyes,' Raff says into my ear. 'I could keep drinking and . . .'

I open my eyes and he's up close to me. His hands are splayed over my ribcage. It's tight and hurting me but I can't stop him – I don't want to stop him. He's lifting me and I tip my head back and I close my eyes and reach for the

211

ceiling but it's not the ceiling in my head but stars. Should this have been what I had done with my life? Should I have been the dancer?

'In a couple of days, Leonie is away at a friend's,' he says. 'We'll see each other again. Yes?'

I look at him. 'But every time I want to speak, you close off.'

'I'm sorry. All this is hard for me too, you understand?'

'I understand.'

He sighs. 'You know something weird?' he says. 'Even though this is completely fucked up, seeing you is the first time in nine years that I've felt something like . . . I don't know . . . like being alive again.'

I look at his face and find it hungry with urgency, desperation. It mirrors my own.

'Will you ask her to call me?' he whispers.

'Cora won't call you.'

There's hurt in his eyes. 'How can you be so sure? If you told her you'd made contact with me – we could talk all together? Make sense of it all. Try again?'

I shake my head and he looks so sad that I put my fingers to his cheek, stroke the coarse stubble.

'I'm sorry,' I say.

I've closed any potential connection down and I feel a pang of guilt. They were in love once. But that was a long time ago. She doesn't need him now, wouldn't want him.

He takes my fingers in his hand, leans in, and kisses me on the cheek. I can taste his tears as they run to my lips.

TWENTY-TWO

CORA

From a distance I see Miss Patricia walking – her back still ramrod straight and her grey hair neat in a tight bun. She's wearing a tailored black coat and the clicky court shoes she has always favoured, and I love how she's kept herself: proper, exact, unwavering.

Despite there being a metal rail to separate the river from the towpath she is as close to the hedgerow as she can get and I laugh to myself about this. Miss Patricia has always hated the water. No changes there.

The towpath of the canal is wide and empty, except for me, but Patricia hasn't seen me yet because I'm on the blind curve of the river, sitting on a tree stump amidst the undergrowth in dark, new-on-this-morning running clothes, and gloves on my hands. It's a cold Tuesday and it feels right that it should be cold when we connect eyes again after so long.

She disappears from my view and I have a couple of minutes until I'm graced to see her, face to face. What a surprise it'll be for her to see me. The last time I saw her was a couple of years ago, here, in Winchester city. I found her address in Granny's frayed black book and I have come to visit her – secretly – a number of times. I take a train out of London and snatch a few hours to watch her, to study the shape of her neck, the way she drinks her coffee when she sits at outdoor restaurant tables, the way she laughs with friends. She has always been graceful and elegant and beautifully stifling. She has always created a complexity of emotions in my heart.

Over the years I've come to know that she walks this way to town from her house, which is a quarter of a mile away. She lives in a pretty red-brick house covered in white wisteria with a little gravel path leading through a front garden dressed in flowers, that no doubt someone else tends for her because she's not one to get her hands dirty. This route following the river is quick and there are no, or only a few, people for her to have to weave around, because she always hated to weave around people. She would march in a straight line if she could, and never have to step aside for anyone.

I hear her shoes before I see her and then she appears around the bend. She's so close and my heart is banging. There are leaves blowing down from the trees like raindrops but they don't touch her. As she nears me, I bend my head and pretend to stretch my legs but as she passes me, I snap straight.

'Hello, Patricia,' I say to her back.

She stops dead, momentarily frozen.

'How are you?' I say.

214

She turns around, registers my face and stares, open-mouthed at me.

'You'll catch flies like that,' I say.

'Goodness,' she says. 'What are you . . . What are you doing here?'

'Surprise!' I walk up to her, link my arm with hers. 'Walk with me a while.'

'This is . . . very unexpected,' she says. 'How did you know I would be here?'

'Oh, Patricia. I *always* know where you are.'

I can see her confusion. She licks her lips; she's wearing coral lipstick, which is chalky in her lip lines. I would tell her that it's unbecoming on her but it would upset her and no one should ever upset Miss Patricia.

'But . . . Why are you here?' she says again.

I skirt us round a wet pile of leaves, draw us towards the water's edge and she goes to pull away from me but I hold her tight.

'I came to find you,' I say. 'Because I want to talk about what you're *doing*.'

She blinks. 'What I'm doing?'

'Granny tells me you're nannying again. Is that right? And opening a dance school. I missed all that. That's a big undertaking.'

I start to drag her forward then and she goes with me. Sixty-five now and not as strong as she was.

'I – I am,' she says.

'Are you going to teach all the little girls *Mirror, Mirror*?' I say.

215

'You remember that play?' she says.

'How could I forget it?'

'Well, quite,' she says.

I pull her close to me again, so close that I can see myself in her eyes, once so stern and fierce, eyes that I looked up to, but which are now old and watery.

'You're hurting me.'

'Why are you trying to contact Margo?'

'What?' she says.

I walk us closer to the water's edge and I feel that she squirms and I'm happy to feel it because now I want to make her worry.

'Margo could have made something of her life but you're stirring it all up, aren't you? You don't think you did enough harm all those years ago? Telling our mother it was Margo's fault? *You're* the reason Mother did what she did.'

She sniffs. 'I only told your mother what I saw.'

I press her against the rail as we walk and she stiffens. 'Is it you that's sending all this shit?' I say. 'Because it can't be Annie and it's not Mother either.'

'I don't know *what* you're talking about,' she says. 'And I don't appreciate you coming here out of the blue.' Her voice changes. 'You could have been something, dear. Is that it? And you're not? You were always an incredible dancer but you didn't fulfil your potential. You've been tracking me to give me the sob story? Is that why you've come?'

I tighten my grip on her so that my fingers are digging into her frail tendons.

'You're going to break my arm!'

'What happened to having a strong body?' I say. 'That was your mantra, remember? *Your body is your weapon.*'

'Please,' she says and I startle at that because I don't think I've ever heard her say 'please' in all the years I've known her. 'I don't understand.'

'You sent Margo my book of dance? But you don't get to play games with us any more.'

'I've not been playing any *games*,' she says.

'Oh, but you were always so fond of them,' I say. 'Remember? Always watch the quiet ones, Patricia.'

'I don't understand,' she says again and there's genuine confusion in her eyes.

'I've come to eliminate threats,' I say. 'Are you a threat?'

'Do I have to call your father about you?'

I shove her, hard, so that she crashes into the canal railing.

She tries to steady herself but I kick her legs from underneath her and her footing falters on the slippery siding. She folds inelegantly between the gap of the edge and the middle rail, smashes her face on the concrete edge as she goes and then the water whips her dangling legs away. Her arms are outstretched on the concrete, her hands trying to grapple something for a hold, but there is nothing but loose gravel and mushed leaves, and the strength of the river pulls her in.

She doesn't even scream, there's no time for it. I see the purple lining of her coat plume upwards around her as she's carried away by the fast-moving water, watch as her head comes up to the surface, her eyes glassy and dark like stones, and back down again, her hair plastered over her scalp. I see her stringy limbs thrash against the pull of the water as she goes fast downstream into the deep, her mouth open in panic, and her fingers splayed in front of her as she tries to reach for low branches dipped in the water. Maybe she's trying to shout, perhaps she *is* shouting, but I can't hear her over the sound of my own rushing heartbeat.

I wave her goodbye.

TWENTY-THREE

MARGO

I remove the green caps from the strawberries, and then cut them into halves. This morning I've made French toast with maple syrup, yogurt, and three fresh fruits, and my stomach aches for some, but I'm too wound up to eat.

When I woke this morning I saw that Raff had texted me, wants to see me so we can talk properly, and when I read it, I wondered if we'd go somewhere to dance again, wondered if he would kiss me again, and then I felt ashamed because my intention to talk about Annie was immediately shunned into second place. All my waking hours have been spent in a dreamlike haze thinking about Raff since our meeting – how he took me into his arms and danced with me, the brush of his lips on my cheek.

There was a moment when I was seventeen where I nearly kissed him.

The three of us – Cora, Annie and I – were standing on the steps at a house that belonged to one of the boys in mine and Cora's year. The house was called Juniper Hall and it was a huge and intimidating red-brick place with small windows and uneven stone steps leading up to a white door. I remember hearing thumping bass music from within and fearing to go inside, but Cora reached up to the brass horse head and rapped it. I had looked to her and then to Annie and they had beamed at me, excited, before Cora had laughed. The setting sun caught the gold in her hair.

'You're at a party, Margo, not a funeral,' she said. 'Why are you looking so worried?' She leaned over to me, unbuttoned my shirt by two. 'Is that Mum's shirt?'

'Yes,' I said. 'It's got sparkles in it.'

'Jesus,' Cora said and the two of them burst out laughing. 'There's no saving you.'

She and Annie were both wearing short summer dresses. Annie's dress was white and floaty, virginal, and Cora's was canary yellow, ruched at the sides with a scoop neckline and no bra. Their legs were tanned and silk-smooth, they had matching freckles scattered over their noses and perhaps I did too but I hadn't wanted to look too closely at myself in the mirror before we left.

I wanted so much to turn and go home because, as always in situations like this one – and I'd been forced to go to many – I felt unsafe. I looked behind us at the sun setting over the ridge. The moon would come up soon, bright and full, and I remember thinking that I could just sit on the steps and wait out the party, dusk until dawn and beyond. But as I was thinking it, the front door opened by a boy called Lior threw his arms around Cora, hastening us inside, where we were handed plastic cups of home-made punch. I was left by Cora and Annie within seconds and I drank the punch for something to do, to make me look normal, but it stung my throat.

Alone, I wandered the house, shrinking back against the walls when people passed me by. Everything in Juniper Hall was beautiful and elegant; the curtains were heavy velvet, the dark sofas were soft leather. The artwork on the walls looked regal and some of the sculptures were works that I had seen in magazines. Everything was so fragile and I was on a knife-edge each time someone spun past them, tilted their glass or dangled their cigarette. It wasn't my house but I was emotionally taking care of it, like I do with everything.

'Hi, Cora,' someone said.

I looked to see a couple of girls in our year coming towards me, smiling and waving.

'Love your top,' one of them, Clarissa, said.

'Thanks,' I said, and decided to play along. It would be easier now to pretend to be Cora than to be me and for them to suddenly sneer at my appearance and walk away.

'You want a smoke?' Anvi asked.

'Great,' I replied, and I took a cigarette from her, put it to my lips and she lit it for me.

'You seen Lizzie King?' Anyi said. 'She's a right mess. I took her down the hall to the bathroom. Think she'll be in there all night.'

'She was going to try and hook up with Clinton,' Clarissa said.

221

'Guess I might instead,' Anvi laughed and I laughed loudly alongside her.

'Raff looks hot tonight,' Clarsisa said to me. 'You lucky bitch.'

I pointed to the painting above my head, a hunting portrait full stride. 'I'm going to ride him tonight like the man on that horse.'

They shrieked with laughter and I smiled.

'I need another drink,' Anvi said. 'You want something?'

'No, you're all right,' I said and I watched them walk away.

I still had the cigarette in my hand and I stubbed it out on the floor, feeling bad for the wood, and shuddered out a breath.

'What do you think you're doing, Margo?'

It was Cora's voice behind me and I turned around, my heart thudding. She came out of a dark corner.

'I – nothing.'

'It wasn't a bad impression of me.' She was smiling but her eyes weren't.

'Cora, I'm sorry – I just . . .'

'You just wanted to be me for a while?'

I looked down at my feet, ashamed.

'Some of us are playing spin the bottle,' she says. 'Come with me.'

'Oh no,' I said quietly. 'That's not for me.'

'It's a game, Margo,' she said and grabbed my wrist. 'Don't be a wuss.'

I tugged against her. 'But I want my first kiss to be special.'

She laughed then. 'Special? Are you kidding? The girls are going to demo blow jobs on the bottle in a few rounds. Maybe you'd want to try that instead?'

'Please, Cora,' I said. 'I don't like things like that.'

She stopped yanking me, leaned close to my ear. 'I could tell you what one tastes like,' she whispered. 'I could tell you what Raff tastes like.'

My heart jumped and something else too; something in the pit of my stomach at the mention of him.

She dragged me again, to a room with high ceilings and a magnificent fireplace where twelve of them were sitting in a circle on the floor – all of Cora's girlfriends, and Raff and his friends.

Cora sat me down next to her. 'My sister needs a snog,' she declared and sat me down beside her.

I calculated that I could stay a couple of minutes and then excuse myself, find a bathroom somewhere and lock myself away to wait out the party alone. I watched with my heart in my throat as people spun the bottle, held my breath in hoping it would never land on me. But then came my turn to spin it.

'Girl or boy,' Sabine stated. 'Doesn't matter who it lands on. You *have* to kiss them.'

They were all looking at me, smiling. I leaned towards the bottle, knew that people could see that my fingers were trembling. I spun it, then leaned back on my heels, and watched with a sickening dread as it decided my fate. My first kiss. It came to a standstill, and I looked up at who it was pointed at – Raff.

'Pearl!' he laughed.

My heart started to flip over in my chest.

'Why do you call her that?' Cora's voice was clipped.

'That's what her name means,' he said.

'Go on then,' someone called. 'Kiss!'

'Pearls are made up of parasites, did you know that?' Cora said. 'They grow from a parasite inside a clam.'

They all laughed but my heart felt like it had been splintered by a shard of ice.

'Better not go there,' Cora said to Raff and then she looked at me. 'Spin again.'

'Those aren't the rules—' one of the girls piped up but Cora silenced her with a look that could have killed.

'Spin again,' she said.

I looked at Raff who winked at me. 'You nearly had me there, P,' he grinned, and in that moment, I ached for him with all my being.

I looked at Cora, and clenched with rage at her for denying me.

Choose me.

'Margo?'

I blink, come out of myself. David is standing next to me.

'Sorry,' I say. 'Yes?'

'I said there's someone here for you. She's waiting on the porch.'

My heart jumps. Immediately I think it's Cora because she must be able to smell my guilt.

'Thank you.'

224

I go to the door but it's not Cora waiting for me, it's the woman that I saw in Raff's house, his girlfriend, Leonie. She's dressed in a grey coat over a figure-hugging red rib-knit jumper and has glossed her lips into a sheen. I have a fleeting thought on whether Raff would lick it off as he kissed her and this thought shocks me, like it's not come from me. I'm thinking too much of him.

Leonie speaks first, answers the question that forms on my lips.

'I followed you home,' she says. 'After you went to the pub together.'

My ears have snagged at the accent in her voice.

'You're – you're French?'

'Swiss-French,' she says and frowns. 'Why is that relevant?'

Like me, I think, like Cora and me.

'I saw you dancing,' she says. 'You and Raff.'

I start to explain but how can I? How can I explain an old lifetime of wanting a person but never reaching him?

'I saw how you *move*,' she says and the hurt in her eyes is undeniable and I feel ashamed. 'Like a dancer.'

'I'm not one.'

'This is your house?' she asks and her voice is suddenly unkind. 'It was your husband who answered the door?'

'No,' I start, but she talks over me, angry.

'You have all these nice things,' she says. 'So why have you come back for him? For Raff?'

I look back at the house. 'I have to drop the children at school,' I say. I'm wearing only black jeans and a grey cashmere cardigan and bare feet. I turn to grab shoes in the closet by the front door. 'Perhaps we should talk outside,' I say.

'You don't want your husband to hear me?' she says. 'Is that it?'

'I'm a nanny,' I explain. 'That's not my husband, it's my employer.'

But she's already walking down the street and I don't know if she's heard me. I jog to catch up with her, wrap the cardigan around myself as the wind swirls through the houses.

'There's a photograph of you in his wallet,' she says, not looking at me as she walks. 'He doesn't know I found it last year but it's you. Obviously.'

'No, it's not me,' I say. 'It's not of me.'

'You think me stupid?' she says. 'Don't you see how alike we are?'

I do, of course. I almost mistook her for Cora, after all.

'He likes dancers.'

I stare at her. 'You're a dancer too?'

'I teach it,' she says.

I think how strange, how *constructed* these similarities between the three of us are. I wonder if Raff ever closes his eyes when he's with her and whispers Cora's name, privately in his own head. I think of our closeness in the pub and wonder if he would ever whisper mine.

'I found this,' she says and pulls a piece of paper out of her pocket. 'He wrote it last night and then got drunk, fell asleep.'

The paper is thin, torn at the edges and on it are scribbled, lopsided words.

I wandered the silence of blank pages,
Until you walked into my life like a song.

'He loves you,' she says and pins it to my chest.

I hold it close. The piece of paper flutters between my fingers.

'We've only been together for two years,' Leonie says. The pitch of her voice raised with emotion. 'And Raff's struggled on and off with mental health issues.'

'I – I didn't know that.'

'Please don't take him from me.' Her voice is imploring and I think it could have been me asking Cora this exact question for so many years.

Leonie's eyes are filmed with tears. 'I know he was obsessed with you.'

'Not me,' I say softly. 'He was never mine. He was with my twin, with Cora, for years at school.'

She pauses. 'Your twin?'

'Yes,' I say. 'Not me.'

It could have been me. It should have been me. Raff had more in common with me than he did with Cora.

'But it was you in the pub?'

'Yes,' I say, feel embarrassed. 'Yes, that *was* me. But he never loved me.'

'So why are *you* here?' she says. 'Please, I love him. But since you've turned up . . . It's all he's doing.'

'What? What's he doing?'

'Dreaming of you – or, or your twin, I don't know. But he's spiralling again into a place where I can't reach him.'

I'm at a loss for words.

'It looks like you have money and a life here,' she says. 'But he's struggled with the past – with *you* or with your twin, I don't know. He told me that he hit rock bottom, lost everything, his money and his family because he was depressed, turned to alcohol, but then dragged himself up and he's been so good but now . . . now he's up all hours of the night talking to himself.'

'I'm sorry,' I say. 'I didn't know he had been unwell . . .'

She takes my hands. 'I don't want you seeing him again. Promise me. He's fragile.'

'But he has answers about what happened to my little sister, Annie. She died years ago. And Raff was there. At the theatre.'

She's quiet a moment. 'A theatre?' she says. 'Which theatre? Where did your sister die?'

'It was near our school. Out of London. A theatre in Windsor.'

She makes a sound, a small animal-like moan, covers her mouth with her hand. She has beautifully long, slender fingers.

'Are you – are you OK?' I say.

She breathes deeply, drops her hand to her side. 'I'm sorry to have come here,' she says. 'But I'm glad I did. I'm glad I know.'

She strides across the road and away from me.

'Leonie?' I call but she doesn't turn back.

TWENTY-FOUR

CORA

Every sense is heightened; I can feel every last droplet from the shower run down my bare arms and legs, I can taste Nav's hairspray like he's here next to me even though he left the flat hours ago; I can hear birdsong over the sound of the bin lorry down the road.

I sit on my bed, hair in a towel, scrolling my phone. Over the last forty-eight hours I've been refreshing the South West local news to glean the information as it's unfolded but there's been nothing, *zero,* about suspicions of foul play. How long do I have to keep refreshing this page for? A week? A month? Forever?

The body recovered from city-centre canal after police respond to 999 call has now been confirmed as sixty-five-year-old Miss Patricia Bergen, a resident of Winchester and ex-prima ballerina with the Zurich Company.

A local dog walker made the tragic discovery at five in the evening on Tuesday 12 October when their dog raised the alarm.

Superintendent Amy Nealon spoke to the press this morning. 'As of yet, there have been no witnesses that have come forward to shed light on what happened to Miss Bergen, but her friends have confirmed that this was her usual route from home into town. At this present time we believe her death to be an unfortunate accident, however we are urging anyone who might have been around this area – between the hours of ten in the morning and five in the evening – to contact the police.'

Miss Bergen leaves one sister, Penelope Bergen, and previous spouse, Andras Varga. Both say that they are devastated by the news of Miss Bergen's death.

I text Margo.

Sorted everything. No need to worry. Cxx

I throw my phone on the bed, take the towel from my hair, and then dance around the room, naked. The wound on my side pulls, but I don't care.

'Yes!' Jean-Luc cries from his seat and I hold myself strong in the lift. 'Your expressions, Cora! This is heaven!'

Zdravko places me down to the ground again and I spin away from him and there are lights in my eyes now but they're not from the room or the pain. They're from euphoria, deliriousness.

'Cora,' Jean-Luc says. 'Are you all right? Cora? *Arretez!* Stop!'

'What?' I say, panting. 'What's not right?'

But I'm right in the corner of the room, perhaps I would have spun into it had he not called to stop. Sweat is pouring from my face and my whole body feels like it's electric. I dosed myself up to the eyeballs on Nav's secret party drugs that he doesn't know I know about. It's giving me jets.

'Let's take five minutes,' Jean-Luc calls to the room and then he looks back at me. 'Are you all right?'

'I'm fine,' I say.

'*Oui,*' he agrees. 'Better than fine but the space here is too small for such big turns. Save them for the stage.'

Zdravko comes towards me. 'That was great.'

'Do you think that lift was better?' I say. 'That lift was stronger, wasn't it?'

'Yes,' he smiles. 'You're on fire today.'

'I know.' I wink at him, wonder what he'd be like in the bedroom? Moody and sensitive? Or is he the type to pin me against a wall? I like those types.

Joanna and Jean-Luc are talking quietly from their chairs in the middle of the room. Jean-Luc takes a coke from the floor, sips it and looks at me, smiles and my heart soars. My injuries won't stop me from making this show my debut performance into the world, and nor will Margo.

We carry on for another hour and I'm high as a kite, dancing like my limbs are injected with liquid adrenaline, dancing like I used to. My feet have wings. Is this what all murder feels like? Like I could touch the sun? I've sorted it all. Fed Margo the line that it was our mother who sent the photograph, and fixed Patricia. I will dance this play and I will fucking shine and no one will stop me.

'Rosa and Cora, you're needed here tomorrow at nine until midday,' Joanna says. 'Zdravko and Cal, Sophie and Ivana, you're here all day.'

'Before you go,' Jean-Luc says. 'I've had confirmation that we have a very important rehearsal on Thursday night. I've invited Kaito Kobayashi for a private showing of Act One. I want you all here at five-thirty. Do not be late.'

I walk out into the fresh air, call Nav.

'Come party with me,' I say.

'Some of us have to work.'

'So bunk off.'

'I can't,' he sighs. 'I have things to do.'

'You work part-time in Harrods, Nav, you're not a criminal lawyer,' I say.

'Harrods pays well,' he says. 'Who once came back with those diamante knickers for you?'

'They were on sale,' I say. 'And massively chafed my flaps.'

'Whatever,' he says. 'If I remember, those pants got you in a broom cupboard with Matthew Moriarty and landed you that role for *Big Girls Don't Cry*.'

'True that,' I laugh and hang up.

I call Guy Harris.

'Hello, gorgeous,' I say when he picks up. 'I'm in need of a good time. Are you my man?'

'I could be,' he says and I can hear the wolfish smile in his voice.

TWENTY-FIVE

MARGO

I've tried all day today to distract myself with household chores and batch cooking, but I'm anxious. My head is banging, more so than ever before with coming off the pills, and I've been sick three times, and I think that I should cancel tonight but know that I won't.

I shower, take my time with dressing, put on make-up, curl my hair and then lastly I open the drawer of my vanity, reach to the back of it and take out a bottle. It's blue glass, square and heavy in my palm, and I've never used this perfume though I've had it for years. I remember that I loved it from the moment I smelt it. I spray it at my neck on my wrists and almost immediately I'm hit with an explosion of images behind my eyes – racing footsteps up a staircase, a piano rolling across the floorboards, a billowing curtain.

'Are you going out?' Marie says.

I face her and the images melt from my mind's eye. Marie is in her pyjamas, her feet in gorilla slippers.

'Yes, sweetheart,' I say.

'Are you wearing perfume?'

'Yes.'

'I've never seen this dress,' she says, comes over to me and strokes the softness of the one I've chosen.

'No,' I say.

It's an emerald green and I can't remember where I bought it – when I bought it, even. It matches his eyes and, I think suddenly, matches my envy for my sister. I'm wearing her perfume.

'Why have you brought me here?' I say.

I stare up at the building, it's frontage floodlit in the drawing dark. I thought we were meeting in central London for a late coffee, a dinner, somewhere we could talk. I wasn't expecting this. The hotel rises four storeys tall in majestic white stone with classical lines, columns at the front in a Greek revival style.

'You don't like it?' he says.

'It's beautiful,' I say as we walk up the stone steps. 'But why are we here?'

'Because my place is a mess,' he laughs. 'And I'm guessing we can't talk at your place because it's not your place.'

'No,' I say.

'I booked a room.'

I stare at him.

He laughs again. 'So we can *talk*.'

I catch a note of alcohol on this breath, realise he's been drinking. He takes my hand.

'It's somewhere neutral, comfortable,' he says. 'You didn't like the pub I took you to.'

'No,' I say. 'But there are other places.'

'Not like this!'

A white-gloved and black-tailed doorman opens a glass door and Raff puts his hand to my arm to steer me into a lobby that dazzles me with its white marble flooring and bright shining lights.

'This is . . . amazing,' I say.

'I know,' he grins.

'I thought you said you didn't have any money?'

'I don't,' he says. 'But I have a credit card, unless you want to pay because you're rolling in it?'

'I'm not . . .' I begin but I suppose I am. I know there's always plenty of money in my account because I never spend it. I should be investing it properly, should securing it for the future, but that all feels too exhausting to think about.

'I'm kidding,' Raff says. 'I just thought this would be nice. You asked me why I kept shutting off. It's because we needed to talk in a better place. This is perfect place! Cora loved places like this. She was always such a magpie for glamour.'

I'm not Cora, I want to say, but I don't. I also want to say that Leonie came to my house, that she begged me not to see him again, but I don't say that either. Instead I stand and stare upwards at the brilliant white ceiling and dripping crystal chandeliers while he checks in at the reception desk, then waves a key card at me.

'I wrote a new poem,' he says and he walks over to a lift, presses a button. Floor three. That's where we're going. What's going to happen in the room on floor three?

'That's good,' I say.

'I stayed up all night,' he says. 'And I'm really happy with it.'

'Can you read it to me?'

He smiles, blushes, and I see that he's so happy and like the boy I knew, and I smile back at him. We stand close to each other in the lift and I wait for him to speak but he just takes my hand and squeezes it.

'I'll read it to you another time.'

The lift pings and the door opens into the corridor, and suddenly it's too quiet. I can hear the sound of Raff's footsteps on the plush carpet, can hear a hoover somewhere in a room nearby, can hear my own pulse crashing in my ears. Here I am, alone with him.

Choose me.

He flicks the key card through the door lock and it opens into a beautiful, lamplit room. The bed is the main feature, a pristine white duvet with a fawn-coloured silk bed runner and pillows, but there is a small sofa too, blue-and-cream striped, and a cream chair facing it. I sit down on the chair, promptly, because to sit anywhere else would feel wrong when this already feels so wrong.

'Are you nervous?' he says.

I look at him. 'Sorry?'

'You're scratching your hands.' He nods to my busy fingers. 'You did that when you were worried.'

I stop. Had he observed this habit at school all those years ago? Had he been so perceptive to know when I was stressed? I was so rarely with him.

237

'Cora told me you used to make your skin bleed.'

Cora had told him. I clear my throat, embarrassed. 'Yes,' I say. 'I did. I do. I don't know why.'

Now I don't know what to do with my hands, or indeed any part of me. Did Cora also tell him that I suffered from constipation, paralyzing anxiety? Did she tell him all the bad, embarrassing things about me and none of the good? Or perhaps she did share some of the good, like how I used to stroke her hair when she was unwell, and when I'd buy her nail varnish and lockets and soft toys with my pocket money. I've never thought that she'd bother talking about me to him. I'm both terrified and thrilled at what he might know.

He walks to the minibar, opens it and takes out a small vodka. 'Shall we enjoy ourselves?' he says.

I see how lopsided his smile is, and how unfocused his eyes are.

'Leonie is a dancer,' I say because I should mention her right this moment. I'm in a hotel room with her boyfriend. 'And she's Swiss-French.'

He looks at me, as he's drinking the vodka, straight from the bottle. His joy is shaded by a frown. 'How do you know that?'

My heart jumps. I don't want to tell him that she came to see me because I'm worried he'll turn tail and go to her. 'I – saw you both together that day I was outside your flat. I heard her accent.'

'How do you know she's a dancer?' he asks.

'I – saw . . .'

238

I don't have an answer but instead of pressing me, he sighs in resignation. 'I like dancers,' he says. 'Like some people like blondes.'

'She's blonde too,' I say. 'Like Cora.'

'Yeah,' he laughs, and looks back to the minibar, selects a gin. 'What are you drinking?'

'Nothing,' I say because I don't want to add another layer to my confusion. I need to think clearly and process what he's going to tell me. I need to be prepared.

'Alcohol is a poet's fuel.' He uncaps the bottle and drinks it straight. 'Drinking alcohol, and in the stairwells of crowded house parties – that's where the writers are. Overhearing and salivating over all the confessions and the shame.'

I'm doing something shameful.

'I might just go to the bathroom,' I say.

'Go for your life.'

The bathroom is white and gold and it blazes my eyes. I don't want to use the toilet – I'd be fearful anyway of making a noise with Raff standing on the other side of the door – so I sit on the bath edge, and try to gather my thoughts. I put my wrist to my nose, breathe in Cora's scent and I'm transported back in time, to a narrow staircase where I'm running up the stairs to the dressing room. Cora's dressing room – the one with the piano, the vanity, the window and the smell. There was noise behind me. There had been someone chasing me.

I unlock the door.

'Raff, someone was—'

I pause because Raff is kneeling on the plush carpet, his fingers in my opened bag.

'What are you doing?'

'Your phone was ringing,' he says, pulling the phone out. 'Or do you have a vibrator in there?'

I blush, and he laughs and holds the phone out to me. I look at the screen but there are no missed calls. I look at him and he smiles at me before unscrewing another bottle. I lay my hand on his arm.

'I was in the dressing room,' I say. 'That night.'

His face changes, becomes very serious. 'Yes. That's where you put on the dress.'

I'm suddenly confused. Had I been wearing the dress when running up the stairs? 'Where was Cora?' I ask.

'She was on stage before the show. Taking direction.'

'I don't understand?'

'You wanted to be her,' he says. His voice sounds tight. 'Didn't you? Because sometimes you liked being her.'

'Did I dance that play?'

'No,' he says. 'Why don't you have a drink?' He pours the small whisky bottle neat down his throat.

'I'm so lost, Raff—'

'Look!' He jumps over towards the window. 'What a view!'

He's so drunk, too drunk to talk sense to me.

'I can see St Paul's!' he says and tries to open the window.

'No!' I yell and I pull him back with such force that we both fall to the floor.

'Sorry,' he says. 'Whoa, I'm sorry.'

He's so close to me. He puts his arm around my waist, lifts me up towards him so we're sitting, and then suddenly his lips are on my cheek and then seeking my mouth and his hands are on my breasts, in my hair, on my thighs and I think that I could be in real danger except that I'm not. I'm responding to him – without even my full consciousness – kissing him back, dizzy with the effort to keep myself present.

'What about Leonie?' I say when we both know I mean Cora.

'I shouldn't have brought you here . . . it was selfish. I'm not myself and you're . . . you're not . . .'

'Please,' I whisper but what am I saying please for? Please, it's OK, don't worry? I won't tell Leonie? I won't tell Cora? Please don't stop?

'She didn't come back for me,' he says. 'Cora didn't come back and that breaks my heart but *you* did and you're beautiful, Margo. You're beautiful. And I *felt* something that night – I felt something even when I didn't know . . .'

He trails off and I see that tears are standing in his eyes.

'You let *go*,' he says. 'You were like someone else.' He comes towards me again, takes my hands. 'Here,' he says and he guides me to the pristine bed.

'Wait,' I say because Cora will know, she always knows, somehow.

But he's not listening to me. 'And your smell . . .' he says. 'That perfume. You smell so beautiful.'

He's kissing me and I force Cora's thunderous face from my head.

'You'll remember,' he says. 'If you just let go.'

'Raff,' I try again but it's not said with protest this time, but with surrender. Finally, I'm playing the leading lady, I'm the girl tangled with him in the dark. I'm centre stage.

It's early. I've woken from a dream where I swam in gold but I was drowning. I turn over in the bed – in these crisp white sheets that aren't mine – and I look at Raff asleep next to me and I feel a sickness creep up my throat. Not through guilt or shame, even though I *should* be feeling those, but because being with him last night has woken me.

I dress quietly so as not to disturb him and then I close the door gently behind me with a click. I keep my head down as I walk across the lobby, like I'm a mistress that should be shamed – I suppose I am – and only when I walk the wet pavements of Kensington Gardens do I look up, face the world. Low sunbeams spotlight the ground from the clouds above and light up the tarmac path. The horse chestnut trees have dropped their conkers. As a child I used to peel them from the spiky encasement and then thumb the red-brown waxy orbs inside and it made me feel calm. I'm not calm right now because shards of memory are gluing together and making me feel sick. I sit on a bench, dizzy with the memory roiling inside my head.

It was opening night and there was an hour before Cora was due to get ready. She was on the stage with the rest of the cast, stretching and getting last-minute notes from the director and I went up the stairs, to the top floor, to her dressing room.

It was empty but for the little vanity table and mirror, the piano in the corner. Dust particles glittered in the last of the sun's summer beams through the tall glass window. It was a perfect room for Cora. Here she would transform into Eliza and I could smell her excitement even though she wasn't in the room. This show was going to be her defining glory; what she had waited for since she was a girl, and, after this performance, she would be catapulted out into the world of dance and become the star she was born to be. There were agents in the audience and I would finally be relinquished of the guilt I had held for pulling her back from Tring.

I laid flowers for her at her dressing table; dusty pink roses and tiny heather-purple chrysanthemums with green stems. I traced my fingers over her black leather jacket slung over the chair at the dressing table, her waiting make-up bag and her black dance bag, and there my fingers stopped. I knew what would be inside; the dress she'd wear in the show – silken and dazzling. I unzipped it, gathered the skirt of it in my hand and the material melted through my fingers. I took it out and hung it on the rail where it blazed in my eyes, and I thought how my sister had always loved this colour because it was her all over – the winner, the taker, the sun.

I looked to the door. Did I dare, just once, to feel as she might feel walking out on that stage? It could have been me too if I'd been brave enough, if I'd been passionate enough. If I'd been better. Could I be brave now, if only for a private moment?

I walked across the wooden floor, shut the dressing room door and undressed. I felt embarrassed but excited, kept looking at the dress on the rail like it was a lover waiting for me and then, in nothing but my knickers, I took it from its hanger and slid into it. It felt like a glove around my body; my skin prickled with gooseflesh and my nipples stiffened under its hold. I felt like a queen. I turned in it, felt it slide along my legs, my hips, and then I tipped my head to the ceiling, closed my eyes in ecstasy and started to spin across the wooden floor in bare feet.

'You look beautiful.'

I stopped suddenly, seeing Raff at the door. His camera was around his neck and he held an enormous bouquet of pink and white flowers.

'Oh!' I said, alarmed.

But he walked towards me, put the flowers on the dressing table, and then took my waist with one hand and pulled me into him and I held my breath through absolute terror and embarrassment.

'You look better than you've ever looked,' he said. 'Let me take your picture, right here.'

Before I had a moment to protest, he raised the camera, clicked its shutter, and then smiled at me like I was the most beautiful thing he'd ever seen. I looked into those green eyes and I saw the boy I'd met four years ago in that meadow, saw a life where I could have had him if it had not been for her.

Before I could register what I was doing, I leant forward and my lips found his and my tongue was searching out his mouth. I knew I had only minutes but still I pulled him down to the hard wood floor where I positioned myself underneath him and his fingers hitched up the golden dress. He put himself inside me and in seconds both of us were breathless and out of control and I loved it because I was leading this moment. At school I had imagined him up close to me but the reality by far surpassed my fantasies. I knew that I'd remember the contours of his taut body under my fingers, the childlike freshness of his hair, and the sound of his breath in my ears, even though I knew it was the worst thing I'd ever done and probably would ever do. But I hadn't ever taken control of myself or my body and I liked it – I liked him responding to *me*. Me and not her. I utterly surrendered myself to the moment, arched and moaned whilst he pulled my hair and grabbed at me and I put my hands under the shirt on his back and raked my nails down it.

He climaxed inside me and I went to kiss his face but on his lips he spoke one word that shot through my body like a lightning bolt.

'Cora,' he breathed.

I knew that he'd mistaken me of course, from the moment he'd walked in with the flowers, but her name aloud bit its teeth at me. I stared up at him in horror and shame and he smiled back at me with those perfect teeth and I pulled his head down to my shoulder and we lay there for a minute, our sweat cooling on my skin and I began to feel a terrible suffocation; of fear and by the weight of my own humiliation. I pushed him away from me as gently as I could and slipped from underneath him, pushing down the golden dress with fumbling fingers, my teeth chattering with sudden cold and shock and the enormity of what I'd done.

'I need to get ready,' I said.

'Sure,' he said. 'Fuck, that was amazing.'

He stood up, buttoned his shirt where I'd undone it and then he drew towards me again, caught my chin with his fingers and kissed me. He was doing up his trousers when she came in. Annie. She saw us together and she knew immediately that it was me and not Cora in that dress. She knew what I'd done.

'Margo?' she said.

'What?' Raff said and the three of us stared at one another in silence.

Oh God, that moment. A few precious minutes where I'd felt truly myself, and it was shattered in an instant. Nothing would ever be the same again.

What happened after? Did Annie leave? Did she stay? Did we argue? Where was Raff and what did he say? I've blanked it all out. I must have taken the dress off and folded it back into the bag, slipped out of the room before Cora entered it and gone down to the stalls, because I *know* that I watched Cora dance the first act in the gold dress, didn't I? I can see her in my mind's eye, her performance was electric, full of fury and passion, and I watched her in awe and also in terror because of what I'd done. I kept looking for Raff and for Annie in the audience because they were in the same row as I was and I wanted to try to read their faces. Would they tell her? What would they do? I remember, as the first act neared the end, I turned my head and saw a face already turned to me and the feeling of it overwhelms me now. Not the memory of who the face belonged to, because I can't see that, but only the feeling associated with it. That person was filled with hate. Was it Annie staring at me with utter loathing, and contemplating telling Cora everything at the interval? Was it my mother or father and she'd told them? Or was it Raff, the only man I'd given my heart to, looking at me in utter disgust?

Or it could have been Cora. She could have found out what I'd done and hadn't gone on stage because she was so upset. Her understudy could have gone on instead while she had watched from the audience, heartbroken and bereft of the chance she should have had. My heart throbs with worry. My brain won't work to unscramble that face. It won't work at all.

I should go back to the hotel, scream at Raff to tell me what happened after that, but I'm afraid. I hated Annie, all my life, and that night Annie knew something that could sever my already-fragile connection to Cora forever.

I'm scared of what I did to Annie.

TWENTY-SIX

CORA

Something is making a noise. I look to the floor, see that my phone is lighting up the darkened room. I must have dropped it last night and it's ended up in a greasy-smelling pizza box. Did I order pizza last night?

From bleary eyes I see that it's Nav calling me and I should answer but my phone goes to black before I have time to think about moving my arm and I'm relieved until about a minute later when my bedroom door flies open with a bang. I scream in fright, pull the duvet over my head, but feel a cold whip of air as it's torn from my body.

'What the bloody hell are you doing, you absolute twat?'

'Nav?' I say.

'Who did you think it was?'

'What's the problem?' I say. 'Why are you shouting at me? Why did you *call* me?

'I had no idea you were here,' he cries. 'You've been AWOL and I've been worried sick—'

I put my hands to my ears. 'Jesus, Nav, stop *shouting* at me.'

'I've been calling you for fucking hours!'

'I've been here, bellend,' I say.

'Look!' he says and brandishes his phone at me. 'Look!'

I glance at the clock on my bedside table. 'Shit, I'm going to be late for rehearsals.'

'No, you need to see this first.'

'It can wait,' I say, swing my legs out of the bed. 'Did I order pizza last night?'

He throws the phone at me and it hits me on the arm.

'Ouch!' I look at him in surprise. 'What the fuck, Nav?'

I freeze with terror. Someone has come forward to the police. My body convulses with terror. 'What, what, *what*?'

'*Read it*,' he hisses.

There's a creeping dread stealing into my consciousness. Someone saw me, someone saw what I did to Miss Patricia. I was careless, nervous, fucking *stupid* to do it.

I look at the web browser, see that he has it up on *The Stage*. Relief floods through me. 'What's this?'

He points at it wildly. 'The column by Hazel O'Mara.'

'The article?' I say. 'Jesus, Nav, I thought you were going to tell something awful had happened.'

'*Isn't* this awful?' He swipes his finger so the screen scrolls down.

'Oh, they used Gisele's picture,' I say, frowning. 'Why did they—'

'Oh God, Cora,' he moans. 'You don't know, do you? I didn't think you did.'

I scan the copy and my heart lurches. Gisele Wu's name is listed as dancing *Eliza*. I put my fingers to my temple. 'What the holy fuck is going on?'

'I thought dancing *Mirror, Mirror* was all you wanted?' he says. 'Why did you miss that rehearsal last night? Kaito Kobayashi was going to be there, right?'

'Tonight,' I say. 'Thursday. Tonight.'

'It's Friday.'

'No, it's not.'

'It fucking *is*,' he says.

'I missed the rehearsal?' I say. 'Last night with Kaito Kobayashi?'

'Where have you been?'

Who was I with the last few days? What did I *take*?

'Guy,' I say.

Wasn't I with him? Did we really go that big?

'Why did you do it?' Nav says, dismayed for me. 'This was your dream!'

I scramble up and strip from my pyjamas and throw open my closet.

'Where are you going?' he says.

I'm flinging things from the back of my wardrobe, clawing at boxes long unopened. 'I've got to go!'

'Go where?'

'To the rehearsal!'

I find what I'm looking for. The slick of material like molten gold, *the* dress, and I throw it on over my head.

'What the hell are you wearing?' he says. 'What's that – is that blood? Why has that dress got blood all over it?'

I grab my bag and my bike helmet from the hook on my door.

'Did you not hear me?' Nav shouts, following me down the corridor. 'They've given it to Gisele!'

I slam the door.

Frost has kissed the streets overnight and brushed the bark of the trees silver and I should be careful but I cycle hell for leather along the icy roads. My foot and side scream in pain but I grit my teeth through them and I'm at the studio in twenty minutes. I leap from the bike, leave it crashing on the pavement, and then I run through the lobby and push the studio door open with such force that it crashes on the wall and all heads swivel towards me.

'I'm sorry, I'm sorry,' I say and I dump my bag, my water bottle. I try not to notice the fury on Jean-Luc's face or the looks of confusion from the other dancers. I don't let myself look directly at Gisele but I can see out of the corner of my eye that she's in hold with Zdravko and that their bodies suit one another. Fuck, *fuck*.

'Cora?' Joanna says, rising from her chair. 'What are you doing?'

'I'm here! I was ill, and I fell off my bike, and I had some personal stuff going on—'

Joanna gets up, comes to me. 'No, Cora. I'm sorry but you've been late, had falls, been injured, whatever else has happened, but last night you missed a crucial rehearsal.'

'I know,' I gabble. 'And I'm sorry and thanks for stepping in to fill for me, Gisele, but now I'm here and so I can pick up and—'

'And we are sorry,' Jean-Luc interrupts icily. 'But we have filled your role. I told you from the beginning, no? That this schedule was tight, that we needed absolute commitment and you have failed us. Kaito Kobayashi was here last night and you were not. Do you know how embarrassing that was for me?'

Failed. I am a failure. I will never dance this play.

'Please, Jean-Luc,' I say. 'I'm sorry.'

'It is a pity,' he says. 'Because I had told him that you are skilled and this could have been the making of you – I told Hazel. She *agreed* with me but you have, for want of a better word, fucked up, *oui*?' He turns again so his back is to me. 'Goodbye, Cora.'

'Please,' I say. 'Give me another chance!'

'I don't believe in second chances,' he says. 'Leave the studio. You've wasted my time. And what are you *wearing*?'

'No!' I scream now and he looks back at me, shocked. 'You can't do this!' I roar. 'This is *my* part! It's mine!'

I push past Joanna and stride towards Zdravko and Gisele and pull them apart roughly.

'What are you doing?' Gisele says. 'Is that – is that blood on your dress?'

'This is *my* part,' I spit at her. 'I was chosen! Get the fuck away!'

Zdravko moves to block me from her. 'I think you need to go.'

I push him with all my might and he staggers backwards and into the mirrors.

'Get out!' Jean-Luc roars, stands now. 'Get out!'

Joanna strides over and takes my arm firmly. '*Cora*,' she hisses. 'Get some air.'

'No!' I shout. 'I need this! You don't understand, I need to do this! This is *debt* to be paid!'

Joanna bends her head to mine and her fingers dig into my arm. 'You're embarrassing yourself,' she whispers. 'Come with me.'

'I won't!'

'*Now.*'

She steers me towards the door, looks over at Rosa. 'Bring her things to the lobby,' she says and then she removes me from the room, through the reception and out of the main doors.

'What was that in there?' she says when we're alone. 'And this *dress*? What is this?'

'Why won't he let me back?' I wail.

'Because that's not how things work,' she says. 'Who do you think you are? Some celebrity who can waltz in and out of commitments as you chose? We all believed in you!'

'I've had some real shit hitting the fan,' I say. 'But I can fucking *do* this! Please!'

'You're hyperventilating,' she says. 'Slow down.'

'You can talk to Jean-Luc, can't you? You can get my part back?'

'Cora, listen to me,' she says. 'It was too much for you to take on, wasn't it? You look so tired. Perhaps you need to talk to someone? A doctor perhaps?'

'A doctor? Is that what you think I need to do? Because that's what *she* does, not me! Fucking Margo!' I shout.

Joanna looks startled. 'Margo? Who's Margo?'

Rosa comes into the lobby and I snatch my bag from her. 'Thanks for nothing,' I snarl at the both of them.

I fish out my phone, see a message has come through from Margo. It was sent early this morning and I never saw it. Two simple words.

I'm sorry.

My heart stills. What is she sorry for? What's she done? I call her but she doesn't pick up so I try again and again until I'm stabbing her name on my screen.

'Answer me!' I scream into the voicemail. 'Where the fuck are you? What have you done?'

I kick my bike with my bad foot and it hurts like hell. I scream some more.

It's night. My feet are getting wet from the damp rising up from the lawn and into my trainers. I'm cold, freezing in fact because I'm still only wearing the thin golden dress, and my bones hurt, but I can't move from this spot because I need to get into this house.

Is she still hunting out the truth about Annie? What more can I do to steer her away from all this? I thought I'd dealt with it but clearly I've fucked up, I've missed something, and *she* must have the answers. From the darkness of their Kensington back garden, I watch as the window lights turn off, one by one, and know that soon everyone will be asleep and I can get in.

An hour passes before I allow myself to enter the house because I can't be caught – Emmeline believed me to be Margo before but how would I explain creeping around the house in the dark if she were to see me now?

It's one in the morning when I finally turn the key in the lock, walk softly across the spotless tiled conservatory, and into the beautiful living room. Up the stairs, pause only when the headlights of a car illuminate me for a moment before fading again. I go to one of the rooms, see a little boy asleep in his bed, and I walk up to him, put my face up close to him and breathe him in. I smell all the promise his life holds, all the magic of his years ahead.

Mine was a life of a thousand possibilities.

I wonder what this kid dreams about, I wonder if I blew into his ears and told him everything about me and what I know, a nightmare would seep into his head, but I would never do that to a child. I hold some terrible memories, I hold all the cursed secrets, know the fragility of being a child, a butterfly in a dangerous palm.

I go out of the room, stalk the corridors. I know this house in the dark because I've been here often, have grazed the walls with my fingertips, have rifled through their most private things, have eaten their good cheeses in the kitchen, but tonight I'm here for a very specific reason. I'm going to work out what Margo has been doing in her waking hours and how on earth she's managed to keep all these secrets from me. She tells me everything, doesn't she? I thought she did. I go to her room, this neat tomb, and study the bulking, crumpled bed linen in which she lies.

'You carry on sleeping, motherfucker,' I whisper to her as I rummage around her drawers.

I know she won't hear me because although she's always had trouble sleeping, once she *is* asleep a train crash won't wake her. She's dead to the world and good job too because I can't have her waking up unexpectedly.

I catch sight of myself in her mirror, see that the gold is tinted blue-grey in the darkness. I have dance clothes in my bag and I should take this dress off and get warm but I belong in it right now. The bloom of red-rust blood in the middle of it seems to be growing larger, and I wonder, not for the first time, whose blood it is. Oh, if this dress could talk.

I skulk around Margo's room, rummage and then I see a familiar package high on a shelf behind a lamp. It's an unopened pack of the pills – she hasn't taken them.

'You little fuck face,' I hiss at the bed but I should have realised, should have questioned her when she was starting to question it all herself. I ball my fists in anger. Somehow my tricks have been turned on me.

I go over to the bed, feel like I want to smack it hard, when I notice an origami crane sitting on top of one of her bookshelves. I tilt my head at it. The paper looks soft, faintly lined. It looks like the paper we used at school. I cross the room, snatch it up and unfold it.

> *Sweetheart, let's lay under this embellished sky,*
> *Under the way and atop the scent of flowers,*
> *Cosy up to me like I'm the bonfire of your childhood*
>   *years,*
> *Kiss me on this endless night for hours.*

Raff's poem. How did she get this? I feel sick as I fold it back up to a crane and then go to replace it when I see what it was sitting on. A scrap of paper with a phone number written on it – a phone number I *know*.

I run down the stairs and shut myself into the kitchen, breathe deeply before I dial 141 and then the number on the paper.

'Hello?'

The voice crackles with sleep but I would know it anywhere.

'Hello?' Raff says again.

I hang up immediately and pocket my phone. I want to scream. Has Margo been seeing *Raff*? What would she tell him about Annie? What would she tell him about *me*? What more do I have to do to protect myself? Do I have to take care of Raff the same way as I took care of Patricia?

I am a quaking mess in this perfect, still, kitchen that Margo works so hard to keep pristine.

The parents are on the third floor.

With a sudden lurch I throw my fist into a picture on the wall. The glass cracks, falls to the floor, and then I spin around, sweep my arm across the dresser shelves and make contact with a vase, the tiny china espresso cups, stacked papers. They all bunch together, topple, smash to the ground and to the sound of their miserable endings, I dance around the room, punch and kick and smash and carve and swipe and tear with wild abandon and recklessness. Shards of glass jar into the skin of my arms but I don't feel them; I feel serene, ethereal, like some sort of ferocious composer. This, this is the beautiful soundtrack to her demise. She deserves broken things because she's broken, but I won't let her break me.

TWENTY-SEVEN

MARGO

The mess is astronomic.

The conclusion that we all came to when coming downstairs was that the house was burgled but on closer inspection, nothing was taken, and there was no sign of any forced entry.

The police officer slurps the coffee I made him. 'Whoever it was either knows how to pick locks,' he muses, 'or perhaps found a dropped key.'

'We don't lose our keys,' Emmeline says sharply. She's switched from weepy to angry several times this morning. 'You haven't lost yours, have you, Margo?'

I pull my cardigan around myself. 'No.'

'Do you have a key safe out the front?' the officer asks.

'Yes, but we don't use it—' David says.

'But you have one,' he interrupts. 'So someone found it, got lucky with the combination or they've been watching one of you use it.'

'We *never* use it—' Emmeline starts.

'Maybe one of the kids was messing around with it,' David says to her.

'They *wouldn't*,' she snaps.

'You got a personal security system so we can take a look?' the police officer says.

'No,' David says.

'Well,' he says. 'However it happened, you don't need me to tell you that you'll need to change the location of your safe and the digits, of course.'

David rubs his fingers over his stubble: he hasn't shaved this morning. 'But they didn't take anything so why the mess? The *destruction*?'

The police officer shrugs. 'Some people don't like others to have nice things,' he says. 'And this is a nice house.'

'That's horrible,' Emmeline says.

He nods. 'Yup. People are animals.'

He isn't taking in the heartbreak of a family home, the violation and exposure. This is a minor incident to him. He slurps the coffee again, stares around the room. I move close to Emmeline.

'I'll clean it up,' I say.

'Thank you,' she says, touches my shoulder. She's teary again. 'We'll take the children out for breakfast so they don't have to see this. It might upset them. We'll bring you something back?'

'That's fine. I don't need anything.'

'We'll check the local CCTV of course,' the police officer says. 'And keep you updated. It might be that whoever it was is scouting out the neighbourhood. Looking to have a bit of fun.'

'OK,' David sighs. 'Thank you.'

'Either that or you have enemies.' The officer laughs and then stops abruptly, realising his joke is off colour. 'Anyway,' he says. 'I'll be in touch.'

He hands me the cup and leaves the house.

'Ouch!'

My forearm is bleeding; I've cut it on glass whilst cleaning the tiny shards from the grooves of the wooden floors.

I'm grateful that everyone has gone out, grateful for the quiet, because every ten minutes for the last two hours I've rung Raff but it's gone straight to voicemail. Since I left the hotel on Thursday night, I've felt sick from worry about Annie and shame at what I did with Raff and consequently, what I've done to Leonie and to Cora. Now the word *enemy* is bouncing around my skull. Was it Leonie who came to our house and trashed it?

Blood drips onto the wood next to me and I stop scrubbing. I have to address these cuts before I can carry on. I fold a clean kitchen towel around my arm, walk upstairs to my bathroom and get a plaster from under the sink but as I bend to get it, I see that the long-loved origami crane sits next to my ensuite sink with a note next to it which reads—

Don't you dare go walking into his arms.
Love from Bad Penny.

I gasp. No one else but Cora and Annie ever knew about Bad Penny. It was *Cora* who ripped the kitchen apart. How did she get in here? Has she watched me with the key safe, and let herself in? I stifle a sob between my fingers. Was it her all those years ago, too, at our childhood houses? Cold hurt floods my body; she let me take the blame all those times. Twenty-seven years old and I'm still being played as a fool by my sisters.

The one thing I can be certain of is that she knows I've contacted Raff and she's furious.

'Holy Mother,' the man says when he opens the door to me. 'You look *exactly* the same as Cora!'

'Yes,' I say. 'We're twins.'

Cora has given me her address before – she must have – but this is the first time I've ever come. I took a thirty-minute tube and walked the rest. I've felt sick the whole way.

'I mean, yeah,' he grins. 'I know, but like, *exactly* the same. People must get you confused all the time.'

'Some people, sometimes,' I say. 'But not when they get to know us. Are you her housemate?'

'I'm Nav.'

'Have you seen my sister?' I ask.

He frowns. 'No, and I've been ringing her. Do you want to come in?'

I hesitate but don't want to seem rude. 'OK, thank you.'

I feel awkward about stepping inside but I do and, at once, I'm met with brightly painted walls and vibrant posters.

'Tea?' Nav asks.

'Er . . .'

'I have to say, I've been *dying* to meet you!' he says. 'Does that sound weird? God, now I sound like a stalker or something. I'm not, I'm a fan! Actually that sounds weirder, doesn't it? Whatever, I don't care. The things she's told me about you are *amazing*.'

'What things?' I say.

'Do you really turn coins over so that the Queen is upright?'

I swallow. 'Yes,' I say. 'Because there's a bad side—'

'Ha! I thought Cora was kidding!'

I don't know what to say and I feel silly, but he doesn't seem to notice my discomfort.

'Builder's tea, then?' he says.

'Maybe I should come back a bit later . . .'

'No, stay,' he says. 'I'm a bit worried about Cora because she's lost a part in a show she was desperate over. Did she tell you? And she's injured herself. She does tend to go on these rampaging benders, right?'

I smile tightly, think of the chaos of the kitchen that is now in order. David and Emmeline wouldn't even know anything had happened except for the fact that there are several photographs unframed and flowers without a vase. I've hung the bunch upside down by the range: it'll dry there and look pretty. I'll take the pictures to a framer. I'll make it all better because I have to. I owe them.

'And she got hit by a car,' he carries on. 'Honestly, does everything happen to that girl?'

'She didn't tell me,' I say but I feel a hit of instant pain and my fingers touch my ribcage.

'There, yeah,' he says. 'On her ribs. Wow, being a twin is *loopy*.'

'She didn't tell me she'd got a part in a play?'

'It was called *Mirror, Mirror*,' he says. 'You know it? Apparently she danced it forever ago.'

I steady myself against the kitchen counter, feel beads of sweat forming in the crooks of my elbows and my knees, on my hairline, all the places that a fever strikes.

'She's in *Mirror, Mirror*?'

'*Was*.' He grimaces.

The room begins to swim in front of my eyes. This play is haunting us. The past and *Annie* are haunting us and Cora blamed me for opening it all up but she has been digging it all up too.

'Can I – can I lie down?' I ask. 'I think I might pass out.'

His eyes widen. 'Oh, really? Shit, yeah, come on.'

I see the blur of him move towards me, see an extended arm and feel him pull me gently from the room.

'Lie down in Cora's bed,' he says. 'I'll get you some water and do you still want the tea? I'll keep ringing her for you.'

I can't speak as he guides me and sits me down on a soft mattress. Blood rushes to my head as I lie flat and my eyes fill once more with colour and sharp focus. I'm alone in Cora's room.

It's an explosion – clothes draped from every available piece of furniture and open cupboard doors like a still-life art project, make-up pallets and brushes strewn across the floor, books upturned, the mirror of her dressing table grubby, and the curtains pulled so the afternoon light is shaded. There is a smell of old food, the sugary flatness of cola, the sweet tang of perfume. It feels disorderly but at the same time oddly reassuring. My sister has, and will always be, this beautifully messy, wild spirit.

'Here's the water,' Nav says coming back in and handing me a glass. 'Are you OK?'

I sit up. 'Yes, sorry.'

'Hey, no problem,' he says. 'I'm going to nip to the shop on the corner to get some milk for tea.'

'Oh, please don't worry,' I start but he talks over me.

'We need some anyway,' he says. 'I'll be five minutes. You can chill here.'

'Thank you. That's very kind.'

He leaves and I hear the front door close. I stay on Cora's bed for a moment, breathe in the silence and the familiarity of her, and then get up to open her curtains. She's a sloth, a vampire perhaps, and the light of the day won't last too much longer anyway but I will feel better for the sun. I peer out of the window, see below a small, unkempt garden and a rain-filled ashtray where cigarette butts float like boats. I turn back to the room, absently finger one of Cora's dance tops on the back of the dressing table chair. It's black with gold sequins that spell *DANCE* across it. I open the wardrobe, find a hanger and hang the top on the rail for her and then pause. Because on the inside of the door a calendar is tacked up but it's not her schedule on there but *my* life written out on each day of the week. She's written down where I'm supposed to take the children for after-school clubs, their inset days, where David and Emmeline are taking day trips, where they are holidaying. She's copied it all down, word for word, from our calendar on the kitchen wall. Did she take photographs of it last night? How could she have filled it all in in the short space of a morning when Nav told me he's not seen her here? I swallow down the thought that she might have been in the house before last night, that she's been secretly watching me for weeks, months, but why would she do that?

I stand in the stillness of the room, thinking. If my sister is anything like me, she'll have buried any secrets deep. Nav said he would be five minutes. I reach into the closet, grapple with shoeboxes and hangers before my fingers find something familiar. A trunk, just like mine. Perhaps we're not so different, after all. I drag it out, open the lid. It smells sweeter than mine does, musky with hairspray and old stage make-up. On top of old clothes that I don't even recognise – a lace corset, frilled skirts – is a stack of letters and I take them out, see that they're postmarked from Grindelwald. I open the one at the very bottom, recognise the slant of our father's writing.

Stop writing. You're no longer welcome in this house. The damage that you've caused is unforgivable. Your mother is gone.

My skin prickles with cold and hurt even though I don't know what this means. What damage did Cora cause?

There's a slam of a door, and Nav calls out.

'I'm back!'

I fold the letter hurriedly, shove it back into the stack. How will I explain everything out of Cora's wardrobe?

'I'll make tea, yeah?' Nav says.

I hear him whistle, walk past the door, and bang around in some cupboards.

'I – yes please,' I say, relieved at the seconds he's buying me by being so nice.

I go to close the trunk when my eyes catch something tucked in the corner. Before I know what I'm doing, I'm drawing my hand back out and gripped between my fingers is a slick of yellow material. I have to tug it free – it's wrapped around something big which reveals itself as a heavy black camera. This is Raff's camera.

My heart thrums in my chest as I pick it up and turn it over in my hands. The roll of film in the back of it has been removed and I feel cold; Raff took a photograph of me in the dressing room before he knew I'd deceived him into believing I was Cora. Has Cora seen those photos? Has she always known what I did? Would that mean that she was the one to send the photograph and write the note from Annie? But she's been going to such lengths to get me to leave the past alone. She told me *Mum* had sent them.

'You want chocolate?' Nav calls. 'I got Penguin bars. They're Cora's favourite – obviously don't need to tell you that, ha! Are they yours too?'

'I'm – I'm fine, thank you,' I say, and I go to wrap the camera back again but the gold material keeps slipping in my fingers.

'OK,' he says. 'Oh, hang on, my phone's going, it might be Cor.'

I wind the material around the camera, go to put it back into the trunk but notice there's something on the gold, a rusty stain. I realise at once what it is. It's the gold dress Cora wore – that *I* wore – covered in blood.

It takes everything I have not to scream. I shove the trunk back into the closet, arrange the boxes back in just as Nav comes in.

'She's such a untidy biatch, isn't she?' he laughs as I stand up. He offers me a tea. 'Wait – are you tidying her room for her?'

'Yes,' I say.

'I picked the wrong twin to live with.'

I close the cupboard door. My vision is turning to static. 'I have to go,' I say. 'I'm sorry about the tea.'

I stagger out towards the corridor.

'Are you feeling OK?' he says, sounding concerned.

'Please ask her to call me,' I say and I walk out of the house and into the cold air, gulp breaths like I'm drowning.

TWENTY-EIGHT

CORA

It's late when I get home. I slam the flat door shut, march into my room, and after a couple of seconds I hear Nav's voice from down the corridor.

'Cora? Where the hell have you been? I've been calling you for like, eternity.'

'I've been *thinking*,' I yell back.

I've been to the graveyard, walking around trying to figure out what to do next, but I'm cold now, and tired and angry. So very angry.

'What happened?' he asks, coming to my doorway.

'What the fuck do you *think* happened, Nav?' I say. 'I lost the part.'

'Yeah,' he sighs. 'I mean that much is obvious.'

He watches me pull boxes down from the shelves.

'Your sister came looking for you this afternoon.'

I whirl to face him. '*Here?*'

'Yes, *here*,' he says.

'Fuck me,' I say. 'She found her way here, did she?'

'She seemed a bit agitated.'

'Well, that's better than her usual zombie state.'

'I invited her in—'

'You did *what*?'

He looks taken aback by my reaction. 'What? She's your sister,' he says. 'It's called *manners*.'

'Fuck *manners*,' I say. 'Don't you dare do that again.'

He looks affronted. 'You can't cold-shoulder a sibling, Cora, right? She was pretty upset. I gave her a cup of tea.'

'A cup of tea?'

'She didn't drink it though. I said you'd call her.'

'She'll be waiting a long time for that,' I say.

'I guess now isn't the time to tell you she lay down in your bed?'

'Are you serious?'

'She almost fainted.'

'Jesus. She ruins everything and then lies on my bed like Goldilocks? I hope you've cancelled all your plans tonight, Nav, because you're going to be my wingman. We're going on a charm offensive! And not only tonight, yeah? Every night until I get a new part! No, wait. I'm going to put on that play. Me. I'm going to hire a studio, a director, a choreographer, a musician—'

'Oh yeah? With whose money?'

'*Her* money! Margo's money! She won't even notice I've taken it! I take it all the time!'

He stares at me. 'You steal from her?'

'I use her passports and spend her money,' I say. 'How do you think I get by? How I pay you rent?'

'Wow,' he breathes. 'There are dark little corners of your head I knew zero about . . .'

'Fuck!' I scream. 'Why now? That was my part! It's like history repeating itself, Nav!'

'Bloody hell, mate, calm down, yeah?'

'I could have *been* something!' I cry. 'I could have made it! But I was *stopped*! *She* stopped me!'

'Who stopped you?'

'MARGO!'

'I'm not following—'

'She stopped me from going to the rehearsal with Kaito,' I say.

'Right,' he says disbelievingly. 'And how did she do that?'

'She's fucking me up. I'm disorientated because I can *feel* something.'

'Like, a twin thing?'

'You know what I think? I think she's been with him. Margo has *been* with Raff. She can't open it all up again. It'll *hurt* her!'

'Are you unhinged, woman?' he says. 'I have no idea what you're on about. Take some responsibility here, yeah? You went out and got off your tits again and you missed your big chance. Sorry to tell you but this is on *you*.'

'Fuck off.'

I pull open the closet door, fling one of the boxes to my bed and it comes apart halfway through the air, spills photographs all over the floor.

'What are all these?' he asks.

'Memories,' I say.

He picks up a photograph. 'You and Margo? Who's this in the middle?'

'Annie,' I say.

'Who's Annie?'

'Our little sister,' I say.

'You never said you had another sister?'

'I don't see her any more,' I say bluntly because now is not the time to go into the specifics.

'Who's that woman?' he asks, bending his head to another picture by his feet. 'Your mum?'

It's one of Margo and Annie and Miss Patricia standing in front of our house in Brazil.

'Not Mother,' I say. 'That's Patricia.'

'Your dance mentor?'

'You know, she had a trick with her eyes when she was angry,' I say. 'She made her pupils shake in the whites of her eyes.'

'That sounds sort of freaky,' he says.

'She came so close to us that her face was the only thing we could see, Nav.'

I remember how I could feel the hot sting of spit that rained and gathered in the corners of her mouth as she speared cruel words into our ears.

'She'll not be doing *that* ever again though,' I say.

'What are you doing with all these photos?'

'We're going to have a bonfire,' I say.

'A bonfire?'

'Yup,' I say. 'My life has gone up, spectacularly, in flames.'

272

'I think you're being a *little* dramatic,' he says, stares around the mess. 'Your sister only just tidied all your crap away anyway.'

'She – she what?'

'She tidied your room for you.'

Fuck me.

'Where?' I say. 'What was she doing?'

'She was in the closet.'

'What did she see here?' I say. 'What did she *see*?'

'I don't know,' he says. 'I was out getting milk.'

'Oh, God.'

He puts his arm around me. 'I'm sorry you got kicked out of the play, Cora,' he says. 'But I think you might have a drinking problem.'

I can't stay and put on *Mirror, Mirror*. I need to take drastic measures. We need to leave London but the only way she'll leave those kids is if I make her. Mess it up for her like she's messed up my opportunity.

I laugh. 'I've got bigger problems than that.'

'Like what?'

'The truth,' I say.

And the truth is that it wasn't Annie we buried that day.

TWENTY-NINE

MARGO

It's Sunday and David and Emmeline and the children are visiting friends and will be back late. I should be putting a wash on, polishing David's shoes, cleaning Emmeline's jewellery and taking her autumn clothes out of the wardrobe to make room for her winter ones. I should be with Granny. I *want* to be with Granny but instead I'm in my room, in the duvet chair, trying not to shake.

All I can think about are all the things in that wardrobe – the letter my father wrote to Cora, the gold dress and the blood on it, Raff's camera with the photos that Cora must have seen. I never thought she was vengeful but did I ever know her at all? She's gone to extreme lengths to infiltrate my life. There are still only fractures of memory scratching from inside my head but I'm still in the dark, waiting, hoping that my brain will chase them out.

I blink. It was Annie that chased me up the stairs in the interval. I can hear my breath in my ears, faster and louder. We ran up to Cora's dressing room and I was screaming her name – I was begging her for something. Her forgiveness? Her silence?

Raff answers the door looking tired.

'Is Leonie here?' I ask.

'No,' he says. 'She and I . . . We had an argument.'

'I'm sorry,' I say, but I'm not really. 'Does she know about us?'

'No.'

'OK.'

'Do you want to come in?' he says.

I hesitate because crossing this threshold will be like entering the past and creating a different future all at once but I suppose that's a stupid thing to think – I've already crossed a forbidden threshold in a much more intimate way.

I walk through the door and follow Raff down a dark corridor. The air is close and smells of tobacco, of old books, of fusty carpets and dog hair. I feel along the wall of the corridor to steady myself and the paint is bumpy under my fingertips until a light snaps on ahead of me and I see that Raff is in a small kitchen. It's cramped and messy. There is paper everywhere on the table, on work surfaces. There's an open packet of crisps spilling out from the side of the sink and on to the floor and two fruit flies listlessly hovering above a brown banana in a bowl. The only thing of beauty is a fern in a bright green pot on the windowsill but the window itself is filthy; the dirt and grease picked out by harsh strip lighting. It's so like Cora's flat – they were made for each other. Who was I to ever think that I should have him.

'I know. Leonie and I aren't very tidy people. Creatives often aren't. Do you want a drink?' he says.

He opens a fridge door, takes out two beer bottles and hands one to me. I don't drink beer and, even if I did, it's too early in the morning to be drinking, but I don't say anything as he flicks the cap with a metal tool from his keyring. The caps both clatter to the floor and skitter away, one under a radiator and the other beneath the small kitchen table.

He gestures to one of the tall breakfast-bar chairs whilst he lights a cigarette, the neck of the bottle of beer balanced between the last three of his fingers. I think that it would be easier for him to put it down on the table but it's as if he's too desperate to wait. I don't remember this about him; was he always disposed to dependency? I suppose he depended on Cora, her love and always being his. So did I. I still do.

I don't sit down. He slouches by the bar, smokes and watches me.

'The other night,' he says.

'Yes.'

'You left before I was awake.'

'It's because I remembered,' I say at the same time. 'What happened at the theatre. You and I . . .'

He says nothing, just watches me.

'And I remember that Annie followed me up the stairs in the interval to the dressing room Cora was in. Did Annie tell her about us?'

'I don't know.'

'I've got to ask you something,' I say. 'Has Cora been here to talk to you?'

He frowns. 'No. What do you mean? You told me she was in Switzerland?'

'She knows about us,' I say. 'I think she knows and she's angry . . . I need you to let me know if she comes here.'

He straightens. 'You – you lied to me?'

'I—'

'Oh my God, Margo,' he says. 'What game are you playing? Cora's *here* in London? Now?'

'She's . . . Yes. I'm sorry.'

He looks livid but then he barks out a laugh. 'You know what? You know why I took you to that hotel? It's because it's what I thought *you* wanted – to be with me. I thought that if you let your guard down and I gave you what you wanted, you might tell me where Cora was. I even tried to look in your bag for your phone to get her number! And now you tell me she's here, that I've made her angry without even having laid eyes on her in nine years!'

'Raff—'

'No! You tricked me that night when you put on that dress. That was the beginning of the end for me and Cora, and you know what's fucking weird? You turn up in my life and everything turns upside down again. Do you know what I saw in the news today?'

'What?'

'I read about your old nanny. She died in a canal last week.'

I frown. 'My nanny?'

'Miss Patricia,' he says.

'Who?'

'The one who looked after you all when you were little,' he says. 'She taught you all to dance.'

'I don't remember,' I say.

'How can you not remember her? Cora told me she lived with you for years!'

I shake my head. 'Please, if you see Cora, you have to call me, OK? Straight away.'

'Leave,' he says. 'I think you've done enough damage. You owe me Cora's number so text it to me when you get out of my flat, OK? I need to speak to her myself.'

'Please, Raff—'

But he refuses to look me in the eye, concentrates on gathering things up and so I look down too. There's a beat where he's closing up a photograph album and hasn't realised that I'm looking at his notebook, but when he does, he slams it.

'That's private,' he says.

'I read your poem,' I say at the same time.

The dilemma is loving you. The dilemma is the laughter on your lips and the wind in your hair. In the mist of my own heart I search for those things still. I'm guilty for loving you, for leaving you. Guilty of so many things.

'What are you guilty of?' I say.

He closes his eyes for a moment, resigned that I've read his words, before snapping them open and walking towards me. I shrink back from him because there's anger in his face but he grabs me and kisses me with such force that my head cracks against the wall.

'From telling you the whole truth even if it's the wrong one?'

'What do you mean?'

'Maybe I should have loved you from the start,' he laughs coldly. 'You're a tortured poet just like me.'

He lets go of me, spins sideways so that he's next to me against the wall before sinking down to the floor.

'Go,' he says but I'm already running down the corridor.

THIRTY

CORA

We buried someone else that day; a person that Margo will not want to think about, *cannot* think about. Someone I have helped protect her from thinking about for years.

Annie is not dead but I never thought she would manage contact.

I guess I grew complacent. Margo and I agreed not to talk about the accident and Margo sees Granny rarely enough for it all to let slip. Granny is so away with the fairies most of the time anyway that Margo would never bring Annie up in fear of upsetting her. And if Granny herself ever said anything Margo would have taken it with a pinch of salt. Occasionally I've had to pluck the odd letter from our father that's come via Granny but until now, we've never had anything from Annie herself. I went to great lengths to keep all this from Margo. We were out of the country at the time that papers went to print but I contacted all the local newspapers to take down their stories online about the accident and fuck me, there were plenty. I used my father's money to buy them off and after a while

I successfully erased the entire night in case Margo ever went looking. But what I didn't bank on was Annie coming back. She's been trapped in the Grindelwald, for Christ's sake. How has she managed to learn to *walk* again? How has she managed to hold a pen and write?

I've booked Margo and me train tickets to Paris, a city big enough to be lost in, somewhere I can perform on stage and where Margo can find wealthy families to nanny for. I can convince her, I'm sure of it. I just need to get her to the train station and then we can talk. She'll be upset, mad at me, but what's the alternative? I need to keep her safe and that means having her kept in the dark about Annie.

I'm standing slanted with one hip out and with my arms folded. I'm chewing gum, I'm wearing huge sunglasses, my hair is in a wild bun and I can see people looking at me. I know what they're thinking; they're wondering why I look so different. I should have dressed more appropriately and not in a leather jacket and revealing top.

At three-fifteen children flood out of the school gates, hungry and buzzing. The twins run over to the spot Margo's always at and I lift my sunglasses at them.

'Kids,' I say, 'we're going to do something a bit different today.'

'You look strange,' the girl says. Her name is Marie.

'Do I? Do you mean awesome?'

She giggles.

'October is National Pizza Month, you know that?' I say. 'So we're going to go to my flat to eat pizza.'

'We're going to *your* house?' Marie says.

'I know, right? And then we're going to watch a movie. And eat ice cream on the sofa.'

The boy, Jonny, jumps up and down. 'Yes!'

'Have we been good?' Marie asks.

'You've been perfect.'

I take their bags from their shoulders and then put my palms against the softness of their heads and I'm about to waltz them down the road and hail a cab.

'Where do you live?' asks Marie.

'You'll see,' I say. 'You want some gum?'

'We can't have gum, Margo,' Jonny gasps.

'I'm not Margo.'

They frown, confused and I reach over to them both.

'I'm the Wicked Witch of the West,' I laugh and they squeal as my fingers grasp to tickle them.

I give them gum and for the half an hour it takes the taxi to drive to my road, we take it in turns trying to blow the gum into bubbles. When they go pop, we laugh over and over hysterically and when the boy gets it stuck to his hair, I tell him I'll lop it off and give him a proper cool cut because I'm not a fan of his long fringe anyway.

'Mummy likes it,' he says when we get out of the cab.

'Yeah,' I grin. 'But it's time for reinvention.'

He smiles then as I open the door and lead them to the kitchen, turn on the light.

I see it how they see it. A poky square kitchen with the utensil drawers half out, cupboard doors hung at lop-sided angles. There is grease on the cooker hood, there are encrusted pans piled up in the sink and the floor is crumby underfoot.

'I mean, it's seen better days,' I say. 'I haven't cleaned today.'

Have I ever really cleaned this kitchen? Nav has never complained but he's an equal slob; we've been in stalemate over a dead fly in the bathroom for three months, maybe more. 'We didn't know you lived here.' Marie stares around.

'I am full of surprises!' I say and take scissors from the drawer. 'Come here, kid,' I say to the boy.

He bows his head obediently and I snip the gum out of his hair.

'Let's jazz this up a bit,' I say and give his hair a few more strokes of the scissors. His soft dark hair falls to the floor.

'Can you cut my hair, Margo?' Marie asks.

'Sure!' I say and she tilts her neck so that her dark hair falls in a cascade over one shoulder. It's long, halfway down her back. I lop it straight so it sits at her chin. 'Fringe?'

'OK?'

I gather and smooth the front of her hair and then shear it deftly.

'You look ace,' I nod.

She smiles though there's no mirror but I haven't done a bad job. Dramatic but not bad. I sweep her beautiful tresses under a chair with my foot.

'My haircuts usually take longer than that.'

'But I'm magic,' I say.

283

I show her in the camera screen of my phone.

'Oh,' she says and her voice is small. 'It's short.'

'Bang on trend,' I reassure her.

'Is this a new phone?' she asks.

'Nah,' I say.

'You have two phones?' Jonny says.

'I'm a spy,' I say.

'Are you really?'

'I'm whatever I need to be,' I say. 'Come, come.'

I open the freezer and they peer inside.

'Oh!' they exclaim, delighted.

'Oreo ice cream or Cookie Dough?' I say.

'Can we have both?' asks Jonny.

'I love your thinking,' I reply and I give them a tub each and I rattle in a drawer for some spoons. 'To the lounge!'

They follow me like the Pied Piper and we all flop down onto the sofas. The lounge is also messy; the coffee table is covered with magazines and glasses that are half filled with coke. There are clothes drying on the radiators, a tall plant in the corner with dropped dead leaves at its base. I turn the TV on.

'What channel?' I say.

'Have you got Netflix?' Marie asks.

'Yeah,' I say, put my feet up on the coffee table. 'Let's watch something cool.'

I put on a film that's rated a fifteen about a high school dropout and his band. They're too young for it because there's a lot of swearing but I don't care. They snuggle into me, eat their ice creams. They smell of vanilla shampoo

284

and sugary sweetness – Margo looks after these kids. It's going to be a shame for her to lose them but lose them she must.

'Why haven't we been here before?' Marie asks after ten minutes. She's lost interest in the film already.

'Because it's messy,' Jonny says but not in a judgmental way and this is my kind of kid and I reach over, muss his hair.

'I like the pictures on your walls,' Marie says.

I look over to where she's pointed at my crumpled posters of Alessandra Ferri, Maria Alexandrova, Katherine Dunham and Sammy Davis Jr that I've had since I was a girl.

'You want to dance?' I ask.

'Yes!' she beams.

I stand, move the coffee table to the wall.

'Get up,' I say to them and they dig the spoons so they're upright in the tubs and then they stand in front of me like little attentive soldiers. They're quite sweet actually.

'Let's do the five positions together,' I instruct.

They giggle, go from first to fifth with ease. Has Margo taught them these?

'OK, let's do fouetté en dehors,' I say. 'Turn on one leg with the other making a whipping motion to create the turn. Good! Then extend the leg to the front, pull it quickly back in – yes! – and then finish in second. Like this, see?'

I show them. Jonny claps me and then they both try it.

'You've got it!' I say, though their moves are clumsy. God, they are sweet.

'Can we try jumping?'

'Here, I'll show you a diamond jump,' I say and I spring up, make a diamond in the air. My ribs scream at me to stop and I land awkwardly on my foot but what does it matter any more? What does anything matter?

'I can do that!' Marie says and they both start leaping up around me and laughing like we're all at a party with a bouncy castle.

They remind me of us at their age, Margo and I. Full of life. I remember how Miss Patricia used to pace as we did exercise repetitions but no more. No more. I ended a life. The gravity of it hits me like a hammer to the head. I *killed* a person.

'You know what, kids?' I say, falling onto the sofa.

They stop spinning and they fall onto me and their bodies are warm and nice. 'What?' Marie says, nestles into my arms.

'Let's sit down a while so I can order the pizzas.'

I fish my phone from my pocket and order online; two huge cheesy pizzas, garlic bread, dips and coke.

'We're not allowed coke at home,' Marie whispers.

'But we're not at home,' I say with a wink. 'Are we?'

The kids watch the television and the pizza comes and we drop grease onto the cushions and BBQ sauce over our laps and I laugh and wave away the concern on their faces. They choose a different film – something Disney – and I pick up a trashy gossip magazine from the floor. It's dark now and Margo will be worried about where they are and I'm pleased because I've put Margo's job, her security, on the line. That's what I need.

'Cora?'

I jump, look to the door in surprise and the magazine drops to the floor.

'Margo!' I say. 'How did you get in?'

The twins look at me, look confused.

'My sister is here!' I groan. 'Perfect timing.'

'Why did you take them?' Margo says and she pulls roughly at the Jonny's arm.

'Ouch!' he cries. 'Margo, you're hurting me!'

'Your hair!' Margo breathes and then she looks at Marie. 'And yours!'

'They look funky, right, kids?' I say.

Margo's hands are shaking, all of her is shaking. I've never seen her so vibrant. About fucking time.

'I can't believe you took them!' She kneels to the children, strokes the chopped fringe out of Marie's eyes. 'Has she hurt you?'

'I wouldn't hurt the children,' I snap.

'Can we go home?' Marie whispers.

Margo stands, eyes blazing at me. 'You're angry with me. I know why and I'm sorry. I'm sorry about Raff. But you broke into their *house*?'

'Desperate times called for desperate measures,' I say. 'But you'd know all about that, wouldn't you?'

'I saw the calendar,' she says. '*My* calendar. The family one! What are you doing?'

'What have *you* been doing?' I answer. 'You've been hiding things. Hiding *Raff*. He makes you feel special? Is that it? And because you always loved him you think you're entitled to him now, after all these years?'

'I was never allowed to love him.'

'Well, guess what?' I say. 'You're *still* not allowed to love him. I know what you've done with him. How *dare* you keep this from me. You've caused so many problems, you know that?'

'Margo?' Jonny says. 'What's happening?'

Margo puts her arm around his shoulder, and he starts to cry but I don't give a shit. They're not cute any more, they're an inconvenience.

'Can we go home now?' Marie asks again.

Margo looks down to them. 'I'm sorry, I'm sorry,' she says. 'Let's go, OK? Your mum will get so worried. You shouldn't be here.'

'They can go home, Margo, *if* you agree to leave London with me. We need to get out of here and go to Paris'

'Paris?' she says. 'What do you mean?'

'We have to leave because you have been fucking things up.'

The children look shocked at my language and Margo starts scratching at the back of her hand.

'Can we go?' Jonny tugs at Margo's arm.

I watch as her chest heaves up and down, her fingers flutter to her neck. 'But – but the children. I have to look after them. I can't go to Paris.'

'I want Mummy!' Marie is crying now, properly wailing.

I spin round to her. 'Shut up!' I shout at her and she's stunned into silence. 'Margo, we will be going to Paris and you have no one to blame for it but yourself. This is all on you, hear me?'

'I can't – no. I can't listen to this,' she says.

'You will listen to me,' I yell at her.

'Where are your bags?' Margo says to the children.

'Margo?' I say. 'You get what I'm saying? Leaving these kids will be all your fault.'

'Your bags, Jonny?' she says, ignoring me.

'Are you fucking ignoring me?' I say.

'In the – in the kitchen,' Jonny stammers.

'You understand?' I shout.

She doesn't respond. This is the first time she's never listened to me, the first time she's not backed down when I've been insistent, and I'm so shocked that I'm rooted to the spot, stunned into silence by her anger. I hear them in the kitchen, I hear her exclaim at the hair on the floor and then I hear them opening the front door.

'Ah, you're here,' I hear Nav say from the doorstep. 'Wait, whose are those kids?'

It's only when the front door crashes with the wind and the phone rings that I look down and I see there's one in my hand but it's not mine. I've picked up Margo's by mistake but how have I done that? I answer it anyway.

'Where the hell are my children!' a woman is screaming. It's Emmeline, the mother.

'Fuck you,' I say and I hang up.

THIRTY-ONE

MARGO

It's early Tuesday morning, only just breaking dawn and too early for the children to be up even though they have school, but the three of us – Emmeline, David and me – are wide awake. We sit at the kitchen table, both of them on one side and me on the other. There's birdsong outside. I placed a cafetiere of coffee on the table between us with three delicate white china cups like some sort of peace offering, an attempt to be normal and to act their subservient helper again but no one has touched them and the tension is knotted and heavy above my head.

'Let's talk about yesterday,' Emmeline says.

'I'm sorry.'

'From what I understand from very garbled accounts,' she says, talking over me. 'You took the kids, you gave them pizza and ice cream and cut their hair and then you started shouting in front of them and scaring the life out of them. It's completely unacceptable.'

'Yes, I know—'

She raises her hand for my silence. She's furious. 'I've never been so worried in my life about where you'd taken them,' she says. 'I called you so many times and when you did eventually pick up, you swore at me and hung up.'

'I know,' I begin. 'Except, it wasn't me. I left my—'

'It wasn't you?' David cuts over me. 'What do you mean?'

'I promise it won't happen again,' I say. 'I won't let her take them.'

Emmeline narrows her eyes. 'Her? Who?'

I shut my mouth, search my head for the best possible answer. Either I let Emmeline believe that Cora abducted the children or I let her think it was me and that I was irresponsible. Either option is bad.

'Emmeline and I have talked at length about all this,' David says. 'And have come to no other conclusion than to terminate your contract.'

I stare at them.

'We've decided,' Emmeline continues, 'because quite simply, we don't trust you any more, Margo. Over the last few weeks you've been acting very strangely. And that language on the phone to me was . . . inexcusable. Do you swear like that in front of the children?'

'No,' I say. 'I can try and explain all this.'

But can I? I bite at my bottom lip.

'I blame myself,' Emmeline says to David. 'I've been distracted by my sister. I haven't paid attention to what's been going on.'

'We've contacted your agency,' David says, looking at me, 'and explained that your contract will be terminated because of health reasons. You deserve a good reference for the years you've had with us but you need a break or to see someone. A doctor.'

'But I am seeing a doctor!' I say. 'A therapist—'

There's a heavy pause above our heads.

'So there *is* something wrong?' Emmeline asks. 'And you didn't tell us about it?'

'No, I mean there's nothing wrong with me,' I say hurriedly. 'Not where the children are concerned. I'm safe, they're safe with me! Please, you'd never think I'd hurt them?'

'We're giving you twenty-fours hours' notice.' David's voice is cold. 'I think we've heard enough.'

I feel myself tip, like I'm floating above myself. My security is being ripped from underneath me and I can only look on, like I'm watching a film where a character hurtles towards disaster and I can't do a thing about it.

'But you need me, Emmeline?' I say. 'Your work, the school runs?'

She shakes her head sadly. 'I'm sorry, Margo. About your contract. About all of it.'

'But this house,' I plead. 'And the children . . . You're all I want. The only things in this world that make sense to me! Please, I'm begging you. I can't live without those children. It's like – it's like they're mine—'

'But they're not yours, Margo,' David reminds me like I need reminding that I have nothing.

I close my eyes and tilt my face to the ceiling. The downlights are bright through my lids, warm, and for a microsecond I could be somewhere else and believe that this could all be a bad dream. I've lost them. I won't get to hold Marie and Jonny, smell their hair, watch them grow up. My twins.

'Please read this,' Emmeline says.

I feel rather than see something being waved at my face before coming back to myself. Emmeline places a folded piece of paper on the table, right in the middle of us.

She nods at me. 'Go ahead.'

I snatch up the letter, run my eyes over the words.

Dear Mr and Mrs Andrews, I am hoping that you can help me. I have recently come across information that my sister, Margo, lives with you in Kensington. Perhaps you find it odd that I'm contacting you directly and not Margo herself but I wish to make contact with her in the right way because our relationship is extremely sensitive. Please could you pass on my contact information and tell her that she has family wanting to get in touch? She should have this contact information already but here it is again, AnnieGMalone@gmail. com phone – 07859599610

My sincerest regards,
Annie Malone

I feel my pulse throb in my ears and my vision skews as I clutch at the table to steady myself even though I'm sitting down.

'When did you get this?' I breathe.

'Yesterday,' she says. 'And then everything happened with the children and—'

A moan escapes me. 'But this isn't possible! Annie is *dead*. Can you call the police? I think I need to speak to someone.'

'The police?' David says. 'Are you in some sort of trouble?'

'There's a stalker because this *isn't* Annie, OK?'

They look confused, mirror my own expression.

'Can you call the police?' I ask again.

'Do you know something about our kitchen getting torn up?' says David. 'Because if you think you know who might have done that, you need to tell us right this moment.'

Cora, Cora, Cora. Bad Penny.

'You're going to have to leave here right now.' David stands up. 'We'll take you to your house.'

I shake my head, their words tumbling through my ears but making no sense in my head. 'My – my house? What do you mean? I live here.'

'Your house in West London,' he says.

'I don't have a house in West London!'

'Where do you go then?' Emmeline asks. 'When you're not staying with us?'

'But I always stay with you,' I say. 'What do you mean? Has she been speaking to you?'

'Who?' David frowns.

'Cora!' I say. 'She's got my phone! What's she been saying to you? She's making out like I'm mad! Has she been here? In the house? Has she pretended to be me before?'

David looks over my head at Emmeline. 'Maybe we should take her to the doctor?'

'Or her grandma?' Emmeline says.

They're talking about me like I'm a child and I feel like one because I don't understand. I stand up, too quickly because I immediately feel faint, and I grip the edge of the table.

'Maybe we should call the police, Emmy?' David says. 'Do you think—'

'It's OK,' I say. 'It's OK. I'll go and pack a bag and I'll – I'll make arrangements with the agency for the rest of my things. Can I – can I say goodbye to them? Marie and Jonny?'

'They're asleep—'

'I'll kiss them,' I say. 'Can I kiss them?'

They don't know what to say and I use their hesitation to get to the door and run up the stairs. They follow me, hover by the door frames as I go inside and kneel by each of the children.

'I'm sorry,' I whisper into each of their ears. 'I'm sorry I wasn't better. I tried to be the best nanny. I tried to give you everything.'

I go to my room, pick up my phone except it's not mine in my hand but Cora's because I took hers by mistake. How did I do that? I throw it down on the bed and pull an empty suitcase from the top of my wardrobe. What do I do now? The phone bleeps from the arm of the chair – did I move it from the bed? – and I look at the screen.

Meet you at the EuroStar tonight. 7 p.m. We'll go to Paris. Start again. C

Cora has texted me from my own phone. I'm not even angry with her any more. Was I ever? I'll do exactly what she wants because what else have I got here now? I've lost the twins, I've lost Raff, I haven't got answers. I'll uproot myself from my safe haven and go to Paris, but I can't go yet because there is someone else I need to see first.

'Dove!'

'Granny,' I say, and although she was always going to be here, because where else would she be, I could weep with relief. I curl my whole body into her, grip the softness of her warm body. I don't know how I've arrived here in one piece; I'm beyond fatigued.

Granny lets me inside and it's all I can do not to fall onto her sofa, put her tatty beige knitted shawl around my shoulders and sleep for a thousand years.

'How long are you staying for?' she asks. 'For tea, yes? Would you like a jazz apple? Some biscuits from the tin?'

'Yes,' I reply. 'I mean, no, don't worry about the biscuits. Or anything really. It's fine, Granny. Have you heard from Cora?'

Her face folds into concern. 'Cora?'

'Has she been in touch?'

She puts her hand over mine and it's warm, so warm and soft like crepe paper. 'No? What's happened?' she asks. 'You're shaking.'

'I don't feel in control,' I say.

'Are you unwell?'

She leads me straight to the bedroom and she sits me down on the eiderdown. I sink into it.

'Lie down,' Granny says. 'Perhaps you need a little sleep?'

Her pillow smells intensely of lavender and of linen washed too many times. I'm terrified, devastated, confused. I look at the walls. There are framed photographs of Grandpa, of the two of them at their wedding, of our mother as a little girl and of the three of us, Cora and Annie and I at Christmas at Granny's old house. Cora is twirling her girlhood rainbow umbrella over Annie's head. I'm to the side of them and holding a book. I look like I could be in a separate photo – always the other.

With my head on the pillow I look at her. 'Granny?' I whisper.

'Yes, Margo?'

'Where's Mum? She was so angry with me. Why was she angry?'

'Let's not talk about that now,' she says.

'Where do I live?'

'London,' she says. 'Are you all right, darling?'

'What about Cora?'

'Your sister is on her way over,' she says, looks worried.

How did Cora know that I came here? What will I say to her when I see her? I'm too exhausted to feel angry with her. I don't know if I'm even capable of being angry with her. Jealous of her, yes.

'I love you, Granny.'

'I love you, too,' she says and strokes my hair.

And I believe her because I can hear love in her voice. I wish it was my mother's. But that love has long gone and I don't know why. She and my father don't love me any more.

'Your phone is ringing, love,' Granny says.

I startle out of myself. Have I been asleep? It's dark outside, or must be because the curtains are drawn.

'Granny?' My tongue feels thick.

She's not on the bed any more; she's coming through from the door with my handbag in her hand.

'Your phone, Margo,' she says.

I look down at my handbag she's holding, see my phone inside flashing. It fades before I can think of an excuse to give Granny as to why I'm not going to answer it but then it stops flashing with a call and pings with messages instead.

From Nav: *Where are you?*

I've got Cora's phone. I'd forgotten again. Will she tell that him we're leaving? What will I tell Granny?

'Shall I leave it by the bed?' Granny asks.

'Thank you,' I manage. 'Did I sleep?'

'On and off,' she says. 'It's eight in the evening.'

I was supposed to meet Cora an hour ago at the Eurostar.

'I'm so sorry,' I say and I don't know if I'm saying it to Granny or to Cora who will be livid, pacing the long platform.

'Please,' Granny says waving it away. 'You have always apologised for yourself when there's never been the need. You are enough, Margo. You, yourself. No one else. Don't apologise for being *you*.'

I smile at her and I think how much I'm going to miss her. The one person in my life that has been consistently kind.

'Besides, I have Sybil falling asleep here nearly every afternoon. It's no trouble. I like the company! Would you like tea, dove?'

'I should – I should go . . .'

I stare at Cora's phone, move my fingers in an automatic sequence and I unlock it. I'm both surprised and unsurprised that she hasn't bothered to change her password for a decade. I fumble with it, go to answer Nav's texts but delete them by mistake. I should call Cora, placate her because she'll be fuming. But we can leave tomorrow. I'm so tired.

'Come into the lounge, dove,' Granny says. 'Your sister is here now.'

I blink. 'Now? She's here?'

'Come through,' Granny says.

I get up from the bed. 'Cora—' I say as I walk through. 'I'm sorry—'

But the person sitting on the sofa isn't Cora.

I want to speak but can't, want to move, but can't. I feel like I'm beginning to tilt, like I'm entering a dream, and I shake myself away from it. Now more than ever, I need to be awake. This young woman looks like Annie should look at twenty-five; chocolate curls and violet eyes but Annie was always smiling, and this woman is not.

'Annie has written to me for a little while now,' Granny says. 'Haven't you, dove?'

I stare at this woman next to my granny.

'How is this possible?' I whisper.

'I would have come sooner,' the woman says, 'but I couldn't get out of Switzerland. Not very easily, as you can imagine Everything has been difficult.'

I stare at her.

'You blocked me, Margo,' she says. 'All my calls.'

'I – I didn't . . .' But I trail off because I feel numb and my tongue is sticking.

'Annie has had a very tough road back to yourself, haven't you, dove?' Granny says and the woman nods again. 'I'll go into the kitchen and make some tea.'

Granny leaves me with the ghost of my sister before I have a moment to scream aloud. I'm trapped; forced to accept this woman in front of me. I need to look at her again and make sure she's who she says she is, that Granny hasn't been fooled into letting in a stranger. *I* feel like a stranger.

'Sit with me.'

'You're not Annie,' I say.

'Yes I am.'

'But – but you're dead.'

Her eyes glisten and then she starts crying, shakes her head over and over. 'No, Margo! I'm here. Though it feels like some days I *am* dead.'

I take a step forward. 'Is it – really you?'

'It's me,' she says. 'It's taken me years to find you.'

'But – but then who died?'

She looks at me strangely and then I know.

It's why I can't see Mum's face at the funeral. It's why I can't go back to Switzerland – because she's not there – and why our father blames me for her absence. Why did Cora lie about this? I can feel myself start to rock back and forwards. What's happening to my brain?

THIRTY-TWO

CORA

'Why the hell aren't you at the fucking station!' I scream into the phone. I've pressed it so hard against my ear that I'm hurting myself.

She's not answering me.

'Why do you always fuck things up!' I hiss. 'Stupid, stupid bitch!'

I can't get through. It's all going to hit the fan.

THIRTY-THREE

MARGO

There's a crash. I've bumped into something but I'm not sure what.

'Margo,' Annie says. 'Are you OK?'

She's touching me. Her fingers are warm, grounding. I stare at her, can't seem to breathe. Her eyes are wide with concern.

'Please listen to what I have to say,' she says. 'I know it's a shock that I'm here.'

'Oh, Mum,' I breathe. 'What happened?'

'Calm down,' she says. 'Here, sit down.'

I find myself sitting and Annie – this woman that claims to be Annie – sits beside me.

'I've been trying to get in contact with you for so long,' she says. 'You never told me how to get out of there – out of Grindelwald. You just *left* and I never thought I'd see you again.'

She's crying hard now, fat tears down her cheeks and dripping on the carpet like raindrops. I feel like I'm drowning in her tears and my own confusion. I'm travelling down a tunnel and I can see myself with Annie but I'm blank and not present.

'Tell me about Mum,' I say.

'Mum knows I'm here,' she says.

'What? But she's – Mum's gone,' I say. 'She's dead!'

She stares at me. 'No, Mum's in Zurich. She and Dad split up, remember? It was just all too hard, that's what she said.'

'She's OK? She's alive?'

'Of course she is, Margo!'

I'm at once overwhelmed with relief that our mother is alive, and also crushed with hurt. 'Why don't I speak to her?'

'Because Mum blames you for what happened to me . . .'

'Your accident?'

Annie nods. 'She should never have believed anything Patricia ever told her.'

'Patricia?'

'Mum was just too wrapped up in grief, Margo, OK? And Dad . . . he was so angry because she left him. It was all such a mess.'

Her words are claggy, like mud.

'I don't understand. I don't remember any of this.'

'And then you left,' she says. 'You came here and severed all contact with me. You left me, and Mum left and I was alone with Dad. With all his *rage*.'

'But . . . but I must have asked you to come with us.'

She laughs and it sounds bitter. 'It's taken me five years to recover any strength in my legs to even begin to attempt to walk. This is the first time I've managed to fly somewhere – I

303

have sticks now to help me walk. It's been so *hard,* Margo. My education was delayed. I couldn't go back into school so I had to finish my exams from home with a tutor when I was twenty-three because I couldn't pick up a pen properly until recently. Like I could have gone anywhere with you!'

I'm silenced by the anger, stamped into her every sentence.

'I was like a prisoner in that house. I wasn't allowed guests in case I could access the internet somehow and try and find you. I did try once but you never replied – it bounced back. A year ago, Dad went away for the weekend and I broke into his study, and I found an address for Granny. I wrote to her and she told me you'd started coming to visit her on her birthdays. About six months ago, I started to send her things for you – anything that might get you speaking to me.'

I swallow.

'But you didn't respond to those either,' she says.

'But I didn't get anything from you,' I explain. 'Not until recently.'

Unless Cora took them. Did she take them so I wouldn't talk to Annie? Why would she do that?

'I got a photo of Cora in the dress,' I say. 'Was it you that sent it?'

'Yes,' she says. 'It was the one Raff took. You took his camera that night. Or I thought you did. You must have done because it wasn't me, obviously. But I found the roll of film you must have taken out of it and you'd put in the loft in Switzerland. Dad was clearing out some things earlier in the year and I saw it. I sent it away to be developed and when they came back I felt so sad.'

'Did you see . . .' I pause. 'There were some of me.'

'In Cora's dress.'

'Oh, Annie,' I whisper. 'I did a bad thing. You know.'

She reaches for my hands, strokes them. In her eyes are a thousand words. She had tried to find me and I had turned my back on her.

'I thought it was Mum who wrote on the back of it,' I say.

Annie shakes her head sadly. 'I tried to find Raff too but I couldn't. I just wanted to make contact with someone from the world that was taken away from me. Who would understand what I was going through.'

'I'm so sorry,' I say.

'Finally Granny remembered the names of the people you nanny for. I got hold of your agency and they passed my email on. Did you change your name?'

I'm confused. 'Margo Malone. Isn't that my name?'

'Yes,' she says. 'But the agency said you used Devaux so it took me a long time to finally convince them it was you.'

'No, that's Cora,' I say. 'Her stage name.'

She looks at me, frowns. 'All the entries for the book you sign into when you see Granny are signed Devaux.'

She looks at me for an explanation but I don't have one.

'Your phone is on the floor,' she says to me and she picks it up, gives it to me.

I look at it dumbly. When did I drop it? When did I ever even have it out?

Granny comes back into the room. 'Annie is going to stay here a while with me,' she says.

She goes to hand me a cup of tea but I don't take it from her. Instead I tilt my head; try to tip out the confusion that's filling my brain.

'But why didn't you look for Cora?' I say.

They both look at me strangely.

'What?'

'Why did you only look for me?'

'Oh, Margo,' Granny says.

I sit very still. 'Who died? The service sheet that we found when we came for your birthday . . .'

'That service sheet was from Cora's funeral. Cora's, my love.'

The air in the room is heavy. Has time stood still? Their faces are bleary in front of me.

'Cora's funeral,' Granny says again, gently.

I want to laugh at this absurdity, this completely ridiculous thing that they're saying. Maybe I do because Annie takes my hands.

'Margo,' she says. 'Listen. Cora is dead. You understand that, don't you?'

My brain feels electrocuted, scrambled.

'You're not real.' I look at Granny. 'Annie isn't real, is she? There's no one here. It *was* Annie who died. Am I dreaming?'

'Margo, do you need another lie down?' Granny says.

I'm asleep, I must be. Is it the lack of pills? Withdrawal causes delusions, hallucinations, it must be that. I pinch myself on the arm so hard that I yelp in pain because I've pierced my skin with my nails.

'Cora died,' Annie says. 'Don't you remember, at the theatre? Mum and Dad moved her – all of us – to Switzerland and she was on life support—'

'No, Annie!' I cry. 'That was *you*! Cora's fine, Cora's OK!'

'Cora never came out of her coma,' Granny says and Annie is nodding alongside her, like a pair of nodding dogs and I want to scream. What are they saying? They're actors in a play, taking the roles in a nightmare I'm having. Why can't I wake up?

'But I see her! I see her and – Granny! You saw her too! At your birthday! Every birthday she comes with me!'

Annie and Granny look at one another and suddenly I feel not quite awake and the two of them are fading into black like a film when it changes scene. I can hear my feet on gravel, I have my car keys in my hand and the jagged metal is cold and digging into my flesh. I can hear that I've unlocked the car and I'm inside it and I'm reversing the car back out of Willows and into the main road. A horn blares as a car is forced to swerve around me. I realise I haven't put my lights on. I switch them, full beam and then I put my foot to the floor and drive like I'm a woman possessed all the way to London, all the way to Russell Square where I leave the car parked haphazardly in front of the blue door.

Does he live above his practice? When I asked him he never replied because in a profession such as his why would he risk people coming to his house in the middle of the evening like I'm doing? I hammer with my fists.

'Mr Hawkins? Mr Hawkins! What's happening? Mr Hawkins!'

THIRTY-FOUR

CORA

'Hi, Mr H,' I say.

He's opened the door hesitantly and blinks at me like a mole out of a tunnel because the hallway behind him is dark inside. He switches on a light when he sees me properly. He's got a short beard peppered with grey, wears black-rimmed glasses and he's handsome in a geek chic sort of way.

'So you *do* live above the shop,' I say and smile at him.

'Has something happened?' he says.

'I'm in very dire straits,' I say. 'Can I come in?'

He looks reluctant, ever the professional, because I've crossed a boundary. It's nine-thirty in the evening and he's off duty now. I shouldn't be here; he shouldn't have let me in.

'Did my sister tell you that you're kinda cute?' I say.

'I—'

'Well, you are.' I push past him and step inside.

Mr Hawkins closes the door behind us. 'Are you – are you . . .'

I laugh. 'I'm Cora!'

He nods slowly. 'Yes,' he says. 'I see now.'

I walk straight through to his room, snap on the lights and I look around at the charcoal couch, the bright white skirting boards, the green unobtrusive plants in corners and the books on shelves. There's the beautiful ruby jewel-coloured Persian rug.

'Are you all right?' he says.

'I remember you asking Margo if I could come,' I say. 'And I'm guessing you don't do late-night appointments but here I am.'

He sits in his chair, stares at me intently. He's trying to work all this out. 'I'm under the impression that you've come here under somewhat strange circumstances?'

I grin, spread my arms across the back of the sofa and cross my legs. I'm wearing jeans and plimsols, a tatty grey cardigan. 'She could have made an effort,' I say, looking at the shoes Margo put on today. 'Sorry.'

'I'm glad you've come,' he says.

'Are you?'

'I've wanted to meet you.'

I smile. 'That's a lovely vase,' I say. I touch the glass which is cold beneath my fingertips.

'Thank you,' he replies. 'Tell me, Cora, why you've come to see me tonight?'

'She feels very strange, Mr H,' I say. 'Margo does.'

'Does she?'

'I was doing really well for myself and for her,' I say. 'I had protected her a long time and now it's all going to shit. She needs you to explain a few things, OK? I need you to.'

He leans forward. The clock on the wall ticks, echoes around the silent room. 'Can you tell me who you are, Cora? *What* you are?'

'Did you suspect?' I say.

I see him lick his lips. 'I suspected some sort of condition but – no, I don't think I suspected this.'

'I lie dormant in her head but sometimes I'm listening. It's like a theatre, see? Dancers and actors in the wings, not always centre stage but there nonetheless. I'm a dancer, Mr H, you know?'

'Tell me what you know about yourself, Cora.'

I look at him and smile. 'That I'm my own person, Mr Hawkins,' I say. 'But not always in control of the body. I'm the "other".'

THIRTY-FIVE

MARGO

When I come round, I'm on the grey sofa.

'Have I been asleep?'

Mr Hawkins frowns.

'Thank you for letting me in,' I say. 'I'm sorry it's late.'
I look at the clock above his head, see that it's nearly ten in
the evening. I get up hurriedly. 'I'm so sorry! You should
have woken me, I've taken liberty of your kindness—'

'No,' he says quickly. 'Margo, no. Please stay.'

'Did we talk? Before I fell asleep?'

'Yes . . .' he says. 'I mean . . . in a sense. Please sit
down.'

'I'm sorry I'm here so late,' I say.

'Please,' he gestures back to the sofa and I sit.

'I've had – I've had a bad dream or news . . .' I say.
'I don't know which it is. I feel unbalanced. I've lost the
children. I've lost . . . I've lost *her*, Mr Hawkins.'

'Who have you lost?'

'They told me that she's dead. My sister.'

'Yes,' he says and waits for me.

'But not *Annie*,' I say. 'Annie's not dead. She told me – Granny told me that Cora . . .'

'That Cora is dead.'

He speaks it like it's not a question but a statement, and that further panics me. Why is he so sure of this when I am not?

'But that's not possible, is it?' I say. 'Why are they lying to me in such a horrible way?'

'Perhaps we should call a family member to be here with you?' he suggests.

'Why is the world upside down? What's wrong with me?'

'Margo. I need you to listen very carefully to me,' he says. 'I believe that you live with a mental health condition called Dissociative Identity Disorder. Do you know what that means?'

'No,' I say.

'It's the name for what used to be called multiple per-sonality disorder. You might be more familiar with that term.'

He waits like he's expecting me to say something but my mouth won't work and he's glowing in front of me. My eyes aren't working.

'Am I dreaming again?'

'No,' he says.

'Sometimes I can't tell.'

'You told me the very first time you came in that your sister was dead,' he says. 'That you were confused about the night that she died. You told me it was Annie who died in an accident.'

312

Shadows begin to creep from the peripherals of my vision. 'But she – I *saw* Annie! And she told me, she and Granny told me that Cora died! But Cora isn't dead because how could that be?'

'The Cora that you have been seeing and talking to isn't here,' he says gently. 'At least, not how you think she might be. She is an "alter" as they're commonly known, or an "other".'

He's still shimmering in front of me, unreal. Any minute now I'll wake up, won't I? And I'll be in my bed in Kensington. The twins will run into my room and life will be safe.

'Margo?' says a voice. 'Can you hear me? Cora is part of *you*.'

I blink. 'A part of – me? What do you mean? Like a – a ghost?'

'No,' Mr Hawkins says. 'Not exactly. Think of it like she's another part of you that takes over the consciousness or "head space".'

'I've read about this in books,' I say. 'But it's not possible. That's not a real thing. Cora is *alive*.'

'It's very much a real thing,' Mr Hawkins affirms. 'From what I know of it, it can be a very confusing condition for a person to live with. It can cause extreme exhaustion, a loss of sense of reality, acute loneliness.'

'I have . . . I have all of those things,' I say. 'But it's anxiety.'

'You *are* probably anxious,' he says. 'Because it's stressful on the mind. Do you lose time?'

'Yes. I have blackouts. But I thought . . . I thought it was the panic attacks . . . Do you think it's true? Is Cora really dead? Does this make me insane?'

'No, it makes you a survivor. You've likely suffered extreme trauma and have protected yourself by creating "Cora". DID is most often caused by trauma during childhood and it's a very new field of exploration, and I'm no expert, but I can try to explain the basics of it. Children see the world very black and white. When they're little it's not unusual to hear them say things like "that was bad me" or "that me was sad". There's a new theory that states that children do not have one fully formed personality until around the age of seven, and before that, they have connected "states". For example, they have a desire for attention, affection, food. All these "states" are in flux until their personalities are solid. The integration is usually an automatic process, unless it's disrupted by trauma.'

Choose me.

'If a child is consistently traumatised, and has no stable attachments before this pivotal age, DID can be a result.'

'But I'm not a child. I'm an adult.'

'Your disorder may always have been there,' he explains. 'When you were younger you might have experienced mild disassociation from yourself, perhaps triggered by feelings of sustained alienation from the world and loved ones.'

I think of the fantasies I had as a child, how strong I'd felt as George from the Famous Five, how fierce and omnipotent as Aslan from Narnia. A memory surges into my eyes. There *was* a girl called Penny that I read about in a book. No, wait. Someone *told* me about a girl called Penny. She was a bad girl.

I inhale sharply. Cora left me that message the night she ripped David and Emmeline's kitchen apart – Bad Penny. But it had been *me*. A terrible animal moan reverberates around the room and I shrink inside myself.

'What was that?' I say but as I look at him I realise that it came from within me. 'I can't do this,' I say and I black out.

THIRTY-SIX

CORA

'She can't do it because it's too painful,' I say. I lean back against the plush cushions, flick my hair behind my shoulder. 'You got a stiff one, Mr H?'

Mr Hawkins looks shocked.

'A drink?' I say with a grin.

'Cora?'

'That's right,' I say. 'You got something hard?'

He hesitates a moment so I stand, go to the cabinet behind him and open the door. Inside there is a neat little row of bottled water on one of the shelves and, below it, a decanter.

'I love sherry. You want one too?' I say, pulling out the decanter and a glass.

He watches me but doesn't intervene as I pour. 'I'm fine,' he says. 'I wouldn't recommend a strong one.'

'Fine, just a little one then,' I say, pouring three fingers. 'For her shock.'

Mr Hawkins is sitting up and very straight, like some of sort of animal on sentry. I imagine he's worried that I'm going to disappear any moment, and maybe I will because I do so enjoy a cliffhanger.

'How long have you been with Margo?' he asks. 'As her alter?'

'A very long time,' I say and sit back down. 'Since we were children. But I never had the reason to come centre stage until the real Cora's accident when she was eighteen.'

'Centre stage?'

I sip at the sherry without taking my eyes from him. 'I never came forward. I stayed in Margo's head and watched. Stored things. I didn't have a name for a long time but sometimes they called me Bad Penny.'

'Margo said she was often the bad side of the coin. Is that what you mean too?'

'Yes, the bad side of the penny. Margo has a lot of anger,' I say. 'Anger and fear and hurt. I'm in charge of all those emotions.'

'You were created by Margo to protect her? To help her with them?'

'Correct,' I say. 'I kept the bad memories for years, the hurt, the rage, and I keep them still so she doesn't have to see them.'

'When did you become "Cora"?' he asks.

'When the real Cora died I needed to step up to protect Margo in a different way. I needed to *become* Cora. I needed Margo to believe *Cora* was safe.'

'Why?'

'Because Cora had always been Margo's constant, you understand? Even though their relationship had been strained at times, they were born from the same womb and Margo loved Cora more than anything. To rip away Cora was to rip away all the unstable rocks that Margo had built her life on. If she remembered Cora was dead and *how* she died, she might have fallen apart completely. So I came forward into the role.'

He nods. 'And you convinced Margo that it was Annie who had died.'

'That's right. I was sure Annie would never make contact. I shifted things in Margo's head to suit my narrative. I even hold memories of being in Doha and Margo cutting herself in a swimming pool, and of Annie in the snow. I wasn't there but the real Cora *was*. I've taken those memories as if they are my own because they suit Margo, make her happy. Margo loved playing in the snow with Cora that night. She loved Cora taking care of her in the swimming pool.'

'Margo is in a strange place,' he says. 'She's been exposed to a truth that she wasn't ready for. Do your extended family know of this condition? Do we need to alert someone? For your – her – safety? Her parents?'

'Hell, no. They're in Switzerland,' I say, crossing myself jokingly. 'I took her away from our parents. They're *unfit* for purpose.'

'What about your sister, Annie? Could we invite her here?'

'Oh, no, no, no. Margo needs to forget all this nonsense. I'm going to take her away.'

'Away? What do you mean?'

'I'm going to take us to Paris,' I say. 'At least, I had planned for it. It used to be easy to take over her body and keep her safe at the house, being a nanny. But Annie obviously learnt how to write again and she found Granny. And then Margo stopped taking the pills I convinced her to take to keep her going and she became stronger with the hunt for the truth. It opened doors that I didn't see.'

'She prevented you from seeing them, even unknowingly,' he says.

'I guess so! I didn't think she had it in her!'

'Will you let her gain some more understanding about this condition?' he says. 'She's extremely distressed.'

'Well, she needs to know more tonight, Mr H,' I say. 'And you can explain it to her. Because how can I? But be quick about it, I'm going to rebook for the Eurostar first thing in the morning and I need some beauty sleep.'

THIRTY-SEVEN

MARGO

I wake on the sofa again and Mr Hawkins is still there but the clock has changed and the hands say it's midnight. On the coffee table between us beside the crystal vase flowers there is a glass with rust-coloured liquid inside. I pick it up, smell it.

'Sherry?' I wrinkle my nose. 'Why have you given me this? I don't like sherry.'

'Ah,' he says. 'Margo.'

I put the glass down. 'I feel so tired, Mr Hawkins.'

'Do you remember what we talked about?' he says. 'Earlier?'

'Before I went to sleep?'

He pauses. 'You weren't asleep, Margo. You were awake but not quite yourself.'

I start scratching at my hands and he watches but doesn't chastise me as Cora would.

'Please,' I say. 'I don't understand. Tell me what's happening to me?'

'You're safe here, I promise. Do you remember what happened before you came here to my office?'

'Annie,' I say. 'She was at Granny's.'

'Do you accept that it was definitely Annie?'

'Yes,' I say. 'I saw Annie and she told me – she told me Cora was gone.'

'That's right,' he says. 'And do you remember what I said about your condition?'

'I – I can't remember.'

'Margo, this is a lot for you to take in for one session. And especially at night when you're stressed and tired, but I can help explain this to you, all right? I'm going to explain DID.'

'DID?'

'That's the condition I am certain that you have,' he says. 'Dissociative Identity Disorder. Would you like some water?'

'Yes,' I nod. 'I have a headache.'

I watch him stand, go to a cabinet across the room and open the door. Inside there is a neat little row of bottled water on one of the shelves. I feel I've seen him do this very recently.

'Is Cora – do you think she *is* dead?' I say. My tongue feels fat and stung. I cradle my head in the palms of my hands. 'Could she be somewhere else, like Annie was? She's so real.'

'To you, she *is* real,' he says. 'This alter that you have called "Cora" has become so real to you that you have come to believe she really is your sister.'

I drink the water and I can taste all the components of it, metals and minerals, fluoride. Water has never tasted like this before.

321

'Your real sister Cora had always been your strength,' he says. 'Or, at least, a dominant part of your childhood. Is that right?'

'Yes.'

'On days where you can't handle life, your alter Cora might take over control of your body. It's called "fronting", I believe, where she is in charge of your consciousness, or the "headspace" if you like.'

'Like in a theatre? Actors on stage.'

'Exactly like that. Cora, your alter, becomes your mouthpiece, but she also serves her own needs. I've met her and she's vivacious, needs only to flick on a smile to get the results she wants. Am I right?'

I stare at him. 'You've met her?'

'I have.'

'When?'

'Whilst you were "asleep".'

I look around the room. 'Where is she?'

'Margo,' he says. 'She is *you*. The condition means that you switch *into* her.'

My brain feels like it's fizzing. I think of Cora, how she's always told me that she has her hair cut and coloured regularly, has eyelash extensions, spends money on good dance clothes because that's her life. And I look *exactly* like her. There have been times where I've come out of hair salons and gyms and I've felt good for it but I could barely remember the classes, couldn't remember talking to the hairdressers, never remembered paying for any of the clothes I bought. I thought I was doing those things to keep up appearances for my job but was I really doing it for her because that's what her life demands? Does she spend all my money? How does she live? I think of Nav, a man I've only just met but no – I've lived with him for *years*.

'All her things,' I say. 'I text her, I leave voicemails on her phone.'

'It's quite possible that you have her belongings and keep them separate from your own.'

I *do* have her phone. Have I always had it? If what Mr Hawkins is saying is true then I have carried all her belongings with me since she died – her phone and laptop, her awards and her love letters from Raff in my suitcase, and her childhood bike because she had never learnt how to drive. I took all those things from Switzerland.

Somehow I've buried Annie from my memory of my parents' house. How could I have done that if we were living together and when she obviously needed me so badly? She suffered a traumatic injury and I merely blanked her from my mind. I am a terrible person, a horrible sister.

I shift and hear a crackle in my trousers. I put my hand into my pocket, dig out a scrunched piece of paper with Raff's number. Cora had it: she must have taken it when she messed David and Emmeline's house up.

Mr Hawkins tilts back into my vision.

'Are you all right, Margo?'

'No,' I whisper. 'I'm not OK.'

I look down at my hands, at my knuckles that are red from clawing at the skin.

I feel afraid of myself. How can Cora be me? She's confident and brave and strong and nothing like me at all. Surely there must be another explanation for this?

'Cora told me we should leave Switzerland,' I say. 'And we did. We came here and she helped me find work as a nanny. I live in Kensington and she lives in a flat with a man called Nav . . . But how can I be in two places at once?'

Emmeline's words flit across my mind.

Where do you go then? When you're not staying with us?

'Am I not living with Emmeline and David the entire time?'

'Possibly,' Mr Hawkins says. 'It would explain how Cora could live her life.'

'She's a dancer.'

'And *you* danced when you were a child,' he says. 'So you have been able to take her to many auditions and been successful for her.'

'How could that be when the children and the family would change their schedules?' I ask. 'When they took holidays? How could she know—'

I stop. The calendar. Cora has always known where I'm supposed to be.

'You have the same brain,' he answers. 'She would deliver you in a particular place if she needed to. It was in her interest to keep you functional and safe as long as you could take her where she wanted to be.'

'Safe from what?'

'We talked, earlier, about trauma in childhood.'

The skin on the back of my neck shivers and I reach for it, touch the scar that I've had for so many years. It's why I always wear my hair down.

'I'm scared,' I say. 'I'm so scared and I don't know why, and that's even more terrifying.'

'It's OK to be scared,' he says. 'I'm going to help you. I can organise for a specialist therapist to talk to you too.'

My lip trembles. 'I don't want Cora to leave me.'

'She won't leave you because she *is* you.'

'But how can I live like this?'

'With your permission – and Cora's – I'd like to ask my colleague to come and we will continue these sessions to align you and Cora into the same consciousness again. This will take time and for you to work through some very difficult conversations but we'll get there. I'm confident that we'll get you there.'

His words are weaving a web of disorder above my head.

'How did she die?' I say. 'Did she tell you that part?'

'No, she didn't tell me,' he says.

Annie and Granny must know. It's all connected to the night of the dress and what I did with Raff.

"This is a huge shock to come to terms with,' he says. 'I have all night. I'm here for you.'

'She's dead,' I say. 'Cora is dead and I need to find out why she died, remember *how* she died. I owe it to her, don't I? This is what I've been trying to do for weeks! To find the truth!'

'Margo, please sit down—'

'I need to get out!' I scream and a there's an almighty crash.

How am I standing up when I can't remember doing so? There's glass, shards of it all over the coffee table and skimmed across the floor. There's water too, up the wall and puddling on the rug, and flowers are strewn here and there, individual stems thrown like onto the stage for a dancer. It's the vase, that beautiful vase smashed into slivers.

'Oh!' I say. 'Mr Hawkins, what happened?'

He's up too, looking alarmed and reaching his hand out to me. 'Please, stay. I think we should phone someone—'

'Margo,' someone says. 'Go back to Granny's, pack your stuff away and get a cab, hear me? Go to the Eurostar. Camp out for the night if you have to. We are *leaving*.'

It isn't my voice but it's loud in my ears so it must have been me. No. It's *Cora*.

I blink, refusing to let myself slip into blackness. I run to the road, wrench the car door open and reverse the car. I bang into a parked one behind me and its alarm goes but I pull out and I drive.

'Cora? What happened to you?' I say.

'You know,' she says. She's here in the car with me but I can't see her. 'You know, but you're not ready to see it. Let me in, Margo, and I can deal with this. We're going away to Paris! To another city, to opportunity, to freedom and a new beginning—'

'No,' I say. 'I have to know what happened to you.'

THIRTY-EIGHT

MARGO

I've come to him for answers; to Raff and not back to Willows Retirement. If Cora never saw me with Raff, it must mean that my feelings for him have always been so strong, a pull like the tide, and have surpassed her taking over our body. Perhaps she isn't strong enough to yank me backwards when it comes to him – the one thing I always wanted. I can feel myself trembling. I'm cold, freezing.

'Please open the door!' I shout.

It's late, past one in the morning, but after a moment, he's standing in front of me in the glow of the streetlight that streams through the crack in the door.

'Margo?' he says.

'Can I come in?'

He looks over my shoulder. 'Is that your car?'

I glance behind. I've left the car diagonal and haphazard in the residential street. 'Yes,' I say. 'But we need to talk, Raff. Something's very wrong!'

'What's happened?'

'Can I come in? I've got to say it quickly—'

'Wait a moment,' he says as I push past him and into the blackness of the corridor.

'It's Annie!' I cry. 'She's, oh God Raff, how do I say it?'

'Stop,' he says, following me. 'Don't go through there, let's go out—'

But I'm not really listening and I grapple at the kitchen doorway, feel for a switch.

'Wait!' Raff says as my fingers find it.

The kitchen is flooded with light and I see them, hundreds of pictures of Cora. Tiny hacked cut outs, huge blown-up photographs, black-and-whites of her dancing, photocopied official photographs of her at school in her uniform. There are close-ups of her face, of parts of her body, there are lots of her laughing, there are pictures of the gold of her hair and they're all tacked up and covering the walls, the fridge, the cupboards and littering the table like some sort of swarm.

'Leonie left me,' he says. 'Obviously.'

I gaze around the kitchen. 'What is this?'

'Cora was my muse,' he sighs. 'She still is.'

The photos close in on me and I can't breathe properly.

Raff reaches for me. 'Please,' he says. 'I'm sorry you saw this. I'm sorry for so much.'

He picks up a bottle of whisky from the side, a glass from an open shelf and carries them both with his fingers inside the glass and puts them on the table.

'I need to tell you something,' I say and wonder how on earth I'm going to tell him that Cora is dead. The sentence in my head clangs.

'You want some whisky?'

'No—'

'It's always helped me,' he says with a thin smile. 'As you know. You look like you could use one.'

I stare around the room again, at this shrine to my sister and think how much he must have loved her, no – *worshiped* her.

'Raff—'

'Here.' He hands me a glass. 'It will help.'

I look at it and then at him and I gulp it back. It strings the back of my throat before flooding my mouth with heat. There's something comforting about this warmth. We stand, quiet for a moment until there's a blaring horn outside the front door and makes me jump.

'That'll be your car in the road,' he says. 'You'll have to move it.'

I nod but my hands are still trembling. He throws on the black jacket that hangs from the back of a chair and then reaches for my hand, walks down the corridor with me and opens the door. Outside there's a rusted blue Audi behind mine and a woman leans out of the driver's window.

'What the fuck is this?' she shrieks.

'I'm sorry,' I say, stumble out of the door and take my keys out of my bag and drop them immediately. I can't seem to bend my body to retrieve them. Everything seems to be in slow motion.

'Christ's sake,' she yells. 'You pissed? Hurry up!'

Am I drunk? I only had half of the whisky that Raff made me. I blink once, twice, three times to try and focus.

'Hang on,' Raff says, closes his front door. 'Back the car up, will you?'

The woman shoves the car into reverse. I can hear her muttering through the open window.

Raff picks up the keys for me. His hair is blown forward by the wind. I wrap my cardigan around myself. 'You OK?' he asks.

I'm not OK; I'm barely conscious. Is it her taking over my mind? Is it me? I'm not sure who I am. Where is she if she's the strong one, because at the moment I have never felt weaker.

'I'm watching,' she says.

'What?' Raff says.

'What?' I echo.

'You want me to drive?' he asks.

'Yes.'

'OK, get in the passenger seat, we'll have to park down the road a bit. There's no space here.'

He opens the door for me and I get inside, sit heavily and the relief of sitting down is overwhelming.

Raff puts the car in gear and starts to drive slowly down the road, his hands momentarily off the wheel as he lights a cigarette. He breathes in the smoke, winds down the window and it escapes his mouth again in a fast thin ribbon, curls outside.

'How far down do we have to park?' I ask as we pass an empty space.

'This is a different permit zone,' he replies.

'OK,' I say. I look at him as he drives. 'Raff, Annie is alive. Cora is dead.'

He inhales sharply and slams on the brakes. I lurch forward, reach my hands out to prevent myself from hitting the dashboard.

'What?' he says.

'I didn't lie,' I say. 'Well I did, but I didn't *know* that I was lying—'

'What are you talking about?' The anger in his eyes is giving way to distress. 'You told me she was here, in London.'

'I can't explain it,' I say. 'I swear to God, Raff, I swear. Something happened to make me forget. I have – I have a condition, a disorder.'

'So she's . . . I'll never see her again? There was never a chance?'

'I made a mistake,' I whisper. 'She's gone.'

His jaw sets. 'A *mistake*? A fucking *mistake*? What the hell? What's *wrong* with you?'

He revs the engine and we fly into movement again. I grip the edge of the seats.

'I've got so much wrong, Raff! But that's why I need you. I've come here to know the truth of that night.'

'I don't want to do this,' he says. 'But I'm going to have to.'

And then I don't hear any more. I feel my head tipping back and then I feel nothing.

THIRTY-NINE

MARGO

When I wake the car has stopped and Raff is sitting beside me. My tongue feels swollen, my throat irritated, and I cough into my hand.

'Have I – have I been asleep?' I ask.

Or have I been her? A lump of fear rises in my throat but he nods.

'Yeah,' he says. 'I gave you a sleeping pill. In the drink.'

Fear prickles my skin.

'Why?' I say.

'Because I decided it's better that we come here,' he says. 'To where it all happened and so you can remember for yourself. Because there will be things that happened up there in that room that I can't tell you.'

I look out of the windscreen, see that we're parked in a dark, quiet street.

'Where are we?' I ask but he's already getting out of the car. I hurry to unclick my buckle and open the door.

'Look,' he says.

I follow his eyes to the other side of the road and am stung at the sight of this enormous white-brick building in front of me, lit up, skull-like, by blue moonshine and white street lamps. Raff has brought me to the theatre where Cora performed *Mirror, Mirror*. Its white columns and sweeping staircase lead to a lobby and I recall it now, mahogany panelling and a spotless marbled tile of cream and gold which reflected the bright lights of the elegant chandeliers above it.

'I want you to take me back, Raff. To London. I can't – I can't do this.'

'You *wanted* to remember,' he says. 'So here we are.' He walks around the car to me. 'You've turned my life upside down so here we are. This is for you.'

'Go back,' I say but the voice isn't mine.

'We're not going back,' he says.

He lights another cigarette, stares up at a tall window several floors above us and I follow his eyeline and feel horribly seasick all of a sudden. I close my eyes to steady myself because I'm swaying and then I feel his hand in mine. He leads me around from the front of the theatre towards the stage door, a small opening within a giant-sized scenery one.

'It's OK,' he says. 'Maybe this is what we both need.'

I stare at him. 'How are we going to get in? It'll be locked.'

'I have a key,' he says.

'What?'

'Leonie teaches here.'

I gasp. 'She teaches dance at Cora's old dance school?'

'Yeah.'

I understand now why Leonie was upset when I told her that Cora's theatre was outside Windsor. She must have put two and two together, realised that this building was Cora's before it was ever hers, and that Raff was bound to it for that reason and that reason alone.

'Oh, Raff,' I say.

'Yeah,' he says. 'I kept coming here when you all disappeared. Is that crazy? Pathetic? I don't know. I ached to be in the space Cora loved most, where I used to sit and watch her.'

He exhales smoke into the air and then unlocks the door.

'In the years after the accident I sat in the stalls and I wrote her poems,' he says, punching in an alarm code at the wall. 'It was a way to keep in contact with her because, fuck me, Margo, you can't imagine how hard it was for the love of your life to disappear off the face of the earth.'

I'm silent whilst he walks inside and looks to me to follow. Do I want to follow him? I step forward gingerly.

'I went to all the shows that the school put on,' he continues. 'I met Leonie two years ago and she didn't know my connection with this place, just thought I was an avid dance fanatic, and I don't know how really, but I got involved with some of the props management so I wouldn't look suspect . . . like a fucking creep.'

He waits as I join him so we're standing side by side and he clicks his phone so its torch shines into the darkness.

'Why didn't you tell me any of this?' I say.

'Because it's fucked up, isn't it?' he says. 'I watch the girls and I find myself attracted to the blonde ones who have the same fury to them as Cora had. The raw, animal passion to just be alive that she had. I sit and I watch and I wonder how it could have gone so wrong. And now, to know that she's dead?' His face twists in grief. 'More than ever you have to remember what happened, Margo. For all of us.'

My fingertips graze the bare brick walls as we wind through the bowels of the building, through snake-like corridors behind the theatre until we get to the stage.

'You want to go up there?' he asks.

Before I can make a conscious decision, I step out of the wings and onto the stage. My footsteps echo on the wooden flooring that my sister danced so effortlessly on, that the two of them made love on. I swallow a lump in my throat. The barrenness of the empty theatre is like a thing made physical, a ghost that crows its past performances. I walk down past the vast red curtains, glance at the yawning hole of the orchestra pit below where silver musician stands glint from the blackness and then I go to the row I sat in when I watched her in that final performance. I run my fingertips to the back of a velvet chair, feel its inviting coarseness, its realness.

'I sat in this seat,' I say.

'Yeah,' he says.

I watched her dance that first act, clapped her wildly as the curtain fell whilst my heart sang with worry that she would find out about what I'd done with Raff. And then, as I stood to leave the theatre for the interval, I caught the face of someone in the audience, twenty seats or so down the row from me.

'You OK?' Raff says.

I'd almost forgotten he was even here. He stands beside me now, his breath stilling in the cold air.

'Yes,' I say.

'Come on.'

My head is buzzing but I allow him to take my hand. We jump up back onto the stage and go through to the wings.

'I remember,' I say. 'This is the way backstage.'

I remember where to go, along the dark corridor, and I'm confident of my footing, of where I'm going even before Raff shines his phone so it can light my way through the theatre's skeleton up to the stairs.

'Wait,' he says.

I turn around on the stairs, can barely see him behind the phone, but can feel his closeness. The narrow staircase creaks beneath our weight. This is where Annie chased me. The further up we go, the stronger the presence of mildew and stale air in our lungs, until at last I see the door.

We step through it and it's as if we've entered a time warp. Everything is exactly how it was nine years ago. The little white dressing table with its oval mirror, the metal clothes rack. The piano in the corner. I walk over to the mirror, bend down to see myself but a layer of dust clings to its surface. I stand straight again.

'No one really uses this room now,' Raff says.

'The window,' I say. 'It's taped.'

'Yes,' he says but it's barely audible.

The window. An overwhelming desire to cry comes over me, and I must have made a sound because Raff moves towards me with purpose, his arms out to take me to his body. Dust particles catch in his phone's light and billow into clouds as I stand in his embrace.

'They fell, didn't they? They fell out of that window.'

'Yes,' he says.

'What happened?'

'You wouldn't let me in, Margo,' he says in my ear.

I can feel heat creeping beneath my skin. 'What?'

'In the interval. You wouldn't let me into this room.'

I'm staring at him, trying to work out what it is he's saying when his phone goes black and his features melt into nothingness.

'Raff? What are you doing?'

'You were screaming,' he whispers. 'All of you were screaming. You, Annie and Cora.'

I feel his hands around my shoulders, gripping me to him.

'Can you remember? Can you remember the screaming?'

'You're scaring me,' I say and I try to wriggle out of his grasp but he holds me tighter.

'I need to know!' he says.

'Please, Raff. Turn on the light!'

'You need to remember!' he shouts and I'm trembling with the shock of his fingernails digging through my cardigan and into my skin.

Do I remember being here in the interval? Yes. We locked the door and we pushed the piano against it to barricade ourselves inside, but he kicked it down anyway.

'You pushed them,' I say. 'Didn't you? You pushed them out of the window!'

He lets me go then and I can see the whites of his eyes in the gloom.

'You pushed Annie, and Cora went with her!' I cry. 'Because Annie had told her about us? Is that what happened?'

'That's not what happened,' he says.

'You were angry with me! And Annie because she saw us! Yes! And you pushed Annie too!'

'*No*,' he says.

I remember my panic on seeing that face in the audience, and I remember that I ran up the narrow stairs to the music room where I knew Cora would go to prepare for the second act. I was shouting her name all the way up it when I heard my name being called from behind me. It was Annie, but I didn't stop running. I didn't stop on the stairwell to plead with her not to tell Cora about what I'd done with Raff. Why wouldn't I have done that? Were we both running from Raff?

'None of it makes sense,' I moan.

'I didn't push anyone from any window,' he says. 'I wasn't in the room when they fell! I was trying to get *in*! I wanted to know what you were going to tell her!'

'What did I do?' I cry. 'What did I *do*?'

Did *I* push Cora? Have I hidden some awful truth from myself this entire time? I'm gulping because it's as if there's no air in here for me to breathe.

'I don't know!' he says. 'I was *outside* the door, don't you remember? With your nanny.'

I look to the door, fear settling onto my chest like lead. 'With who?'

'Miss Patricia,' he says.

The name is sharp in my ear, causes physical pain on the back of my neck and immediately I start to scratch at my hands.

'I don't . . . I don't know who that is.' I say but somewhere in my head the name is taking the form of a woman, fierce and beautiful, whose fingernails sliced into my flesh like talons.

'Enough.' A voice has entered my head, and I know immediately that it's Cora's. 'You can't see this. Only I can see it. You understand? Only me.'

And everything goes to black.

FORTY

THE THEATRE, NINE YEARS AGO

During the first half of *Mirror, Mirror,* Margo sat, scratching her hands raw, and watching Cora on stage as the gold of the dress lit up like fire with the blazing spotlights. Every movement was precise and expertly executed, and people were whispering in the seats that she was going to be a star, but all Margo could think about was finding Annie at the interval before Annie found Cora.

But as she was about to stand and follow the crowd out of the theatre, Margo was suddenly aware of a person sitting, unmoving, down the row with their face turned towards her, staring. The hairs on the back of Margo's neck rose. She knew that face – she knew that she was afraid of this woman even when she couldn't recall her name.

A fog descended like a veil across her eyes and she ran up the theatre aisle, with an unnamed fear in her heart, even though she didn't know what fear felt like.

'Margo?' Annie was reaching out to her at the stall entrance. 'We need to talk. Margo!'

'She's here,' Margo cried, and she grabbed Annie with her, pulled her along.

'Who?'

'Her!' Margo said. 'Miss . . . Miss . . .'

Annie looked over Margo's shoulder. 'Oh my God.'

They ran, Margo in a dreamlike terror and Annie behind her, shouting her name, and the two of them barged into the room where Cora was sitting at the white dressing table, reapplying her make-up.

'She's here!' Annie shouted. 'Miss Patricia!'

Cora stood up immediately and the chair tipped back to the floor. 'What?'

'We have to get out!' Margo cried. 'We have to get out of here!'

Cora ran to her. 'Margo, it's OK. We're older now. And we're bigger than her. She's nothing, she doesn't matter. We're stronger than we were then, OK?'

But Margo was terrified without really understanding why. She knew only that this woman, Miss Patricia, was a danger to her and to all of them, and that they needed to escape her.

'Stay up here,' Cora said. 'You can stay here, OK? Until the show is finished.'

'You can't go back on that stage, Cora, promise me!'

There was a voice from down the hallway. 'Cora?'

It was Raff's voice, and Cora squeezed Margo's hand. 'It's just Raff,' she said, and started to walk to the door.

'Cora, don't,' Annie said. 'Don't open it to him.'

'Why not?'

'I need to talk to you . . .' Raff said from behind the door. 'But there's . . . there's someone here to see you first. Your old nanny?'

There was a beat of silence and Cora stopped dead in her tracks, snatched her hand away from opening the door. Instead, she turned the key and locked it.

'Cora? Have you locked the door? Are you . . . Are you OK? Is Margo with you? Is Annie?'

'Cora!' Miss Patricia sing-songed. 'Where are you, gorgeous girl?'

The door handle turned. 'What's going on?' Raff said. 'Please, let me explain. Has she told you?'

'We have to get out!' Margo cried again, and crossed the room to the window, began to turn the gold lock at the bottom.

'Margo?' There was a discernible tinge of delight in Miss Patricia's voice. 'That's you in there too, isn't it?'

Cora ran to the corner of the room, and with her weight behind the piano, pushed with all her strength. 'Help me, Annie,' she breathed, and Annie nodded, started pushing so that it rolled fast on its wheels. They butted against the door.

'Cora!' Raff shouted and the door started to tremble in its frame. 'Are you OK?'

Margo raised the glass window and the wind shot through and into her eyes. It lifted the curtains, her hair and Cora's gold silk dress as she ran back over to Margo.

'Margo!' she gasped. 'What are you doing?'

'We have to go! We have to climb down!'

'Are you crazy? We're three storeys up! Shut the window!'

Annie came to Cora's side, reached across her. 'Please, it's OK, they won't get in, she can't get in. They'll go back down—'

'She picked you, Annie!' Margo screamed. 'Cora picked you! She didn't choose me!'

'Close the window!' Cora yelled.

'What's going on?' Raff shouted. 'Whatever Margo said – I'm sorry! I'm going to break this door down unless you open it!'

'Break it down,' they heard Miss Patricia say. 'Break it.'

He started kicking the door and Margo lifted a leg onto the windowsill.

'No, Margo!' Cora shouted. 'What are you doing? Stop it!'

She wrenched Margo down and Margo fell on her back, but twisted on the floor to get up again.

'She's coming!' she wailed.

Annie leaned across the window, spread herself against it so Margo couldn't reach.

'Move, Annie!' Margo pleaded. 'Move!'

'Cora! What's going on?' Raff banged the door and it began to tremble on its hinges.

'Move, Annie, please!' Margo shrieked, looked back at them, desperate.

But Annie was reaching to close the window, and Cora was helping her.

'It's OK, Margo,' Cora said. 'I'll deal with Miss Patricia. I don't have to choose between you any more. We're grown up now, OK, and I can choose the *both* of you.'

'We have to get *out*!' Margo screamed.

'The window's stuck,' Annie said to Cora, who stretched up to tug at it.

She lost her footing.

Cora grabbed at something to steady herself. The something she reached for was Annie. And that was it. They fell from the window together, silent, because there was no time to scream in the shock of the moment. Margo screamed for the three of them as she leaned out of the sill, grappling with thin air, watching their faces becoming smaller, watching their arms find each other and lock in embrace, as they hurtled to meet the concrete below. She heard the thud and crack from their bones as they landed. She saw how the blood spurted from Annie's mouth, bloomed onto the silk of Cora's dress who lay beneath her. She saw in horror as one of Cora's shins splintered out of the flesh of her leg, twisted in a gruesome, unnatural way. She saw the glint of an enormous shard of glass embedded in her left foot.

The door flew open and Raff fell into the room and over the piano.

'Where – where is she?'

He ran to the window next to Margo, who had buckled and was now shrinking to be as small as possible beneath the tall open frame.

'Oh my God.'

Miss Patricia marched over towards her, stared down at her with those blue eyes that shivered in the whites.

'What have you done, Margo?' she said.

'Call an ambulance!' Raff moaned. 'Fuck, call an ambulance now!'

'I didn't, Miss Patricia!' Margo sobbed. 'I didn't! It was an accident! Please!'

'Come to me,' Miss Patricia said and Margo scrambled up and went to fall into her arms obediently, like she always had as a young child.

But the part of Margo that had taken all the childhood memories of Miss Patricia for her, was ready to take the stage and obliterate this one too. Margo pushed Miss Patricia with such a force that she staggered and tripped over those pretty little court shoes, landed on her back, and stared in surprise and shock.

'Go to hell,' Margo said.

FORTY-ONE

CORA

I wrench myself from Raff's grip.

'Let go of me,' I say coldly, and my voice is enough for him to let go of us, of Margo and me. 'I fucking know everything. I dealt with it then and I'll deal with it now.'

He looks at me with confusion on his face.

'You brought Patricia upstairs to see Cora,' I say.

Miss Patricia. The taste of her name in my mouth is acidic. But that's what I'm here for, to protect Margo from all the memories of that woman.

'Margo?' Raff says. 'Are you OK?'

I touch the back of my neck, Margo's neck, and feel the gnarled scar stiffen under my fingertips.

'Take me back to my granny's, Raff.'

'Margo, I showed you the photograph of the dressing room in the pub,' he says. 'But you didn't remember and I got . . . I don't know. I got scared to tell you. I'd only just found you again, I didn't want you to bolt from me. I wanted to contact Cora again. I thought you could lead me to her. Call it selfish. It is. I'm sorry.'

'Take me back,' I say. 'We're going to forget all about this now.'

'I – but I thought you wanted to remember?'

'No,' I say. 'We don't want to any more.'

FORTY-TWO

MARGO

The day has dawned – I can see from the pink tinge out of the window – but I don't know what day it is. I'm sitting on the sofa in Granny's flat, my hands rested in my lap, and I'm aware of both Granny and Annie around me, but I look straight ahead into the mirror and into my eyes – in Cora's too because I am her, and she is me.

I am her and she is me. We are one.

I feel a heaviness on my shoulder and neck, see that in the mirror's reflection that Annie is beside me and she's put her arm around me.

'Raff's going home now,' a voice says and then I remember that it's hers – Annie's – and that she is alive. 'Margo? Raff is asking if you want to say goodbye?'

I didn't realise Raff was here, and I don't remember getting to Granny's flat. Did he drive me all the way in the car? How did he know where to come? Did she . . . did Cora tell him the address?

I look at Annie. 'I . . .'

Does she know what I've seen? Does she know *who* I am?

'I don't think I want to see him,' I say.

'OK.'

'Could you tell him I'm sorry?'

I hear voices in the kitchen, and then Granny's front door closes. I breathe a sigh of relief. He's left and I'm thankful. I chased him because I wanted the truth, but I also chased him because I had always loved him, and look what good has come of it. Cora – or, I suppose myself? – was right – I should have left it all well alone. What must Raff think of me after all this? I wonder what she, Cora, said to him in the hours that followed after I blacked out in that music room? I still don't know the truth. I. Still. Don't. Know.

'He asked me to give you this,' Annie says when she comes back.

She holds a folded piece of paper – an origami crane – and then she turns away, busies herself elsewhere because she respects my privacy, and I think what a kind and considerate gesture that is. My little sister, this woman that I don't know. This woman that I abandoned in her time of need. I never loved her as I should have done and I don't know what to feel towards her now.

I unfold the note, digest the words.

Pearl, I'm sorry for so many things.

I sit silent, stare into the mirror.

'You're bleeding.'

Annie has reappeared in my eyeline, her head bent over my lap, and I glance down at my hands to see that the skin is red raw. How long have I been scratching at myself? Time is passing at a rate I don't understand but it's always done so and now I see why.

'I'll get a plaster,' she says.

'No—' I start, because I'm already an imposition, but she's gone.

I break eye contact with the mirror and watch Annie as she moves around the small flat. She moves the same as she always did, even despite the stick she uses as a crutch. I find that nice – she darts like a little bird with her eyes narrowed in concentration. She used to do colouring in with the same expression. She comes back with a plaster, tenderly applies it.

'There's something wrong with me, Annie. I need to tell you.'

'Sleep first,' she says. 'I'm here now, and we've got all the time in the world together.'

'I'm sorry I didn't write back to you,' I say. 'All your letters . . . I didn't know.'

'But I didn't give up,' she says.

'I'm sorry.'

'It's OK,' she smiles sadly.

'I've been so muddled.'

'There's been someone calling your phone,' she says. 'Mr Hawkins. Granny answered it and we put it on speaker. I hope you don't mind. He's been worried about you. He thought it was important we knew . . .'

'What did he say?'

'He told us about what he thinks you have – about DID. I'm so sorry,' she says. 'I don't really get it but he said it's serious . . . that you're needing to be somewhere safe.'

I hold her hand tightly.

Granny comes into the room. 'Dove, do you want to sleep in my bed?'

I look back to the mirror. *Mirror, Mirror.* 'No, thank you. I'll stay here.'

I don't think I can ever sleep again. How can I trust what I'll do when I'm 'asleep'? I'll stay awake like the young man, Randy Gardner. The side effects of sleep deprivation that he experienced won't make a difference to me because I'm already paranoid, delusional, severed from reality. I think that perhaps, if I stare into this mirror hard enough, Cora will come to me. I'll see her and she'll explain what happened and why she kept her death hidden from me and explain why that name – Miss Patricia – turns my blood cold.

'Do you want a blanket then, dove?'

I don't reply. Or maybe I do? I feel the comforting weight of a knitted blanket placed over my shoulders. It smells of lavender and rose.

'I've been to her grave,' I say. 'I think I've been to Cora's grave. But not . . . not as myself. Does that make sense?'

'Cora's in Highgate,' Annie nods.

A vision bolts through my eyes. A tree-lined graveyard. I'm holding a cigarette. Me? Cora?

'There's a bench,' I say. 'A bench where I've sat. We buried her in the cold, didn't we? But she was summer.'

The light fades. Granny and Annie flicker like fireflies until they too fade away into darkness. Perhaps they've gone to bed. I still stare ahead at the mirror. The moon is bright, casting a pale beam across my face.

'Where are you?' I say.

Choose me.

'Do you know what that means?' she says.

I can see that my lips are moving but I'm not in control of them. I fade out of focus but she stays – more beautiful than I.

'Miss Patricia . . .' I say. 'Who was that?'

'Our nanny,' she answers. 'I've stolen all your memories of her, I've kept them from you. *For* you. It's why you never talk about her; you've forgotten her but I haven't.'

'She wasn't kind to us.'

'She was evil,' Cora says.

'But a nanny should be kind.'

'It's why you chose to be one,' Cora says. 'Because you're kind. You wanted to give children everything we didn't have.'

'What happened?'

The scar on my neck – Cora's neck, too – flares with pain.

'Miss Patricia asked Cora to choose,' Cora says.

'I want to know what she asked.'

'Do you? I'm not sure you're strong enough.'

'I know you're gone, Cora. The real you is gone. How can any pain be worse than that?'

She's silent for a long time and I think maybe she's left me. Except her voice comes, whispers into my ear.

'OK,' she says. 'I'll show you.'

The night was hot – dry and prickly on my skin and the street below our beautiful flat was alight with music and laughter and horns beeping. There was a smell on the air coming from the street stalls set up – *picanha*, the salted meat, cassava chips and *bacalhau*, salted cod.

I was five and we were living in Brazil. Our parents were leaving for a black-tie dinner party that evening and the three of us children sat on the sofa in our pyjamas, looking at picture books and waiting for bedtime. Miss Patricia came in after waving our parents off and, as soon as she entered the room, we could see that she was angry. We were young but we knew – children always know how best to read adults.

'He wants the house,' she said. 'That bastard wants our *house*.'

'What house, Miss Patricia?' Cora asked.

'My house! For *her*!' Patricia roared. '*My* sister! He's moving her in. Wasn't it enough that she took my place? Wasn't it enough that she took *my* stage?'

'You have a sister, Miss Patricia?' I said.

'What's this?' Miss Patricia said, ignoring me, and she ripped a book from Cora's hand.

'*The Tiger Who Came To Tea*,' Cora said.

Miss Patricia flung the book on the floor and pulled Cora up.

'You will dance for me,' she instructed. 'You've been learning, yes? The five positions?'

She crossed the room to Father's drinks cabinet and poured herself something into a crystal glass.

'You will all do them! Up you get, come on. Discipline, always! Straight backs, stand tall. My sister and I used to practise all day, every day, you understand?'

We did as we were told, jumped around like we were in a production rehearsal and Annie was laughing, delighted, because she hadn't picked up on Patricia's tone. Cora and I were not. We'd seen glimpses of Miss Patricia being angry before but it had been nothing like this – she seemed wild with it, marching back and forth along our tiny line and barking instructions like a military general. I remember the hands on the clock moved to the nine, and then the ten, and Annie was all-but falling asleep on the floor by then, but every time she slumped, Miss Patricia would haul her up again, sloshing the drink she kept refilling from our father's cabinet.

'Straight backs!' she snapped. 'Diamonds! Come on! What are your parents paying that stage school for if you can't get this right? Turns, turns!'

'Can we finish, Miss Patricia?' Cora asked. 'We're tired.'

Miss Patricia twisted her mouth. 'Tired? You *wanted* to dance, didn't you? You don't get to be *tired*, my girl. There is no room to be tired. More, more, more. Don't let anyone take what is yours! Look what happened to me!'

So we carried on and the clock hand slipped to eleven and Annie was wired, crazed with tiredness and crying.

'Please, Miss Patricia,' Cora said, holding Annie to her. 'Can we go to bed now?'

'Look at you all,' Miss Patricia sneered. 'You think you share sisterly love, but sisters all betray each other in the end.'

Cora and I looked at each other in confusion.

'We're tired,' Cora said.

'You know what this play was called?' she said. '*Mirror, Mirror*. I danced it, yes! But I fell! Oh, I fell, and then *she* was waiting. In the wings, always waiting like something dark and black and wicked! My sister, Penelope. Oh that Bad Penny! Bad sisters should be punished. Bad Penny took everything, my husband and my life! Bad, bad! Bad Penny!' She grabbed Cora by the hair. 'You can't go to bed until you tell me who's the best.'

'Ouch, Miss Patricia!' Cora cried.

'You tell me! You tell who is the best dancer. The best *sister*. Margo or Annie?'

I was a better dancer than Annie was – obviously, because Annie was only three – and I looked at Cora, expectantly, but Cora was staring at Miss Patricia like she was trying to work something out, the right answer to an unasked question. Cora then looked at Annie who whirled around like a drunk doll, unknowing of what was going on above her head. We didn't know but we understood tone and Miss Patricia's tone was dangerous.

'Pick *one* sister,' Miss Patricia said to Cora.

I looked at Cora again, a note of fright singing through my chest.

Choose me, I willed.

'Annie,' Cora said.

Miss Patricia clapped her hands in the same beat that my heart jumped.

'This way, Margo,' she said gleefully. 'You will be marked as the bad side of the penny.'

She took me by the arm, pulled me roughly towards the door and to the kitchen, where she slammed its door. I heard Cora shouting for me behind it.

Miss Patricia stood next to the oven. 'Come here.'

'You don't need to see more,' Cora's voice drifts into my head.

I'm gasping as if emerging from water.

'You chose Annie,' I say.

'But you know why Cora did it,' Cora says to me in the mirror. 'Annie was so tiny.'

'Yes . . . Yes, I know but – I was five, Cora.'

'You would have done the same thing for Annie. At that point we both loved her more than we loved each other. Our Annie.'

I feel numb.

'I'll always be here for you,' she says. 'But please don't ask me for more of this. Not now.'

She's crying. No, I'm crying.

'Where are you?' I whisper.

'Always here,' comes the answer from my own lips. 'We will survive this. We always have.'

FORTY-THREE

THREE MONTHS LATER

CORA

Mr Hawkins leans back in his chair. 'Who am I talking to?' he says.

'Can't you tell?'

He smiles. 'It's nice to see you again, Cora.'

'Is it?' I say, amused. 'That's nice, Mr H. I did smash your vase after all.'

'Yes,' he says, raises his eyebrows. 'But I understand how it happened.'

'Margo should pay for it,' I say. 'I'll tell her.'

'It's all right,' he says. 'Honestly.'

I flick my hair over my shoulders. I've dressed up for him; my hair is curled, my make-up is subtle, I'm wearing a teal figure-hugging dress and knee-high brown leather boots.

He picks up his pen and notebook. 'Margo and I have been talking about a technique often used with clients who suffer with DID.'

'You've relaxed her mind,' I say. 'To get to me.'

'Correct.'

'So there's more to you than a pretty face, Mr H,' I say. 'You've got a magic tongue?'

'Well, I don't know about—'

'Maybe I'll ask your wife,' I grin.

I see heat sizzle to his cheeks but he doesn't rise to my bait and I like that about him. I like a man who doesn't always say yes to me. I respect them far more.

'I would have come to see you eventually,' I say. 'I've been listening to your sessions over the last few months. Quite intriguing work, I have to say.'

'I wasn't sure if I'd see either of you again after the night you knocked on my door,' he says.

I tilt my head, smile at him again. 'You underestimate how much I like your cute elbow-patch jumpers.'

He gives me a ghost of a smile.

'It was a wild night,' I say. 'Film worthy.'

'Yet Margo still isn't quite sure what happened.'

'And that's for the good,' I say.

'Is it?'

'You're not going to kill me off, are you?'

'No, Cora,' he says. 'My role here is to help align you into the same headspace. Get you both balanced; recognising each other and living with the condition to the best of your abilities.'

'I was doing that fine.'

'Except that Margo was chronically tired,' he says. 'And taking drugs every day to cope with the double life she led but was never aware of.'

'We coped.'

'Shall we talk about Margo?' he asks. 'She tells me she's rented a flat in Knightsbridge.'

'That's right. I'm mostly with her,' I say. 'Sometimes with Nav. But Margo is boring when she's alone. I prefer to be out.'

'She's very withdrawn. She doesn't like to talk much about the real Cora.'

'She's a bit like your vase, I'm afraid. She's been shattered and trying to glue herself back together but doesn't have the energy to find or stick the pieces.'

'She's coming to terms with a very big shift in her reality,' he says. 'But she's still very much in the dark about things. As, I admit, am I.'

'Well, yeah,' I say. 'Because there's someone you need to be aware of to make any sort of sense of Margo.'

He doesn't say anything, just waits for me to speak.

'Our nanny. Miss Patricia.'

'I've not heard this name before.'

'No, you wouldn't have done,' I say. 'Because Margo had all but forgotten about Miss Patricia. Until now, Miss Patricia hasn't existed in Margo's head but the night after she turned up here and she found out about Cora, I showed her Miss Patricia. I showed Margo why she was scared of her.'

'Are you able to talk to me about her?' he asks. 'I would very much like to hear what you have to say.'

I lean back on the sofa, put my arms behind my head and smile up at the ceiling. 'Oh Miss Patricia!' I exclaim. 'She was so beautiful. So deceptively beautiful. That was the key, you know? That's what she used to tell me. "Use your body as a weapon."'

'And what did she mean by that?'

I look back from the ceiling at him. 'She meant that you should always keep your body pristine and disciplined. Your face too. That way you can hide all the ugly bits so people don't see them.'

'And how did your nanny use her beauty?'

'She used it like a gloss,' I say. 'She used it to hide all the ugly parts of herself and let me tell you, Mr H, that she had a *fucking* lot of ugly bits. She had been a prima ballerina but she fell on stage once and broke her leg and had to have metal studs in her femur. She couldn't dance again. Her husband had been her dance partner and he had an affair with his new prima. Miss Patricia's *sister*. Penelope. Bad Penny. Apparently they fell in love. Dancing is very sensual, Mr Hawkins – shall I show you how it can be?'

'Thank you, Cora, but please continue with your story.'

I smirk because he's blushing.

'Miss Patricia's life trajectory was upended and she had to find something else to do,' I say. 'So she trained as a nanny. Ha! A nanny! Why did she do that, Mr H? Of all the things! She came to us like a wounded fighting dog, full of hate. But we didn't know it then, Margo and I were only three, right, and when you're a child you don't know that people can do you harm because you're trusting. You're *malleable*.'

Mr Hawkins nods. 'Yes. Children are very innocent.'

'When we were a bit older we began to see the hate she carried. She started drinking more – never in front of our parents though. Only when she was alone with us and she snapped.'

'Was she violent towards you?'

I laugh. 'Oh, yes.'

'I'm sorry.'

'But you know what?' I say. 'The signs must have been there. Our parents *must* have known she was drinking heavily but decided to ignore it because otherwise it would have been an inconvenience to them. Who knows. They had all the money but no love. I carry all that fucking anger and hurt about them too. It's why I took Margo away from that house in Switzerland. You know what happened after Cora died? You know what Miss Patricia told our parents? That she *saw* Margo push Annie and Cora from that window, and our parents *believed* her because she had been there. Mother moved out after Cora died, couldn't stand to be with Margo or Father, and couldn't care for Annie in the state she was in. Father was stuck in an angry funk – sent Margo horrible letters saying he blamed Margo for Mother leaving him. I took all those letters so she'd never see them. Wicked, stupid, people. What our parents let happen – under their noses – was, and still is, unforgivable. They failed Margo in the biggest way possible. Fuck off to the both of them.'

I'm clenched with anger. Mr Hawkins sits quietly. The clock ticks above his head.

'Will you be able to tell me what happened with Miss Patricia,' he asks.

'Oh, I can talk about it fine.'

'Only if you want to,' he says. 'And you can stop at any time.'

'Are you sitting uncomfortably?' I smile at him. 'Then I shall begin.'

I tell him about Cora's decision to save Annie, and how it cast a spell of protection over her, but how from that day on Miss Patricia had her sacrificial lamb. Margo was now a person for Patricia to hate because she couldn't hate her husband and she couldn't hate what fate had brought her, so Margo had to embody it.

'Annie and Cora had to survive and Margo had to be sacrificed.' I say. 'Do you understand?'

Mr Hawkins grimaces. 'I'm so sorry. What a horrible thing for Margo to have endured.'

I laugh. 'Shall I show you what Miss Patricia did to Margo when Cora chose Annie?'

I bend down, move my hair to show him the jagged three-inch white scar. The skin either side of it is pulled and bunched and knotty.

'She dragged Margo to the kitchen and she opened the oven door that was turned up hot and she forced Margo's head down onto the lip of the oven door and her neck – there was a searing hot pain on the back of her neck.'

I hear Mr Hawkins' intake of breath.

'The skin on Margo's neck was gaping. It felt like it was on fire but Patricia didn't take Margo to hospital. She hauled her to the bathroom and ran the bath full of cold water and ducked Margo's head inside and she then she told Annie and Cora to watch. And then she took a gauze and tried to mend her neck. She panicked, I remember. She had to change it every day. She made Annie and Cora promise not to tell their parents. Oh, Miss Patricia!' I laugh. 'No one should ever have been with Miss Patricia when she was angry. Those shaking eyes! Jesus! She used to put ice in Margo's hot-water bottles. She folded Margo's pyjamas over them so she'd be shaking with cold all night. She'd lock Margo in the cupboard under the stairs or in the attic. She used to hide her toys so she couldn't sleep. She'd drop her dinners on the floor and then not give her any more. She pretended these things were all games or accidents at first but as soon as she realised we weren't telling our parents any of it she started with bolder acts of cruelty. She used to ban Margo from using the toilet, would tie her up to my bedpost and when she would wet herself, Patricia would make her clean it up in the dark. When she was around seven, Patricia started hitting her on the back of the legs, on the back of her hands and, later, in front of the whole family, she'd tell our parents how clumsy Margo was and would stroke her hair, wink at her.'

I feel my fists clench.

'She decided that she would break Margo. And she nearly did except I came and took those experiences from her and kept them from her so she could survive life.'

'The human mind is powerfully clever,' he says.

'I've kept some of it with me,' I say. 'I like being tied up in the bedroom. I like having a full bladder and being in control of it because Margo never could be. Isn't that strange?'

'It's not strange to me,' he says. 'Margo was a victim of abuse. These things leave their marks on us in strange ways. Did she ever blame the real Cora for letting it happen?'

'Margo always felt alone,' I sigh. 'She still feels alone. But Cora was a child too. Margo understands the innocence of children: it's why she was drawn to become a nanny. She's a nurturer despite her history. She folds pyjamas over hot-water bottles, she treats those kids with such *care*. It's heartbreaking actually.'

'Does she miss her work?'

'She's looking at jobs in Paris,' I say. 'Well, I'm looking for her. She's got strong references.'

'Does this mean you won't be returning to see me?' he asks.

'Margo had a lot of shit to deal with, Mr H. It's time for us to move on. The only reason she's been coming to you for three months is because I can't get her out of here until she's processed all this a bit more.'

'But that's exactly what I'm here for,' he says. 'I'm here to help Margo come to terms with what happened to her. Gaining awareness is a huge victory, especially given how it was broken to her, but it will take years to help her further. I would like to try.'

I regard him coolly. 'She doesn't need to remember any of this. Why would I show her any of the memories I have? I'm here to *protect* her.'

'But you *did* show her parts,' he says. 'You know she's getting stronger though maybe not right at this moment because she's processing, but she *can* make progress if you let her. If you make the decision to show her any of your memories it would be planned meticulously.'

I remain mute.

'By your own admission, Margo is unhappy,' he says. 'She hides from life and she doesn't really understand why.'

I roll my eyes. 'Oh, come on. Enough with the emotional blackmail.'

'What about Annie?' he says. 'Seeing her could be so helpful.'

'Annie *is* trying to contact Margo and Margo wants to see her but she's afraid. Annie could trigger something in Margo that could be damaging. She knows our past, what our nanny did to us, you understand? That's why I told Margo that Annie had died – it eliminated the threat of the truth.'

'What about if we had Annie here too?'

I pause.

'We can all do this together,' Mr Hawkins says. 'I don't wish to re-traumatise Margo in any way. Having Annie here will mean that you can both support Margo and protect her at the same time.'

I lick my lips.

'We can let Margo have another chance,' he carries on. 'She's lost one sister – her closest and most treasured – but she has another who loves her so much. They can rebuild something. They have the opportunity to have a relationship.'

I'm quiet. 'Margo would like that.'

'Good,' he says.

'You like her, Mr H?'

'Yes. And I think she's worth helping. Don't you?' I feel pleased for Margo. 'She likes you, too.'

'And I would very much like to see you again.'

'That's what all the boys say.'

'Would you come again?' he asks. 'Would you postpone your thoughts about Paris for a while? I promise that I would treat you all with care.'

'I know,' I say, seriously. 'Let me think about it, Mr H, because Paris is a really fucking great city and I could do well there.' I look at the clock above his head, at the carved leaves and acorns and the snake. 'I should go now.'

'Before you go, Cora,' he says. 'Would you give me the name of your nanny?'

I frown. 'Why?'

'Because I would like to contact the authorities immediately. She will be found.'

'Patricia Bergen,' I say as I watch him write down her name. 'But she was found.'

'Sorry?'

I stand up, look out of the window for a moment. 'She died.' I turn to face him. 'Very recently. Apparently, she drowned.'

He pauses, silent, and I can hear every sound in the room, amplified.

'She drowned?' he says.

I nod. 'A tragic accident. Isn't it sad?'

The clock ticks, and for the longest moment Mr Hawkins studies my face, and I wonder if this is the moment where it all gets even more complicated.

'Goodbye, Cora,' he says, and I see him score out her name on the page with his pen.

ACKNOWLEDEGMENTS

This book is dedicated to Jen Hawkins, and I acknowledge her here first and foremost because of the time and confidence she gave in helping me write this book and understand the breadth of its subject matter. *The Twins* took years to write and years to polish and she saw me through it all. Thank you, Jen. Soon we shall go forth, through rain and roadkill, to distant pubs and drink gin once more!

To Camilla Bolton at Darley Anderson for giving me free rein to explore *The Twins*, and for your precious feedback on how to make it (and every book I've written before and since) stronger and better. So much of my development is down to you and I am so incredibly lucky to call you my agent. To Jade, for boundless energy and passion, to all in the rights department and to everyone else at Darley, thank you so much.

Thank you to Jon Elek, my publisher, and to Rosa Schierenberg, my wonderful editor – you have loved this book as much as I have, thank you for upping its game considerably and sprinkling glitter over it! To everyone at Welbeck and to Emma Dowson at EDPR, I appreciate everything you do to promote, support and believe in me. Huge thanks to

Simon Michele and Joe Mills for another beautiful cover, and to Habiba Sacranie at WF Howes for your passion for *The Twins* in audio. To Celine Kelly – can you please live in my pocket and help me forever and always?

Big thank you to 'R' and 'G' for speaking to me about first hand experiences – your time and the insight into your lives has been truly appreciated.

Thank you to my family – Mum for reading early drafts, Dad for building lists of people to buy it for, and my brother for being proud of me. Thanks to all my wonderful friends for being interested in what I do. Special thanks to Tess for your faces when I need to laugh, Nic for your huga-ma-jiggy when I'm cold, and Amy for your voice notes with feedback on dance terminology!

To Matt, for your endless love and cups of tea, and putting up with me looking like Fagin approx 97% of the time in my dressing gown and fingerless gloves. To our boys for keeping me in the real world when I am slipping down the black hole of the fantastical and need reminding that they need *fish fingers now please, Mummy*.

A sincere thank you to all the retailers who have stocked and backed *The Twins*, to the amazing authors I've met, the bloggers and bookstagrammers and the Twitter community, who have all boosted and inspired me to write better books. And finally to you – the readers – for everything.

ABOUT THE AUTHOR

For over 10 years L.V. Matthews worked in both domestic and international sales for major UK publishing houses, before leaving to pursue a career in writing. Her debut novel, *The Prank*, was published by Welbeck in 2021.

@LV_matthews
@lv_matthews_author

WELBECK

PUBLISHING GROUP

Love books? Join the club.

Sign up and choose your preferred genres to receive tailored news, deals, extracts, author interviews and more about your next favourite read.

From heart-racing thrillers to award-winning historical fiction, through to must-read music tomes, beautiful picture books and delightful gift ideas, Welbeck is proud to publish titles that suit every taste.

bit.ly/welbeckpublishing

WELBECK

ANDRE
DEUTSCH

MORTIMER

MORTIMER

WELBECK